“I thought perhaps we might have someth hip?”

“Yes, we mig e each other very m each other well, d

“Ah…” Jack frowned, for her question was unexpected. “If I were to propose marriage today, Lucy, what would your answer be?”

“I should ask you if I might have a little time to think,” Lucy said, giving him a shy glance. “If you were to discover that your true happiness lay elsewhere I should understand.”

“Would you?” Jack’s eyes narrowed. He suddenly realized what all this was about. Someone had been telling Lucy tales, and the devil of it was that he could deny nothing.

Lucy blushed and looked away. She had begun to regret her answer and the wasted chance. She might even now have been telling her sister that she was engaged to Lord Harcourt!

* * *

Marrying Captain Jack

Harlequin® Historical #265—August 2009

Author Note

Lucy Horne has always been a dreamer. She loves fairy stories, particularly the ones her sister has written for her. Both Marianne and Jo have found love, but Lucy fears that she never will. She once met a gentleman she thought she could love, but he was so much older and thought of her as a child. When they meet again, she will discover that he has a secret, but can she accept his past and find happiness?

I hope, dear reader, that you have enjoyed this trilogy about three sisters in search of love.

Marrying Captain Jack

Anne Herries

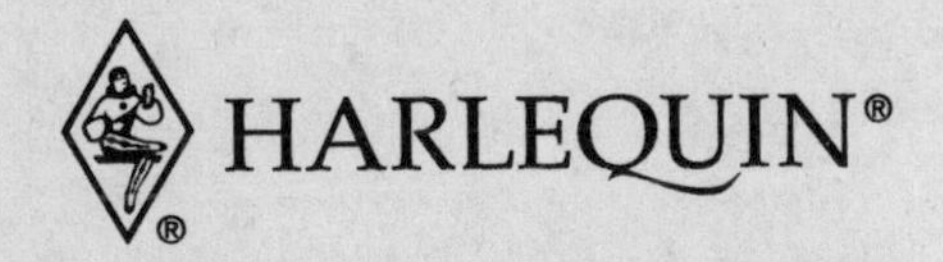

TORONTO • NEW YORK • LONDON
AMSTERDAM • PARIS • SYDNEY • HAMBURG
STOCKHOLM • ATHENS • TOKYO • MILAN • MADRID
PRAGUE • WARSAW • BUDAPEST • AUCKLAND

ISBN-13: 978-0-373-30574-2

MARRYING CAPTAIN JACK

First North American Publication 2009

This edition published by arrangement with Harlequin Books S.A.

www.eHarlequin.com

Printed in U.S.A.

ANNE HERRIES

Award-winning author Anne Herries lives in Cambridgeshire, England. She is fond of watching wildlife, and spoils the birds and squirrels that are frequent visitors to her garden. Anne loves to write about the beauty of nature, and although they are mostly about love and romance, she sometimes puts a little into her books. She writes for her own enjoyment, and to give pleasure to her readers. She invites readers to contact her on her Web site, www.lindasole.co.uk.

Available from Harlequin® Historical and
ANNE HERRIES

The Abducted Bride #135
Captive of the Harem #145
The Sheikh #157
Rosalyn and the Scoundrel #166
A Matter of Honor #173
**A Perfect Knight* #180
**A Knight of Honor* #184
**Her Knight Protector* #188
***Lady in Waiting* #202
***The Adventurer's Wife* #208
††*Forbidden Lady* #209
†*An Improper Companion* #227
††*The Lord's Forced Bride* #231
†*A Wealthy Widow* #235
†*A Worthy Gentleman* #243
††*Her Dark and Dangerous Lord* #249
‡*Marianne and the Marquis* #258
‡*Married by Christmas* #261
‡*Marrying Captain Jack* #265

*Banewulf Dynasty
**The Elizabethan Season
†The Hellfire Mysteries
††Melford Dynasty
‡The Horne Sisters

DON'T MISS THESE OTHER NOVELS AVAILABLE NOW:

#955 THE NOTORIOUS MR. HURST—Louise Allen

Lady Maude Templeton has turned down many proposals with her heart set on one man—sexy, talented theater owner Eden Hurst. He doesn't believe in love, but Maude is determined to make Eden her own. Society is about to see she can be just as shocking as her Ravenhurst friends when she puts her mind to it!

The latest thrilling installment of Louise Allen's Those Scandalous Ravenhursts

#956 SIERRA BRIDE—Jenna Kernan

Sam Pickett is rich, powerful and used to getting his way. So he is baffled when stunning Kate Wells isn't remotely interested in becoming his latest plaything—despite the fact that she's poor, with an aunt and blind sister to support. Since striking it rich, Sam has felt a troubling emptiness and knows that his money can never fill the hole in his life where Kate now belongs….

He'll have the only woman he wants!

#957 THE VISCOUNT'S KISS—Margaret Moore

When Lord Bromwell meets a young woman on the mail coach to Bath, he has no idea who she is—until *after* they have shared a soul-searing kiss! The nature-mad viscount isn't known for his spontaneous outbursts of romance—and the situation isn't helped by the fact that the woman he is falling for is a runaway….

The Viscount and the Runaway

#958 REYNOLD DE BURGH: THE DARK KNIGHT—Deborah Simmons

Tall, dark and handsome, Reynold de Burgh is nonetheless wary of the opposite sex—until he meets beautiful, young Sabina Sexton! That innocent Sabina fearfully begs his help to fight the "beast" terrorizing her village only makes the brooding knight more desirous of her.

The last bachelor of the de Burgh dynasty is single no longer!

#266 FRANCESCA—Sylvia Andrew

Francesca Shelwood was mortified when Marcus Carne reappeared in her life—he had stolen the most magical, illicit kisses from the young, innocent Francesca! Now, on her inheritance, Marcus has returned to offer the unimaginable—marriage! Francesca refuses, but very soon she walks headlong into danger—and the only man ready to sacrifice his life, and reputation, for her sake is Marcus….

Her only temptation!

Prologue

David Middleton walked into his club, glancing round at the company gathered there for an evening of cards and pleasure. Seeing a gentleman he disliked, he hesitated, wondering whether to leave. Sir Frederick Collingwood came from a good family, but he was an unprincipled rogue who would be banned from decent society if David had his way. The man needed to be taught a severe lesson if the rumours were true. However, there was little he could do about it while Collingwood continued to be accepted by others.

'Middleton! Come and join us,' a man called, attracting his attention.

David Middleton frowned. Sir Henry James was a friend. He had won two thousand guineas from him a few days previously and could hardly ignore his invitation, for he must give him a chance to recoup. It meant that he would have to sit down with Collingwood, which he would have preferred not to do, but in the circumstances he had no choice but to accept. He walked towards the small group of gentlemen seated at the table. He would play a few hands and then make some excuse to leave.

Reaching the others, he pulled out a chair and sat down. Collingwood nodded and began dealing the cards, someone mentioned the stakes of a hundred guineas a hand. David reached for his cards.

'You wear an unusual ring, Middleton,' Collingwood said. 'You would not care to hazard it against the cards?'

'No, I should not. It was a gift…' Despite himself, he could not keep the emotion from his voice, and, looking up, saw that Collingwood's eyes were upon him, intent, mocking—as if he had already known.

'From a lady, I dare say?'

'That is my business.'

'So she is married,' Collingwood sneered. 'I dare say one might hazard a guess…'

'Damn you, sir! I will hear no more of this.' David pushed back his chair, on the point of leaving.

'Sit down, Middleton,' Sir Henry said. 'You can't leave now, the cards are dealt. Collingwood meant nothing. It was merely a jest.'

For a moment David glanced across the table, meeting Collingwood's eyes. Some inner instinct warned him to get up and walk away immediately, but his friend was speaking again, telling him that he was glad of the chance to recoup his losses, and David knew it was too late. He must play, even though a sixth sense was warning him that he had been drawn into the spider's web.

Chapter One

Jack Harcourt, sometimes known as Captain Manton and various other aliases, lately of His Majesty's Dragoons, secret agent and aide to Wellington for some years, sat in the library of his London house, staring moodily into the empty wine glass in front of him. Had life no more to offer than this? A full bottle that was there for the drinking, and an inner emptiness that would be eased only by refilling the glass and swallowing its contents again and again, until he could no longer feel the pain.

As Captain Manton, Jack had helped to defeat Napoleon Bonaparte; he had battled against spies and enemies of the state, but this bitterness, the bleakness that had come upon him of late, was harder to fight. He was a peer of the realm, wealthy enough for his needs, an attractive man in the best of health—but he had tasted wormwood too often and, at this moment, he wished that he had died on the bloody battlefields at Waterloo. Instead of that, he had been heaped with praise and honours, received by the Regent privately, and told that he was the backbone of England, a man the prince was proud to shake by the hand—but nothing had eased the deep grief that lived within.

'Why was I not here when you needed me, David?' he spoke the words aloud. 'Why did I not hear as you lay in a ditch, bleeding of a fatal wound, alone and friendless?'

In life a man might count his true friends on the fingers of one hand. Jack had other friends, men he valued, but there was a special reason why David Middleton's death had affected him so deeply. It was a cruel fate that had led to his friend dying at the roadside, a victim of a highwayman, robbed of the personal possessions he valued most. Jack could not put the picture from his mind, for it haunted him day and night, and he seemed to hear David's voice calling out for justice. But it had happened some months ago, when Jack was in France fighting for his country, and he had known nothing until his return. At the moment he had no leads, nothing to help him discover the truth. The frustration of being so helpless, together with the knowledge of the pain David's death had brought to another, had left him feeling deeply at odds with himself. His hand was reaching for the wine decanter when a knock at the door halted him.

'Come!' he barked and the door opened to admit his butler.

'I am sorry to disturb you, my lord, but there is a letter.'

'At this hour?' Jack's brows rose. 'Who brought it?'

'I am not sure, my lord. It was given to the maid Rose, as she went into the street to buy some eggs from the dairymaid.'

'Very well, you may leave it, Henshaw.' Jack dismissed it with a flick of his hand. 'I may read it later…'

'Rose was told it was urgent, sir.'

'Was she, indeed?' Jack picked up the note, which was sealed with wax but did not bear the signet of any man. He was frowning as he broke the wax and unfolded the paper, reading what was written there. 'Good grief!' he shouted and jumped up, striding over to the window to look out. However, the street was ill lit and he could not see beyond the pool of light outside his house. He turned to look at his butler, who still hesitated by the door. 'Fetch Rose to me. I would hear more of this messenger.'

As the man went off to do his bidding, Jack read the few brief lines again, frowning over their meaning.

If I came in person, you would not see me—but I know David Middleton was a friend you valued. If you seek his murderer, you need look no further than Sir Frederick Collingwood. Collingwood is a cheat at the card tables and Middleton found him out after losing to him. This much is certain, for it is well known. I can give you no proof, though I am sure of Collingwood's guilt. There may be more to this, a deeper motive, but for the moment all I know is that the murder lies at Collingwood's door. The rest is up to you, Harcourt. This warning comes from someone who was once proud to be your friend.

The letter was unsigned, and might be malicious, but somehow Jack sensed that it was genuine. He knew his friend well enough to be sure that if David had discovered he had been cheated, he would not slink away with his tail between his legs. He would publicly denounce the man who had cheated him. It was very possible that he had been murdered to stop him doing just that...and yet the letter hinted at something further—a more sinister reason for his friend's murder. Yes! Jack had not been able to accept the facts of David's death, and the letter confirmed that he was right to be suspicious. He got to his feet with a new sense of urgency; his mood of despondency had lifted as swiftly as it had come to him that night.

He would think no more of seeking solace in a bottle of wine. He had been given what he needed. If this message were true, he would seek out the murderer and bring him to justice one way or the other. He wondered who had sent the letter...it was not a close friend, for it had said that he would not see the writer in person.

Jack frowned, because it might well be a false trail, but something was telling him it was not. The writer might be someone who felt that he owed Jack something...someone he had helped at some time. It did not matter! He would seek for the truth of his friend's death first, and discover the identity of this mysterious writer after...

'Mama! There is a letter for you.' Lucy Horne ran into the parlour where her mother and great-aunt were sitting at their embroidery. 'It is from Marianne!'

'I have been expecting it,' Mrs Horne said, looking fondly at her youngest daughter. Lucy was eighteen now, a beautiful, sweet-natured girl who asked for very little except to be with her family. She took the letter, breaking the impressive seal that her eldest daughter was, as the Marchioness of Marlbeck, entitled to use. She scanned the few lines Marianne had penned and smiled. 'It is as I thought, Lucy. Your sister agrees that it is time for your come-out. She suggests that we all go to stay with her and Drew for the christening of their daughter—and then she and Drew will accompany us to London and we shall stay there for a few weeks.'

'Mama! Is darling little Andrea to be christened?' Lucy asked, her face lighting up. She had seized on what was for her the most important part of her mama's news. 'How lovely! It seems ages since we saw either of my sisters.'

'You know that Marianne did not wish to travel immediately after the birth,' Mrs Horne said. 'But it is no more than six months since we were there and Jo visited with us a matter of five weeks ago.'

'It seems longer,' Lucy said and bent to kiss her mama's cheek. She was happy living with her mama and Aunt Bertha, and she had made many friends, with whom she visited most weeks, but she was never happier than with her sisters. 'It is so good of Marianne to think of it, Mama.'

Mrs Horne nodded. 'I asked for her advice, because I had thought of Bath, but Marianne insists it must be London, my love.'

'Yes…' Lucy nodded. She had been to Bath once or twice with her mama and her Aunt Bertha, but she had not attended the public dances, only private affairs given by their friends. Although she was used to mixing in company, she was not officially out. Lucy wasn't sure how she felt about the coming Season, for she knew that it was usually seen as a chance for girls to find a husband. 'It will be so much better if Marianne is with us.'

Lucy went over to the window, standing with her back to her mama, gazing out at the garden, which was very pretty at this time of year, the herbaceous borders just coming into flower.

'We must start to collect your wardrobe,' Mrs Horne said. 'Though perhaps it would be best to wait until we are at your sister's. Marianne is so good with that sort of thing and she will know what the young girls are wearing this Season.'

Lucy hardly heard her mother's words. She liked pretty clothes, but often clung to things that she favoured long after her mama thought they should be discarded. She still had the blue velvet pelisse that Jo had made for her before they left the Vicarage where they had all grown up; it was one of her favourite things and she refused to part with it, even though she had more stylish ones in her armoire.

She was thinking about someone…a gentleman she had met at Marianne's wedding, which seemed such a long time ago now, but was just over three years. So much had happened since then. Marianne had married her marquis, and Jo was married to Hal Beverley. Yet the memory of Captain

Harcourt's smile and his teasing had remained with her, almost as bright as it was at the first. Of course he was Lord Harcourt really, but he had left the army some months after Napoleon Bonaparte's defeat at Waterloo and only then adopted the title that had become his on his father's death.

Lucy pushed her fine, silky hair back from her face. It was the colour of moonlight, more silver-blonde than yellow, and set her apart from most other young ladies she met. Her complexion was soft cream and rose, her eyes were the colour of an azure sky, but could turn darker when she was distressed or angry. Lucy was not often angry, which gave others a false impression of her nature. She seemed a dreamy, gentle girl, mild mannered and perhaps a little insipid at first sight. In truth, she was far from that, for she had a temper when roused and she was a brave girl, but she took after her father. Papa Horne had always been a mild-mannered man, thoughtful, quiet, peace loving—but Lucy had once seen him thrash the sweep who had dared to set a fire under the climbing boy sent to clean the Vicarage chimneys.

He had not known she was there, and when he discovered that she had witnessed the thrashing, he had looked ashamed and begged her to forgive him for subjecting her to such a disgraceful scene.

'I lost my temper, Lucy,' he had told her. 'I should not have done it. I should have reasoned with the man, restrained him if need be—but what I did was unforgivable.'

'No, Papa,' Lucy told him with a smile. 'I think that what you did was justified. He was a cruel man and needed to be taught a lesson. You were provoked by his cruelty and I think that God would understand your loss of temper.'

Papa had smiled, shaken his head and kissed her. Lucy thought that her papa was the most perfect man ever to have lived and it had caused her terrible grief when he had died and they had had to leave the Vicarage. However, that was in the past now, and she had the future to look forward to—and she would be foolish to let her childish daydreams stop her enjoying her Season in town!

She turned back to her mother with a smile. 'I think I should like a yellow silk dress, Mama. I have seen some very pretty material that would make a lovely ballgown.'

'You will need a great many dresses, Lucy,' Mrs Horne said. 'And, thanks to your aunt and sisters, you will be able to have the wardrobe you deserve.'

Jack came in from the street, tossing his gloves into a bowl on the hallstand, his hat following it. He did not notice that it slid to the floor, or see the expression of his footman as he picked it up and brushed it with his fingers. He was frowning as he picked up two letters from the silver salver, taking them with him as he went into his library.

One was from Lady Staunton, Jack's only sister Amelia. He had no other relatives to speak of other than his sister and her family, and he was fond of her, but at the moment Amelia's problems were not his immediate concern. He had looked for Sir Frederick Collingwood, but the man was not to be found in town, and he had learned this morning that he had possibly gone off to Newmarket. Jack was considering whether to post after him, and settle this thing at once, or give himself a breathing space. He opened the first of his letters, reading the brief lines his sister had penned. It had been sent from her home in Hampshire and told him that she had returned to England alone a month ago, because her son David had been suffering badly from the climate.

Her letter said nothing of her unhappiness, though the tone told him that nothing had changed. The only reason Staunton had allowed her to leave India and return to England without him was that he feared he might lose his heir.

Jack cursed as he tossed the letter down. If he had his way, Amelia would leave Staunton for good, but he knew that there were too many difficulties. The man was a brute, damn him! If there were any justice, Amelia would be able to divorce him and retain her son and her place in society, but the laws were all heavily weighted on Staunton's side.

There was nothing he could do while Amelia refused to take his advice, though he knew that she was desperately unhappy. He opened the second letter, which had come from Drew Marlbeck, inviting him to attend the christening of his daughter Andrea.

A smile touched Jack's face, for Drew was one of the few men he valued and he knew how proud he was of his little girl. As one of the richest men in England and the holder of a proud title, Drew could have been forgiven if he had been disappointed that his firstborn was a girl, but not a bit of it. He adored her and left no one in doubt of it—or his love for his beautiful wife.

Jack smiled, because he retained good memories of their wedding, and of the few times he had stayed with them since. He had not visited as often as he would have liked, because until recently he had been caught up with the business of the State and could not spare the time for personal pleasure—and then the horror and grief of David Middleton's senseless death had taken over, making Jack feel that life was cruel and empty and hardly worth living.

He had thrown off his mood of despair in the search for justice. If Collingwood was truly a cheat and a murderer, Jack would not rest until he was in prison where he belonged. However, there was nothing he could do until Collingwood decided to show his face in town. He smiled as he made up his mind to go down to Marlbeck for the christening. He must think of a suitable gift for Andrea, but he would also take presents for Marianne and Drew, because he had money enough and no one to spend it on—apart from Amelia and one or two others.

Lucy watched as her niece Andrea was christened in the lovely old church where her father had once been the parson. Her sister Marianne was glowing with happiness. Andrea was ten months old, a beautiful little girl with honey-coloured hair and blue eyes. Lucy already adored her and was thrilled to have been asked to be one of her godmothers.

'Isn't she good?' Jo whispered as they left the church after the ceremony. Married to Harry Beverley, Lucy's second eldest sister was increasing herself and clearly happy to be Andrea's other godmother. 'She has hardly cried all through the service.'

'Yes, she is adorable,' Lucy said, smiling as she and her sister followed the other guests from the church to the waiting carriages, which would take them back to the house. 'Marianne looks so happy, doesn't she?' She nodded to one of the other ladies, feeling a little uncertain.

The Marlbecks' large house was brimming with ladies and gentlemen, all of whom seemed very fashionable and sophisticated to Lucy. She was a little overcome at meeting so many new people all at once. Drew Marlbeck's friends seemed to be mostly wealthy men and women of the world, educated, polished and a little awesome to a young girl. They had all been kind to Lucy, especially some of the gentlemen, who paid her pretty compliments, but she could not help feeling slightly unsure in their company. It made her wonder about her Season in London, because she was afraid that she might feel overwhelmed by some of the very fashionable ladies she was sure to meet there.

* * *

Once the guests had returned to Marlbeck and the reception was underway, Lucy took the first opportunity to escape. Marianne's house was beautiful, but Lucy loved being outside, especially on such a pleasant afternoon. It was warm, but not overpoweringly hot as she wandered across the lawn to what was the beginning of a large park. Here, there were wonderful old trees with sweeping branches that offered a perch. Lucy had discovered that she could climb up into an ancient oak tree quite easily and watch what was going on around her without being seen. It was a favourite place, and she gathered her white muslin gown up so as not to catch it on protruding branches, climbing into the canopy of leaves and settling down on a thick branch.

From her vantage spot she could see the back of the house. One or two ladies had come out to stroll on the terrace, their delicate lace parasols raised to protect their fair skins from the sun. Lucy was for ever being scolded for going without a hat, as she had today, for, as Mama had often told her, freckles were not admired.

Lucy had a faint sprinkling of them across her nose. Mama had prepared her own lotions, and even bought some Denmark Lotion from the apothecary, but nothing had worked. It seemed that she was doomed to have them as soon as the summer came.

Lost in her dreams, Lucy was not aware of the dog until it barked fiercely. She looked down, dismayed as she saw the huge black hound at the foot of the tree. It was growling, its front paws against the trunk, as if it were considering climbing up after her.

'Go away!' Lucy said. 'Do not growl like that, you horrid thing! I do not know how you came here, but you do not belong in this place. Go away!'

The dog barked louder than ever. It had heavy jaws and looked as if it were some kind of hunting hound, trained to attack. Lucy felt a flutter of nerves in her stomach, because she knew that she dared not climb down while the dog continued to stand guard at the base of the tree. A similar animal had once bitten her as a child, and, though generally not afraid of dogs, she was frightened of this particular beast.

'Lucy...where are you?' Jo had come out on to the terrace at the back of the house and was clearly looking for her. Lucy hesitated to call her, because if the dog was wild it might attack her sister. 'Lucy, Mama wants you.'

Jo returned to the house, obviously thinking that Lucy was not in the gardens. Lucy moved gingerly, wondering if she could get down, but immediately the dog started barking its head off once more.

'Oh, do go away, you horrid creature! I want to get down.'

'Come down if you wish, Brutus will not hurt you,' a voice said from somewhere behind her. Lucy glanced over her shoulder and saw a gentleman riding a horse in her direction. As she watched, he halted a few yards from her tree. 'Here, boy! Down, I say. Come here!'

The dog immediately obeyed. It sat at its master's command, and though it turned its head to watch her as she climbed out of the tree, it neither barked nor sprang at her—though she was sure that it would have done had the man commanded it to do so.

'I was alarmed,' she said, settling her skirts about her and realising that he must have had a clear view of her legs as she climbed down. Indeed, she suspected that he might even have caught a glimpse of the lace garters that held up her white silk stockings. 'He is a fierce-looking creature.'

'I fear his looks do not pity him,' the man said, a smile on his lips, for he had been treated to a view not often granted by properly brought-up young ladies, as he was certain she actually was despite being in the tree. 'But I promise you he has the softest mouth. He is trained to retrieve game when it has been shot, and it is unlike him to behave so ungallantly towards a lady. I dare say he thought you were up to no good up there.' He glanced up at the broad branch on which she had been perched. 'You must admit, it is rather an unlikely place to find a young lady of breeding.'

'Yes…' Lucy's cheeks were on fire. She was well aware that her behaviour was not what it ought to be. 'Mama would scold me if she knew. I have been asked not to climb trees in future, though I often did so as a child. I am too old for such larks now.'

'Indeed?' He gave her an indulgent look, clearly thinking her still a child. 'How old are you—sixteen?'

'I was eighteen two weeks ago,' Lucy said and hardly dared to look at him. He would think her a hoyden, and in truth she was. 'Mama is to take me to London in a few weeks for my first Season.'

'You surprise me. I had thought you younger. You will need to curb your inclinations for tree climbing once you are introduced into London society, young lady, otherwise you will incur the censure of its hostesses, and that would be a shame. It would be a pity if you did not meet with the success you deserve.' He turned to look at the dog. 'Brutus, follow!'

He gave his reins a flick and rode off, following the drive round to the stable block, which was away to the right. The dog trotted behind obediently and Lucy drew a breath of relief as she fled back across the lawns to the safety of the house.

She was certain she knew who the gentleman was, though she had not seen him since Marianne's wedding. Her pulses raced, because she had not expected that Lord Harcourt would come to the christening. He was, of course, one of Drew's best friends, but she had not met him here before and had not thought him in the habit of visiting.

Oh, why did it have to be he who found her in the tree? Lucy bit her lip in vexation, because she knew that he had thought the incident amusing. And, indeed, she did feel very foolish. She wished that she had not been caught in such an undignified situation. He must think her a foolish little girl—and in truth she had behaved like one! Lucy's cheeks were warm as she went into the house, running upstairs to her own room. She must make sure that her gown was not dirty or torn before she rejoined the company! But she feared that the damage was already done.

Lucy did not see Lord Harcourt again until she came down for dinner that evening. He had changed into formal dress and looked impressive in his black coat and breeches, his shirt a pristine white rivalled only by the snowiness of his cravat, which had been tied in an intricate design. Since she knew he had arrived alone, she wondered if he had tied it himself, but of course his valet might have come on with his baggage in a coach.

She felt nervous as he looked in her direction, but gave no indication that they had met earlier. He was standing with Drew and Marianne at that moment, clearly at home with them, laughing at something Marianne had said to him. She hesitated, afraid to join the little group, though she longed to know if she was right about his identity.

'Ah, there you are, my dearest,' Mrs Horne said, smiling at her. 'Have you met Lord Harcourt yet? He arrived too late for the service, but Marianne said he has been very generous. He gave her some beautiful pearls to keep for Andrea's sixteenth birthday and also a piece of silver for herself. Was that not kind of him?'

'Yes, it was,' Lucy said, trembling inside. She watched him as he moved away from Drew, going to speak to some of the other guests. Her memory of him was not quite accurate, because she had remembered him as very handsome, but he was not truly so. He was tall and strongly built, and there was no evidence of fat; his hair was dark, cut short and brushed forward in a fashionable peak. His features were classical, a little harsh perhaps, his nose aristocratic. No, not as handsome as either Drew Marlbeck or Hal Beverley, but attractive just the same. She did not know what it was about him that had made her remember him until he suddenly looked at her with his serious grey eyes and her heart jolted. 'Very kind, Mama.'

'Come and meet him, dearest,' her mother said. 'I would not wish you to be backward in any attention to Lord Harcourt. I know Drew thinks very highly of him.'

'Yes, Mama. I remembered that he was of service to both Drew and Hal.' She understood from her sisters that Captain Manton, as he had been known then, was a very brave and clever man. Manton was one of his family names, for as a peer he had many, and if what Drew had told her was true, he had not hesitated to use others that were false in the pursuit of his duty as a secret agent.

Lucy was trembling inside as she followed her mother to join the little group. The ladies were smiling and laughing up at him, especially Miss Angela Tremaine. She was a redhead, extremely beautiful, and a considerable heiress, and she seemed much taken with Lord Harcourt.

Lucy stood silently as her mama made the introductions, her cheeks slightly pink. She knew that people said she was a very pretty girl, because of her silvery blonde hair and azure eyes, but she felt at a disadvantage beside the vibrancy of Miss Tremaine. Surely he would think her an insipid child against such ravishing beauty?

'Miss Lucy Horne?' Lord Harcourt smiled down at her. 'I seem to recall that we might have met at Drew's wedding. I believe you fetched me a piece of wedding cake and then ate it yourself.'

Lucy flushed but gave him an indignant look. 'You told me I should eat it, for you did not eat cake, sir!'

'So I did,' Jack Harcourt said and gave a husky chuckle, which sent little shivers winging through Lucy's entire body. 'Do you still eat two portions of cake, Miss Horne? If you do, I cannot see where it goes, for you are a sylph and as pretty as a picture.'

Lucy smiled at the compliment, and yet it was the way an indulgent uncle would speak to his young niece, which gave her a sense of disappointment. It was obvious that he still saw her as a child and not a young lady about to make her début in society. She knew that he must be several years her senior, but she did not see why he should treat her as a child and it touched a raw nerve. Just because she had climbed into a tree, it did not mean she was a little girl!

Fortunately for Lucy, she was spared the necessity of making a reply, because dinner was announced and Lord Harcourt offered his arm to Miss Tremaine. Lucy accompanied her mother into the dining room, stifling the little pang of jealousy she felt as she watched Lord Harcourt being attentive to his dinner partner, holding her chair and smiling as she settled down.

Lucy found herself sitting opposite them, between two elderly gentlemen, both of whom were great friends of Drew's. They went out of their way to engage Lucy in conversation and after a few minutes she had forgotten her embarrassment earlier and was laughing and answering their teasing questions. Her eyes were alight with laughter and she could have had no idea of how enchanting she looked, nor did she consider that, seated as she was, it gave Lord Harcourt a perfect view of her.

Hearing a sudden burst of laughter from across the table, Jack's eyes were drawn to Lucy's face. She had seemed an awkward child earlier, but now she sparkled, responding to the gentlemen on either side of her in a way that was entirely charming. Jack thought that she reminded him a little of his sister as she had been when she was a young girl, innocent, full of the joy of living and lovely. The thought brought a frown to his face, his eyes narrowing, making him look severe. Amelia had lost the joy of living some time ago.

When Lucy glanced across at him what she saw was disapproval and it made her cheeks warm. What had she done that he should look at her that way? She had always remembered him as being charming and kind, for at Marianne's wedding he *had* been kind to her, but now he looked as if he disliked her. She raised her head, pride coming to her rescue.

She knew that she had behaved badly earlier; she ought not to have climbed into a tree, and must have revealed much more than was decent as she climbed down from it—but surely she did not deserve to be looked at in that way? She turned to her neighbour, who was asking her what she thought of Lord Byron's latest poem, determined not to let anyone see that she was hurting inside.

What a fool she had been to keep Lord Harcourt's image in her mind all this time! He had been her hero, the prince she had dreamed of as a child when she had read all those fairy stories. Now she decided that he was proud and cold, and she decided that she would not think of him again.

Lucy had been lying awake for some time. Realising that she would not sleep, she threw back the covers and got out of bed. She slipped on a heavy silk dressing gown and slid her feet into a pair of soft leather slippers.

Taking her lighted candle, Lucy went downstairs to the little parlour where she had sat with her sister and mother for an hour or so earlier that day. She had left her book there and hoped that reading it would help her fall asleep.

As she entered the room, she felt a cool breeze; looking towards the French windows, she saw that they were open. That was odd, for it was unlike the servants to leave them open when they went to bed. She walked towards them, intending to close them, and then gave a little jump as a man's figure loomed up out of the darkness.

'Lord Harcourt!' she cried as he entered and she saw him clearly. 'I am glad it was you. I thought we might have an intruder.'

His eyes narrowed, going over her, taking in the fact that she was wearing a dressing gown over her night attire. 'What are you doing down here, Miss Horne? I thought you retired long ago?'

'Yes, I did,' Lucy agreed. 'But I could not sleep so I came down to fetch my book.'

'Then we were both restless,' he said. 'I could not sleep either. I went out for a walk—and to smoke a cigar...' His gaze was intent on her face. 'I think it was fortunate for your sake that it was I you met on this nocturnal expedition...otherwise it might have proved embarrassing for you, to say the least.'

'Oh...' Lucy blushed, becoming aware that she was behaving in a decidedly improper manner by talking to a gentleman she hardly knew when she was dressed in her night-clothes. 'I must go back to my room, sir. I hope you will find it easier to sleep after your walk.' She turned and walked from the room clutching her book, her heart racing.

'Goodnight, Lucy…' His voice seemed to float after her, making her feel a little odd as she fled up the stairs to her own room. Once again she had the feeling that Lord Harcourt thought of her as a foolish young woman.

Jack Harcourt frowned as he sought his own room, taking a candle from the hall, where several were still burning, though the night porter had fallen asleep in his chair. He was thoughtful as he walked upstairs to his room. He had been startled to find Miss Horne wearing only her night attire. It was often his habit to walk for a while at night, especially when he had something on his mind. He had perhaps been a little sharp with her, for his thoughts were elsewhere, but it *was* unwise of her to wander about in that state at this hour—particularly when there were male guests. Some of those guests might not have been above trying to snatch a clandestine kiss—or more!

She might not be aware of it, but Lucy was a delightful young girl, very pretty, and the glimpse of her legs he had received as she climbed down from the tree was enticing, for she had lovely slender limbs. He thought her an enchanting child, perhaps a little shy still and completely innocent—as his sister had once been! Thoughts of Amelia brought a frown to his face, for Amelia's innocence had been abused and that was the cause of her desperate unhappiness. He dismissed thoughts of his sister for the moment. It was useless to dwell on the past, and he had other concerns.

Jack had many friends and acquaintances, all of whom he was happy to meet at social occasions, but there was no one quite like David Middleton. They had grown up together, sharing their boyhood dreams and adventures, more like brothers than friends.

David's death had been like a blow to the stomach, driving the breath from his body and leaving Jack feeling devastated.

Since receiving that mysterious letter, he had made some inquiries and what he had discovered had led him to believe that David might have fallen in with an evil crowd of sharks and heavy gamblers. If they had tried to cheat him of his fortune, David would not have taken it without a fight, and he now believed that perhaps the gamblers had killed him and dumped his body on the Heath. Collingwood was certainly one of the men David had been gambling with in the weeks immediately before his death, though there was no proof yet that he had had anything to do with his murder. The official view was still that David had been set upon by a highwayman on the Heath and robbed.

Jack frowned, for it made him angry to think that his friend might have been murdered over a card game—and yet was that the real reason? Jack was uncertain. He was determined to get to the bottom of the mystery somehow for he could not rest until he knew the truth. Even here, amongst his friends, he was uneasy, for something was nagging at him, something that made him think that there was more to this affair than he yet guessed, though he could not say why. If Jack was right, it had something to do with an entirely different matter, which meant the tale about a quarrel over gambling was merely a blind.

Oh, damn it! There was nothing he could do for the moment. He had come here to enjoy himself with his friends, and this other business could wait until he returned to London.

A smile flickered about his mouth as he thought of young Lucy Horne once more. In another life, before he had become disillusioned and hardened, he might have found her irresistible, but that time was long past. He knew that he owed it to his family to marry one day, but when he did he would choose an older woman, perhaps a widow who had no great expectations. He needed an heir, but he had become accustomed to being single and did not imagine a life of domestic bliss would suit him. He had a mistress, whom he visited when he felt the need, which was not often, for he had been too busy to indulge himself in the pleasures of life. As for marriage, he had not given it a thought until recently. Even now, it was something that he saw as being a long way off. His experience of personal relationships had not been encouraging and he rather thought that he was better off single, even if at times he was conscious of a great gap in his life. And marriage to a gentle, sweet girl was out of the question! He was mad even to think about it. Charming as she undoubtedly was, Miss Horne was not for him.

Dismissing Lucy from his mind, he walked along the upper landing to his own bedchamber. He would stay three days, as he had promised Marianne and Drew, but then he would return to London and the pursuit of the man who he believed responsible for David's death.

Lucy was up early. She had slept for a while after returning to bed, but the sunshine pouring in at her open window called to her and she knew that she could go for a walk before anyone else was stirring.

She walked as far as the lake, which lay glistening in the early morning sunshine, entirely tempting and mysterious. There was a little island in the middle of the lake, and a temple that looked like something out of a fairytale. Lucy looked at it longingly, for she would have liked to visit it to explore, though of course it was only small and she doubted there were any secrets. However, in her mind the summerhouse was a palace where a sleeping prince lay waiting to be awakened after the wicked witch had cast a spell on him.

Had there been a rowing boat nearby, Lucy might have

been tempted to try and row herself out there. But the boats were kept in the boathouse for safety's sake and she did not wish to disturb anyone this early in the morning, because the servants would be busy with their work. She sighed and turned, intending to return to the house, only to discover that Lord Harcourt was standing a little way behind her. He was staring at the lake, apparently lost in thought.

She breathed deeply and then took a few steps towards him. 'Good morning, sir. I think it will be very warm today. Just right for a trip to the island, do you not think?'

'Yes, perhaps,' Jack replied, focusing on her. 'The water looks tempting—especially if it becomes hot later. At home I should probably go for a swim on a day such as this promises to be.'

'It would be delightful,' Lucy said. 'I have sometimes bathed in the cove at home, though I do not swim—but I like to splash in the shallows.' She gave him a shy smile. 'The island looks as if it might be enchanted, do you not think so? Perhaps there is a sleeping prince—or princess—waiting to be woken from slumber?'

'Ridiculous child,' Jack said in an indulgent tone. 'I can see that you have read too many fairy stories, Miss Horne. I fear that you will discover life is very different. Are you sure you are eighteen? Your mama should think twice before taking you into London society—I think you are too innocent to mix with the rogues you may find there.'

'I know that life can be sad as well as happy,' Lucy replied, lifting her head proudly, because his tone stung her. 'I have helped out with various events to alleviate the condition of the poor—not only of this country, but others abroad. Papa taught us to think of people less fortunate than ourselves, and I am not ignorant of the evils of poverty.'

'I was not thinking of the plight of the poor,' Jack said. It was on the tip of his tongue to tell her exactly what he did mean, but he held back. He ought not to be the one to disillusion her. Her mama would no doubt warn her of the kind of men who led young innocents astray. 'But it is to your credit that you do, Miss Horne.' He smiled at her, his mood relenting. 'Come, let us walk back to the house. I believe your sister Mrs Beverley has written some stories for children, has she not?'

'Oh, yes,' Lucy said, giving him an enchanting smile. 'She wrote them for me, you know, because I had always loved fairy stories—but Hal had them published for her as a wedding gift. She has written a few more, I believe, but she does not have much time these days, for they are always so busy entertaining their friends.'

'Yes, I dare say.' Jack nodded. 'I understand there is to be a ball tomorrow evening? Shall you be there?'

'Yes, of course,' Lucy said, her lovely eyes glowing. 'Marianne arranged it because she said it would be good for me to attend my first real dance at her home. I have danced at the homes of my friends, of course, but this is my first ball.'

'Then you must be looking forward to it?' Jack was caught despite himself. She was a lovely girl, very young and naïve, of course, but with a pleasing manner. 'Tell me, what colour is your gown—or is that a secret?'

Lucy blushed as she saw the teasing look in his eyes. He seemed very much more approachable this morning, and she was reminded of the man who had attended her sister's wedding. He had seemed to be more carefree then and it made her wonder what had changed him, for something had—and it had taken the devil-may-care look from his eyes.

'It is white with silver spangles,' she said. 'And Mama has loaned me her pearls, though I have a pretty pearl-and-diamond bangle of my own that Drew gave me for my birthday.'

'Yes, charming,' Jack said, making a note to send her a posy of white flowers—or perhaps pink ones tied with white ribbons. 'Well, Miss Horne, I think we should join the others for breakfast, don't you?'

Lucy nodded, feeling shy again. She usually waited until her mama came down to take breakfast, but did not wish to tell him that. After all, how difficult could it be to join the other early risers and talk in an easy and companionable way? She lifted her head, determined that she would give no indication that she was nervous, even if her mama and sisters had not yet come down.

Chapter Two

Lucy felt pleased with herself as she went upstairs a little later that morning. Far from feeling out of place, she had enjoyed being fussed over by the gentlemen who had come down early to take breakfast. She had not been allowed to help herself, but was waited on by one elderly gentleman who called her 'my pretty' and piled her plate with tempting morsels from the chafing dishes. Another had filled her tiny cup with coffee and yet another had set her chair.

She had thoroughly enjoyed the sensation of being fussed over, until she had seen Lord Harcourt watching her with what she felt was disapproval in his eyes. However, he had said nothing and somehow the suggestion of boating on the lake and a picnic on the island had come up, which everyone had thought a good idea. By the time Marianne entered the room, it had all but been arranged.

'Yes, that is a lovely idea,' Marianne said when it was suggested to her. 'The island isn't large, but because of all the trees and the temple, it is nice to walk there on a hot afternoon. I shall have a picnic prepared. We will have that by the lake, but the boats will be available for anyone who wishes to visit.'

'Oh, how lovely,' Lucy said, her face lighting up with pleasure. 'I have been wanting to explore ever since we came here, Marianne.'

'You should have said, dearest,' Marianne told her. 'Drew would have been delighted to take you there. The lake was unremarkable until we took up residence here, you know. He had it enlarged and the island created and it has made all the difference.'

'May I be one of your party, Miss Lucy?' General Rawlings asked, smiling at her. 'I should like to explore the island in your company, m'dear.'

'Yes, of course,' Lucy replied, for he had been very kind to her during her stay here. 'But I expect everyone will want to see it.'

'It is an enchanted place,' Jack said, surprising her and himself. 'I dare say there may be a sleeping prince to discover—or perhaps elves and witches.'

Lucy looked at him in surprise, thinking that he must be mocking her, but she discovered that he had a look of mischief in his eyes. Her heart started to race wildly, for in that moment he had become the man she had loved since they first met.

'You would not be the first to think that,' Marianne told him, joining in the laughter. 'We hold treasure hunts there at Easter for the estate children, and it is surprising what tales they tell.'

After that, the conversation had turned to estate matters, and the problems associated with educating the children of labourers. Marianne had recently set up a school for the children of parents who could not afford to pay, and she liked to visit now and then to see how they were getting on with their teacher. Lucy listened quietly, unaware that Lord Harcourt's gaze dwelled on her face for some minutes before he got up and excused himself to the company.

Lucy stayed on for a while, excusing herself only after her mama had joined the company, whispering in her ear that Jo was feeling a little unwell and staying in bed until later. She had asked if her young sister would visit her in her bedchamber, and Lucy was very willing to oblige her.

She tapped at her sister's door, entering after she was invited to find Jo sitting up against a pile of silken pillows, a breakfast tray almost untouched on the table beside her, and some letters lying unopened on the bed.

'Do you feel very poorly, dearest?' Lucy asked, dismayed to see Jo looking pale.

'It is just a little morning sickness,' Jo told her. 'I could not face my breakfast and Hal insisted that I stay in bed until noon. I do not wish to disoblige him for I know that my child is important to both Hal and Lord Beverley.'

'Will Hal mind if the child is not a boy, Jo?'

'He says that he does not care either way, as long as I am well—but I know that Lord Beverley longs for an heir and I hope that I shall have a son. Marianne's little girl is beautiful, and I should like a girl one day—but Lord Beverley's health is precarious, and he already has a granddaughter.'

'Yes, I know.' Lucy said and smiled. 'Lord Beverley dotes on Ellen and little Mattie, but he must hope that you and Hal will give him grandsons.'

'He pretends not to mind, as long as I am well, but I know he hopes that my first-born will be a boy,' Jo said and patted the bed for her sister to join her. 'I do not mind, because I want to have several children.'

'I expect you will,' Lucy said, because she knew that her strong-minded sister usually achieved what she wanted in the end. 'We are going on the lake this afternoon, and I want to explore the island. Shall you come with us?'

'I think I shall stay on shore, but I shall watch you all from a comfortable chair,' Jo said and smiled at her. 'You may have my biscuits if you wish, Lucy.'

Lucy laughed softly, remembering the times she had stolen her sister's breakfast when they were all at home. 'Thank you, dearest Jo, but I couldn't eat another thing. I had breakfast downstairs today and General Rawlings gave me far too much, but I ate as much as I could, because I did not wish to appear ungrateful.'

'General Rawlings?' Jo frowned, because, although he was a pleasant man, he was much older than her sister and she knew that he was looking for a wife, having buried his second wife some nine months earlier. 'Be a little careful, dearest. He is much too old for you—and he has five children by his first two wives.'

Lucy shot her a look of pure astonishment. 'Oh, Jo, you do not think…?' She went off into a peal of delighted laughter. 'Poor General Rawlings! I am sure he has no such idea. He would not want to marry me. I am far too young for him.'

'Some gentlemen like very young ladies,' Jo warned her. 'Be careful not to get caught in a compromising situation with him, Lucy. I do not think he would make you happy—and you do not wish to cast a shadow over your reputation.' Jo's cheeks were slightly pink. 'I know that I behaved a little recklessly when I ran off with Hal and Ellen, but it was different for me.'

'Yes, because you were in love with him,' Lucy agreed and frowned. 'Thank you for warning me, Jo. I had thought he was just being kind, but I see now that I must be a little careful. I shall make sure that there are others present when we go to explore the island.'

Lucy's eyes had been opened by her sister's warning, and when the boats were being made up, she made certain that

Miss Tremaine, Lord Harcourt and another lady were in the same boat as General Rawlings and herself. Once on the island, the little group set off together, following the paths through the trees and tall rhododendron bushes to the centre of the island where the little temple was situated.

Miss Tremaine took Lord Harcourt's arm in a proprietary way, so Lucy followed with General Rawlings and the others walked behind them as the boat returned to the shore to pick up another party.

The rhododendrons were in flower as were some azaleas and camellias, their blossoms a riot of reds, oranges and pinks. Lucy was delighted with all she saw—it was a pretty place, quiet and peaceful, populated by a variety of birds, who fluttered anxiously through the trees as their haven was invaded. She gave a little cry of delight as they came upon the little temple, running towards it to investigate.

It had been built of white marble to resemble a Grecian temple and was open to the elements on all sides, though there were little benches where it was possible to sit for a while if one cared to. Lucy thought it lovely, though in a way it had been more romantic when it remained a mystery at the heart of the little island. She sat down on the bench, smiling at Lord Harcourt as he came up to her.

'I fear you must be disappointed, Miss Horne,' he teased. 'No sleeping prince for you to awaken—or elves and witches.'

'But it is an enchanted place just the same,' Lucy replied, looking up at him. 'Do you not think so?'

'Perhaps…for some,' Jack replied. 'I think the company one finds oneself in is all important…' He turned his head as Miss Tremaine joined them, though she did not sit down on the marble bench. 'Does the island please you, Miss Tremaine?'

'Oh, it is pretty enough,' she replied with an air of boredom and twirled her elegant parasol. 'I have seen others as interesting—perhaps more so. I understand that you have had your own grounds landscaped, Lord Harcourt. Do you have a lake?'

'Yes, though I do not have an island. We have some extensive woods, however,' Jack replied and for a moment his expression darkened as he recalled the old woodcutter's hut that had featured in the games he and David had once played.

'I have heard that you have a magnificent water feature—based on something you saw at Versailles?'

'Oh, it is not anything like as grand, though I like to think it fits my estate rather better than something larger,' Jack said. 'But I also have a wild garden—or a wilderness, as my head gardener is pleased to call it.'

'How exciting,' Miss Tremaine said. 'Shall we go back, sir? I have seen enough of this.'

Jack offered her his arm and they began to stroll in the direction of the landing place. The other lady and gentleman had gone a few seconds earlier, and Lucy suddenly found herself alone with General Rawlings.

'So we have this enchanted place to ourselves, m'dear,' he said, giving her a look that made Lucy suddenly a little uncomfortable. Remembering her sister's warning, she got up to follow the others, but he caught her arm, turning her to face him. 'No, don't run off, my pretty. I have been hoping to get you to myself for a little while.'

'I think we should join the others,' Lucy said her heart beating faster. Something about the way he was looking at her was unsettling. She had thought him a harmless gentleman, but now she was not so sure. 'The boat will have to come back for us otherwise.'

'Let it,' he said, his finger caressing her bare arm. 'You must be aware that I find you very attractive, Miss Lucy. In fact, I have been thinking of making you—'

'Miss Horne!' Lord Harcourt's voice cut across General Rawlings's words. 'I believe we should return to the shore. Miss Tremaine is impatient to join the others.'

'Yes, of course.' Lucy flushed and pulled away from her companion, going to join him. She gave him a grateful smile, but was chilled by the expression in his eyes. He was angry! 'Thank you for reminding us, but we were just coming.'

'Go on ahead and get into the boat,' Lord Harcourt said. He turned to the other man as Lucy obeyed swiftly. 'She is too young and innocent, Rawlings. You would do well to remember that!'

'Damn you for your insolence, sir! My intentions are nothing but honourable. I was about to propose marriage.'

'Indeed?' Jack gave him a hard stare. 'I repeat—she is too young and innocent. You should look elsewhere for your third wife, sir.'

'You are in no position to censure me from what I hear,' Rawlings said, giving him a look of dislike. 'At least all of my children were born in wedlock.'

Jack smiled, but there was a hint of menace in his eyes. 'Listening to scandalous tales is a fool's errand. I would not advise you to pass on lies, sir—unless you are willing to face the consequences.'

General Rawlings turned pale. 'I am not the only one to believe it,' he blustered. 'If I have it wrong, I apologise.'

'Accepted,' Jack said and turned away. His face was dark with anger as he followed Lucy to the landing stage, where the others were waiting in the boat. He did not look at Lucy as he joined them in the boat. Nor did he speak to anyone as they were rowed back to the shore.

Lucy was painfully aware of his anger, and, knowing nothing of what had caused it, she believed that he was angry with her. He must despise her for being foolish enough to find herself in a difficult position; indeed, she blamed herself, for Jo had warned her.

She felt close to tears, but held her head high. She would not let anyone guess that Lord Harcourt's disapproval had distressed her so dreadfully.

'You look very pretty, dearest,' Mrs Horne said when Lucy emerged from her bedroom on the evening of the ball. 'Who sent you that charming posy?'

'It was from Lord Harcourt,' Lucy replied. 'It goes so well with my hair band, does it not?' On receiving the pink roses tied with white ribbons, Lucy had tied her long hair back with a pink-spangled ribbon. She looked fresh and lovely, and very young.

'That was kind of him,' Mrs Horne said, smiling at her. She was very proud of her daughter, for she knew that, despite her innocence, Lucy was a sensible girl and would not let something so trivial turn her head. 'Shall we go down now, Lucy?' Besides, although she had heard rumours concerning Lord Harcourt, she was not yet disposed to believe them.

'Yes, Mama.' Lucy looked at her mother. 'Did you say that it would be proper for me to dance the waltz, Mama?'

'Perfectly proper at your sister's ball,' Mrs Horne said. 'But when we go to Almack's next month, you must wait until you are given permission from one of the hostesses. However, waltzing is perfectly acceptable almost everywhere now, my love.'

Lucy nodded. She had heard her sisters talk of waltzing and had not been quite sure whether it was accepted or not. Her heart beat a little faster as she wondered if Lord Harcourt would ask her to dance. If he should ask her to waltz...but she must not expect it. She was well aware that he saw her as a child and believed that he was attracted to Miss Tremaine, who took every opportunity to monopolise his attention. When the dazzling beauty of Miss Tremaine was on hand, why would he bother with Lucy?

The ballroom was already filling up when Lucy arrived with her mama. Marianne and Drew had been welcoming their guests for the past few minutes, and there were already some twenty couples besides the house-guests who were staying. For a while Mrs Horne moved amongst them, introducing Lucy to people she knew, and meeting others she had not met previously, but after some ten minutes or so the music struck up.

Lucy immediately found herself the centre of attention, and her dance card was soon filled. She danced first with General Rawlings. It was a country dance and Lucy was pleased because it meant that she passed on to other partners. She had already decided that she would not waltz with that particular gentleman if he should ask her.

Lord Harcourt danced the first two sets with Miss Tremaine. He approached Lucy as she returned to her mama's side, asking for the pleasure of the next dance, which she was unable to offer him.

'I fear I have nothing left until...the dance before supper,' she said, looking at him shyly. 'Perhaps...'

'I should not have dallied,' Jack said and looked slightly rueful. 'Yes, that will do very well, Miss Horne—and I believe it may be a waltz, which will be all the better.'

Lucy's heart raced. She had hoped that they might waltz together, never dreaming her wish would be granted. However, she could do little more than smile and promise she would keep it for him before she was claimed for the next dance.

Her partners were all kind, generous gentlemen, many of

them married and much older than Lucy. However, she did dance with four gentlemen who were more her own age, and they stayed with her for most of the evening, forming a little court about her when she was not dancing and making her laugh. She enjoyed herself more than she had expected, and when Jo asked her if she was having a good time she was able to answer quite truthfully that she was very happy. However, she could not control a flutter of nerves as the supper dance approached, and when Lord Harcourt came towards her, she caught her breath. He was so very handsome, so much more assured and worldly than the young gallants who had kept her company all evening.

'I believe this is my dance, Miss Horne?'

'Yes, sir,' she replied and gave him her hand.

As he took it and led her onto the floor, her heart was beating wildly. She hoped that her emotions did not show on her face, because she would not have liked him to guess that his touch affected her so deeply, making her tremble inside. She lifted her head, an unconscious look of pride in her eyes as the music struck up and he took her into his arms.

Dancing with Jack Harcourt was all that Lucy had dreamed of and more. The feeling that came over her was like nothing she had ever experienced before, excelling all her childhood dreams. She had wondered what it might be like to be held by him, but she could never have imagined the swirling emotions inside her, the heady sensation of dancing on air, or being swept away to a magical place. But this was not the magic of her childhood dreams. Lucy knew instinctively that what she felt for Lord Harcourt was love—the kind of love a woman feels for the man she wishes to be her husband.

For the duration of their dance, she allowed herself to float over the floor in his arms, lost to reality. She had never known passion or lust, never been kissed other than on the cheek by her relatives or friends, but something deep within her was responding to an age-old need that she had never even guessed existed until this moment.

She wished that she could go on dancing with him for ever, wished that this wonderful experience might never end, but all too soon the music was finishing and everyone began to make a move towards the supper room.

'Perhaps you would like some supper, Miss Horne?' Jack suggested, but at that moment Lucy's mama came up to them.

'Well, my dear, I am glad to see you looking so happy,' Mrs Horne said. 'Come along, Lucy. I want you to help me choose my supper from the wonderful buffet Marianne has ordered for us.'

Lucy gave her partner an apologetic look. She would have preferred to take supper with him, but could not refuse her mama's request. He inclined his head as if to say that he understood, and she turned away, following in her mother's wake. In the supper room she was invited to sit with a party of young people, and to her surprise her mama indicated that she might do so.

'Yes, run along, dearest. You do not need to look after me, for Jo will help me.'

Lucy was a little bewildered. Why had her mama insisted that she accompany her, only to release her almost at once? Joining the other young people, Lucy hoped that Lord Harcourt would not be offended. However, a few minutes later, she saw that he was at the buffet with Miss Tremaine. He was laughing in response to something she was saying, and Lucy felt a pang of regret. She would have enjoyed eating her supper with Lord Harcourt.

'Is something wrong, Miss Horne?'

Lucy turned to the young man sitting beside her. He was fair-haired, about twenty years of age, and attractive.

'Nothing, thank you, Mr Tristram,' Lucy said. 'I was thinking of something, but it is not important.' She turned her bright eyes on him. 'Have you enjoyed this evening?'

'Yes,' he agreed with a slight flush in his cheeks. 'More than I expected. These country dances are often boring, you know—but you were here this evening and that made all the difference.'

'Oh…' Lucy felt her cheeks grow warm. 'How kind of you to say so, sir—though I do not see how my presence could make so much difference.'

'Do you not?' He grinned at her. 'No, I suppose not. I dare say you have no idea how beautiful you are.'

'Beautiful…' Lucy's laugh tinkled like fairy bells. 'Oh, no, you cannot mean that, sir. I have been told that I am pretty, but beautiful…' Her gaze fell on Miss Tremaine. 'Now *she* is beautiful.'

John Tristram's eyes followed in direction of her gaze and he frowned. 'She is very striking,' he agreed. 'But that kind of beauty is skin deep, for I think she is a little shallow, whereas you—' He broke off, looking awkward as Lucy's brow furrowed. 'I hope I have not offended you, Miss Lucy?'

'No, of course not,' Lucy said and wrinkled her nose endearingly. 'Is she shallow? I think perhaps you are a little critical, Mr Tristram.'

'Yes, perhaps—and I should not have said it,' he replied. 'But in my opinion she cannot hold a candle to you.'

'Oh…that is kind,' Lucy said, giving him a radiant smile. 'I have felt a little awkward in her presence, for she seems so clever…so vibrant.'

'Yes, she is clever,' he acknowledged, 'though sometimes at the expense of others—which I think cruel. You would never be unkind, Miss Lucy.'

The expression in his eyes was little short of adoring,

which made Lucy blush and look away. She liked him very well, and his compliments were a boost to her confidence, but she was an honest girl and she knew that she could never feel anything more than friendship for him.

'Do you hunt, Mr Tristram?' she asked, because it was a subject that usually turned the gentlemen's conversation and it did not fail her now. For the next few minutes he regaled her with stories of his hunting experiences, and then the conversation became general.

The company began to drift back to the ballroom. Some of the guests, who had farther to go, had started to take their leave, but others continued to dance, and Lucy was one of them. She was claimed by Drew and then by Hal Beverley, and was one of the last to leave the ballroom. As she went upstairs, she saw that Lord Harcourt and Miss Tremaine had gone out into the conservatory, and her mood of elation was dimmed by the realisation that there was very likely an understanding between them.

Lucy refused to acknowledge the pain in her breast. She would be very silly to break her heart for a man who hardly knew she existed. He had been kind to her, but he thought her still a child. Miss Tremaine was some years older than Lucy, and an heiress. Why should he look at Lucy when Miss Tremaine was clearly so willing to be courted?

Lucy slept very well that night, undisturbed by dreams. Jack Harcourt was not as fortunate. He had accompanied Miss Tremaine to the conservatory to help look for a diamond earring she claimed to have lost, but when it remained elusive he had become aware of the expectant expression in her eyes.

'I fear I must have lost it elsewhere,' she said apologetically and looked up at him, her soft lips slightly parted. 'How foolish of me...'

'Perhaps it is not lost at all,' he replied. 'You may find it in your room later or caught within your clothing.'

'Oh, do you think so?' She pulled at the lace about her décolletage. 'Do you think it can have fallen down here?'

'I have no idea,' Jack told her, realising too late that his attentions during the evening had led her to expect a declaration. 'I think you must ask your mama to look—or search for it yourself in your room. It is not for me to speculate on such matters, Miss Tremaine.'

'I would not ask any gentleman,' she said huskily and looked at him with a clear invitation in her eyes. 'But you… It would not offend me—'

'It would offend my sense of decency where a young lady of respectable birth is concerned,' Jack replied harshly. 'Even if we had an understanding, which we do not, I should not expect such liberties until after the wedding. As I have no plans to marry just yet, I think we should bring this conversation to an end, Miss Tremaine.'

He had been too blunt, for she had turned bright red and rushed from the conservatory, leaving him wishing that he had chosen his words more carefully. Jack had not meant to offend her, and though she had pushed herself on him determinedly since his arrival, he had done nothing to discourage her. Indeed, she was very much the kind of lady he had been toying with the idea of marrying, because he believed she was unlikely to be easily hurt. She had come out four seasons ago, and had not yet married. He had no idea why, because she was beautiful and in possession of a small fortune, which should have been enough to secure her many offers. Either she had refused them all or for some reason her suitors had held back.

Dismissing Miss Tremaine from his thoughts, Jack went out into the garden to smoke a last cigar. He was thoughtful as he stared at the moon, remembering his dance with Miss

Horne, a faint smile on his lips. There was no doubt about it, she was an enchanting child—much too young for him, of course. Besides, her mama had clearly heard those damned rumours, for why else had she intervened when he had been about to invite Lucy to take supper with him? It annoyed him that the tales should be circulating, but there was nothing he could do to refute them.

She was a careful mother, and he did not fault her for that, because he knew what perils could lie in the path of an innocent whose mother—or rather stepmother—did not care enough to protect her. Mrs Horne would take some convincing that he was a fit person to court her daughter. He could, if he chose, set her mind at rest, but for the moment he did not care to—it was not his secret and he would keep it close to his chest, as he had promised. In any case, he had no intention of paying court to Lucy Horne—even if she was the most enchanting little thing he had seen in a long time.

He had stayed on for the ball, as he had promised Drew and Marianne he would, but there was nothing to keep him here now. He would bid his hosts farewell this evening, and leave first thing in the morning. There was something he needed to do in town…

Lucy did not rise as early as usual the next morning. Her mama had given instructions that she should be allowed to sleep on, and so it was past nine when she woke. She rose, went over to the window and drew the curtains, looking out at the gardens. The sun was already quite warm, and as she opened her window the scent of blossom came to her.

She knew that her mama, Aunt Bertha and Jo would all still be in their rooms. Marianne might be stirring, for she had always liked to walk early in the morning. Lucy decided to dress and go down, though she knew that her maid was waiting for her to ring. However, there was enough cold water in her jug, left over from the previous evening, to wash her hands and face, even though it made her shiver.

Once dressed in a simple muslin gown, she went downstairs, letting herself out into the garden. She had stopped to smell a dark red rose when she saw Marianne coming towards her, a basket of cut blooms over her arm.

'Are you up already, dearest?' Marianne asked. 'Mama said that you should be allowed to sleep in. I think she thought you would not rise before noon.'

'Oh, I like to be up early,' Lucy said. 'As you always have, Marianne.'

'Yes, we are alike in that,' her sister said with an affectionate look. 'Did you enjoy yourself last night, my love? I do not think you sat out one dance, did you?'

'No…' Lucy gave a gurgle of pleasure. 'Everyone was so kind to me, Marianne. I do not know if it was because I am your sister.'

'No, I am very sure it was not,' Marianne replied. 'You are lovely, dearest Lucy, both in form and nature.'

'Mr Tristram said something of the kind,' Lucy said with a blush. 'I danced the supper waltz with Lord Harcourt.' A little smile played about her soft mouth, for it had been the highlight of her evening.

'Yes, I know,' Marianne replied, a little frown creasing her brow. 'He left first thing this morning. I think he had offended Miss Tremaine. I saw her looking very angry after she left him last evening.'

'Oh…' Lucy hesitated, then, 'I thought perhaps he meant to ask her… I mean, that they might have an understanding…'

'I believe she may have thought that they did,' Marianne replied thoughtfully. 'Jack is sometimes unwise in his manner, and she did rather push herself on him, though he did nothing to discourage her. He is a flirt, of course. I have heard people say he is a rake, though I am not sure it is true, at least not these days. He may have his…arrangements, of course, but many unmarried gentlemen do. But it is more than that, I think. I have asked Drew, but he will not say.' She shook her head. 'It does not matter. I like him very well, and he is always generous.'

'Yes, he is kind. I have always thought so,' Lucy agreed. 'I am sorry he has gone. I did not get a chance to say goodbye to him.'

'Well, I dare say you may see him in London when you go up with Mama next week,' Marianne said. 'I believe he spends much of his time in London, though he has a large and very beautiful country house—and he is a wealthy landowner and has a respected title. I dare say that was what attracted Miss Tremaine. She has held out for a title, I believe, but so far none has come her way.'

'Oh…is that why she has not yet married?' Lucy looked thoughtful. 'It must be a consideration, I suppose, but I do not think it would be important if one loved a gentleman—do you, Marianne?'

'When I fell in love with Drew, I did not know he had a title and I did not think him rich,' Marianne said, smiling at the memory. 'He was posing as plain Mr Beck, and the boots he wore were quite disreputable. He still clings to them now, though his valet despairs of them and he has more than a dozen pairs of new ones.'

'Drew is Drew,' Lucy declared with a lilting laugh. 'There is no one like him, Marianne. Harry is very nice and kind, but Drew is wonderful. I am so glad that you fell in love with him, because I like to see you happy—and your little Andrea is gorgeous.'

'Yes, she is, isn't she?' Marianne said. 'Come, Lucy, let

us go in. We can go up to the nursery and see if she is awake, because early in the morning is the best time to play with her.'

The rest of Lucy's stay with Marianne and Drew flew by. Sometimes she caught herself thinking about Lord Harcourt, but she tried hard not to dwell on her feelings for him. After all, she had thought of him as her 'prince' for years without feeling heartache, and if she were strict with herself, she could pretend that nothing had changed, even though she knew that her childish dreams had become something very different. As a child she had dreamed of him, but it had all been far away, remaining just a dream, but now…seeing him, talking to him, dancing with him, had made her so much more aware of him as a man.

During her last afternoon at the Marlbeck estate, Lucy had a visitor. Mr Tristram came to call and she walked with him in the gardens for half an hour before tea. At first they spoke of inconsequential things, recalling the ball and talking of the lovely weather, which had remained fine for some days—and then he stopped walking and turned to look at her.

'So you go to London in the morning, Miss Lucy?'

'Yes, we leave first thing,' Lucy said. 'I believe we shall stop at an inn for one night—that is, Mama and I, of course. Aunt Bertha has decided to stay here and then return to her home in Cornwall. Marianne and Drew are to follow in a couple of days and we shall all be together for most of my stay in town.'

'That will be pleasant for you,' John Tristram said. He hesitated, then, 'May I call on you in a few days? I have decided to go up and stay with my uncle—Sir Michael Gerard.'

'I am sure we shall be delighted to see you,' Lucy said, though she blushed and looked down, because his gaze was rather intense. 'Oh, was that the gong? I think it must be time for tea.'

She was a little embarrassed and relieved that they would no longer be alone, for she was afraid that he might go on to say something that would cause her discomfort. She liked him very well, but she did not wish to hear a proposal of marriage from him.

'Yes, I think it was,' he said, looking relieved himself. She thought that perhaps he had lost his nerve at the last moment. 'Yes, we should go in.'

Several of Marianne's guests had gathered for tea, though most had departed. Lucy knew that the remaining few would take their leave later that day. General Rawlings was one of the last to leave, and he gave Lucy a sharp glance as she came in with Mr Tristram. She had done her best to avoid being alone with him since Jo had warned her that he was looking for a third wife to take charge of his children, and she believed that he had given up his hopes of her.

'Ah, there you are, m'dear,' he said as Miss Tremaine followed Lucy into the room. He stood up and went over to her, smiling down at her before clearing his throat. 'Have I your permission to tell everyone?'

'Yes, of course, Henry.' She gave him what looked to Lucy to be a forced smile. 'I think you should.'

'Miss Tremaine…Angela…has done me the honour to say that she will become my wife,' he announced, looking very pleased with himself as a stunned silence fell. 'I am of course the happiest man alive…never thought she would take me.'

Lucy was shocked, though she did her best to hide it. She had been certain that it was Lord Harcourt Miss Tremaine had had in mind as a husband, and she could hardly believe that she had settled for so much less. General Rawlings was a gentleman and quite respectable, his fortune adequate—but he was not an aristocrat and he could not match Lord Harcourt in looks or manner.

A little buzz of congratulations burst out. Lucy added hers to the general chorus, though she could not help wondering why Miss Tremaine had accepted his offer. She must surely have had others more favourable. However, it was not for Lucy to question and she kept her thoughts to herself.

It was only when she left the company to go upstairs and change for the evening that she suddenly found herself alone with Miss Tremaine.

'I dare say you are wondering why I have accepted General Rawlings,' she said, surprising Lucy by her directness. 'I had thought that I might accept Lord Harcourt—but Mama has heard unpleasant rumours, so I decided that I would marry a man of good reputation.'

'Oh…' Lucy wished that she might run away but it would be rude to do so. 'I was not wondering…'

The older girl frowned. 'I thought that you might rather like him yourself and that is why I decided to warn you. He is not to be trusted. Mama has it on good authority that he is a rake and…' she glanced over her shoulder '…there is something dreadful. I do not know if I should tell you this, but they say he has a—'

'Please do not!' Lucy said at once. 'It is kind of you to warn me, but there is no need—and I do not wish to hear gossip.' She turned away and fled up the stairs, suddenly uncaring of whether Miss Tremaine thought her rude or not.

Alone in her room, Lucy discovered that she was shaking. She felt very angry. How dare Miss Tremaine hint at such terrible things? It was most unfair of her when Lord Harcourt was not here to defend himself. And after she had made such a play for him!

If Lucy had been a different girl, she might have suspected Miss Tremaine of jealous spite, but as it was she crushed the unworthy thoughts. She suspected that Miss Tremaine had been hurt, and perhaps there was something of the rake about Lord Harcourt—for he had flirted with both Lucy and Miss Tremaine. However, she did not wish to listen to spiteful tales and she would not let anyone poison her mind against him!

She still could not quite understand why Miss Tremaine should have accepted General Rawlings, and she asked Jo about it later. Jo had come to her room to give her a little gift and to wish her well in her first Season in London.

'I do not know for sure,' Jo said, looking thoughtful. 'I think she has been on the town for some years and is disappointed. I know that her mama had high hopes for her, but for some reason they have come to nothing. I believe she had offers in her first Season and turned them down, and since then…' Jo shook her head. 'Perhaps it is because she has a sharp tongue and is not always kind. I do not think I envy General Rawlings his choice of a wife—and I pity his children, for I cannot believe that she will be a kind mother to another woman's children.'

'Oh…' Lucy nodded. 'Mr Tristram said that she could be unkind. I told him he should not say so, but perhaps he was right.'

'Yes, perhaps,' Jo said. 'In any event, she has made her choice and I dare say she may have felt a little desperate, for I imagine she thought Lord Harcourt would come up to scratch.'

'He did seem attracted,' Lucy said and frowned. 'Do you think he is a flirt, Jo?'

'Yes, I am certain of it,' Jo said. 'I have heard that he is a rake, but I do not know how true it may be. Drew likes him and so does Hal—and I would trust their judgement.'

'Yes, that is what I thought. If Drew likes him, he cannot be so very wicked.' Lucy smiled happily, taking her sister's arm as they went downstairs together. It would be the last time they would have dinner together for some time, because Hal was taking Jo home the next day. She would probably spend the next few months quietly at his father's home awaiting the birth of her baby, but she had told Lucy that she was looking forward to being with her great friend Ellen again.

Miss Tremaine was not present that evening. She, her mother and General Rawlings had left after tea, and it was just the family who dined that evening. Lucy had enjoyed meeting Marianne's friends, but she thought it was even nicer with just her close family about her.

She felt happy when she went to bed, even though a little shadow hovered at the back of her mind. She knew that she must make every effort to put Lord Harcourt from her thoughts. He was older, a rake and, perhaps worse, he thought of her as a child. Only a foolish girl would break her heart for him. Lucy had decided that she would try to forget her feelings for him, and if she should meet someone else she could love that ought to be easy enough.

Jack walked into the less-than-respectable nightclub. It was frequented by young rakehells and ladies of dubious reputation, though sometimes impeccable birth. He stood watching as one rather raddled-looking lady gambled carelessly at the throw of the dice, her rouged cheeks disguising the ravages of dissolute living. A woman of advanced years, who had buried three wealthy husbands, she bore a name that had once commanded respect. She was with a party of gentlemen, who were encouraging her to gamble ever more recklessly and were, by the looks of them, the worse for drink. His eyes narrowed as he saw that one of her court was the man he sought—Sir Frederick Collingwood.

He strolled towards them, outwardly detached, as careless as they, though inwardly it was another matter. He wished that he could simply have come out with his accusations, but he knew that Collingwood would have covered his tracks well. Before he could bring him to his knees, he needed proof that he had been responsible for David Middleton's death. He already knew that they had gambled on the night David was murdered, but that in itself meant little. What lay behind the events played out in public that night? Several people had spoken to him of a quarrel between David and Collingwood—but was it simply over a card game?

Collingwood turned to look at him as he approached, a guarded expression in his eyes, as though he sensed something. Since Jack Harcourt seldom frequented clubs of this nature and reputation, it was hardly surprising that the other man should wonder why he was there—especially if he had a guilty conscience.

'Good evening, Collingwood,' Jack said pleasantly. It took all his strength of purpose to speak politely to the man he knew to be a shark and a cheat, but he must do so if he were to learn what he needed to know. 'I did not think dice was your game?'

'It is not,' Collingwood agreed, lifting his quizzing glass to look at Jack more closely. 'I did not think that this was your sort of place?'

'It is not,' Jack agreed, resisting the urge to lunge at him and knock the truth out of the lying devil. 'But there are times when a man needs something more…shall we say spiced with danger?'

'Ah, yes.' Collingwood nodded, for he understood that, being a reckless gambler himself. 'So what is your pleasure, Harcourt?'

'I am looking for a game of piquet,' Jack said, because he knew that it had been his friend's favourite game of chance. 'But it seems there is no one willing to oblige me. I win too often, it seems.'

Collingwood studied his face, and then nodded. It was clearly a challenge and one that he could not resist, even though he suspected that something more lay behind it.

'I am otherwise engaged this evening, as you see,' he said. 'However, I should be delighted to take you on, Harcourt—in more pleasant surroundings than these.'

'Good. Shall we say tomorrow evening at White's?'

'We shall indeed.' Collingwood grinned. He was a rake of the worst order, a man careful mothers told their daughters to avoid at all costs, but he was dangerously attractive. His black hair and dark eyes brought women to him easily, and he treated them all with contempt. 'Tomorrow at nine, Harcourt. Now, do you care to hazard a bet on the roll of the dice?'

Jack had noticed a certain tendency for the dice to fall a certain way three times out of six. He reached forward, scooped them up, and blew on them and then called a hundred guineas on sixes as he threw. The dice fell with the six spots showing on both of the dice. He smiled at the reckless lady, who had placed her bet on sixes and was now gleefully gathering her winnings. His gaze strayed momentarily to the disappointed faces of the young rogues who had been hoping to fleece their victim of more of her money. He raised his brows, then turned and walked from the room, knowing that several of them were following him with their eyes, and that they would not be wishing him well.

* * *

Lucy looked about her eagerly as the carriage bowled briskly through the streets of London. It was early in the morning and they were not yet crowded with the traffic of the day. She could see a milkmaid crying her wares, her pails suspended from a wooden pole she wore across her shoulders. A coster was selling fresh mussels and oysters from a barrow he wheeled through the streets, and a brewery wagon was trotting proudly along the road, its horses dressed in shining brasses that jingled.

They had stayed at an inn just outside London the previous evening and come on early this morning. Lucy craned excitedly to see as the carriage came to a halt outside the Marquis of Marlbeck's London home. Although Drew and Marianne were to follow in a few days' time, they had insisted that Lucy and Mrs Horne go ahead so as to begin the task of gathering Lucy's new wardrobe before she was introduced into society.

Lucy was glad that her elder sister would be in town during their stay, for she knew that Marianne had many friends, and she would be sure to introduce her sister to them. As she got down from the carriage, she saw a man walking down the street and thought that she recognised his tall figure, though, as she could not see his face, she could not be certain. She wondered if Lord Harcourt was returning to his home after a night out, or if he had risen early—and then scolded herself for speculating. It was none of her business if he had spent the night gambling or...with his mistress. A little flush stained her cheeks, for she imagined he must have a mistress. It was what Jo had meant by *an arrangement*—and what Miss Tremaine had implied by saying that he was a rake, of course.

A butler dressed in formal black, his manner stately and slightly intimidating, had opened the door. He looked at her in what Lucy thought of as a stern manner as he welcomed them to the house, but as she entered behind her mama, a young footman winked at her. Lucy smiled at him, feeling better immediately.

The housekeeper bustled forward, introducing herself as Mrs Williams and apologising to Mrs Horne for not being there sooner to welcome them.

'Your rooms are ready, ma'am,' she said. 'If you will follow me upstairs, the footmen will see to your luggage, and if you care for some refreshment in the morning parlour, a maid will unpack for you.'

'We have only brought a small amount of baggage with us,' Mrs Horne told her. 'It is my intention to buy my daughter a fashionable wardrobe in town.'

'Very wise, if I might say so,' the housekeeper said, looking at Lucy. 'Would you like me to send and have the seamstress of your choice wait on you here?'

'That is an excellent suggestion,' Mrs Horne replied. 'Lady Marlbeck has given me the address of the seamstresses she uses and I shall write a note, asking them to call tomorrow if it is convenient.'

'I am sure it will be,' Mrs Williams replied. 'The Marchioness is a very elegant and beautiful lady, and her custom is eagerly sought. A recommendation from her would be attended immediately.'

'Yes, I dare say,' Mrs Horne said, looking at Lucy thoughtfully. In her opinion Lucy was as lovely as either of her elder sisters, but there was no denying that she was fortunate to have the Marchioness of Marlbeck as her sister. It would be sure to bring her to the notice of gentlemen and ladies alike, though Lucy's portion was not large. However, her two brothers-in-law had both promised her a dowry, which meant that she would not go empty-handed to her husband. All in all, Mrs Horne believed that her youngest daughter ought to make a worthy match, though she had no intention of pushing her towards marriage. She was young yet and it would be Lucy's choice—providing, of course, that she chose sensibly.

Lucy looked about the house with interest as her mama continued to chat with the housekeeper. It was larger than it had appeared from the outside, for it was in a terrace of houses built at the end of the previous century. However, first appearances were deceptive and Lucy realised that it had considerable depth and width, and there were four storeys—the top being the servants' bedchambers—and the kitchens and servants' hall were in the basement. The staircase was wide and impressive, carpeted in a rich blue Persian design, as were the landings on the first floor.

There were beautiful paintings in gilt frames on the walls, also gilt pier tables interspersed with small gilt chairs along the landing of the first floor, which was where some of the main reception rooms were situated. They had to go up a second short flight of stairs to the guest bedrooms.

Lucy was taken to her room first. Her mama told her to simply tidy herself and go down, because they had not stopped for breakfast at the inn and would take some refreshment in fifteen minutes. As she stepped inside her bedchamber, Lucy gasped with surprise for it was very different to the furnishings at Marlbeck Place, which was all rather grand and formal—though Marianne had begun to change some of the rooms. Here, the furniture was far more modern and fashioned of a pale wood that gave the room lightness and style, blending well with the soft rose curtains about the bed and the windows. Rose and cream with a hint of crimson here and there was a pretty combination that pleased Lucy very well.

She believed that she would be very much at home here and crossed over to the window to look at the pretty writing desk that stood there, taking off her bonnet and shaking out her long hair. The desk had a leather writing slope and drawers that contained paper, pens, ink and sealing wax. She was examining some other pretty items that had been placed there for her use and it was a while before she sensed that she was being watched. She glanced out of the window and saw that a young man was standing in the road below, looking up at her window. When he saw her, he doffed his hat, sweeping her an extravagant bow, a grin on his handsome face.

Lucy felt her cheeks grow warm. The look he gave her had been too intimate…almost insolent, and it made her shiver. She drew back from the window, retreating to the far side of the room. It had not occurred to her that she could be seen from the street for she was used to country houses, and no one would have been rude enough to stare at her aunt's house. She realised that her time in London would open her eyes to many new experiences.

She had taken off her bonnet and now she removed her travelling cloak. Her dress was a little creased from the journey, but she smoothed it down, knowing that she did not have time to change before she joined her mama in the breakfast parlour.

She went over to the dressing table, which was to one side of the room, and sat down on the stool. She dragged a comb through her hair, which had begun to tangle about her face, as it often did, because it was so fine. Some of the gentlemen staying with Marianne in the country had told her that her hair was like spun silk and the colour of moonlight.

Lucy pulled a face. She supposed that she had nice hair, but she had always envied her sister Jo her red locks, which curled into ringlets if allowed to blow freely in the wind. Jo usually brushed her hair back, but sometimes she simply tied it with a ribbon, because it was the way Harry liked to see it.

Lucy's hair was usually held by ribbons, because it was too fine to put up in elaborate styles, though Mama had told her she would be employing a hairdresser in London to dress her hair and style it in a more fashionable look. She made a face at herself in the mirror and sighed. She would do anything if it helped her to look a bit older!

Chapter Three

'Lucy darling, that looks lovely,' Marianne said, coming into her sister's room as she finished dressing for the evening, some four days after Lucy's arrival in town. They were all attending a ball, Lucy's first in fashionable society. She was wearing a new gown of shimmering white silk with an overskirt of gauze trimmed with spangles. Her hair had somehow been teased into a single ringlet that curled enticingly over her left shoulder. It had been fastened with pearl-and-diamond pins– a present from her sister—and she had diamond drops in her ears, a large diamond pendent at her throat. 'I knew Madame Suzanne would make something perfect for you and she has.'

'It is wonderful,' Lucy said, turning to her excitedly. 'I really love it, Marianne. I never thought I could look like this—I look older, not like a child any more.'

'Yes, dearest,' Marianne said with a nod of satisfaction. 'Mama was a little afraid that it might be too sophisticated for you, but I persuaded her that it was just right. You are eighteen and not a little girl any longer.'

'Mama is a little reluctant to see me grow up, I think.'

'Yes, perhaps,' Marianne agreed and smiled at her. 'She does not mean to keep you a child, but perhaps because you were the last of her daughters she has tended to protect you too much. However, I know you will be much admired this evening, Lucy.'

'If I am, it is because of all the lovely things you and Drew have given me—and Jo, of course.' She touched her necklace. 'This was so generous of Drew, because he has already given me so much.'

'He wanted you to have it,' Marianne said. 'I already have far more than I need, and Drew likes to give presents. Now, are you ready to go down? I know Mama is already there with Drew.'

'Yes, thank you,' Lucy said. She picked up a small posy of roses, which had been given her by her brother-in-law and were tied with yellow silk ribbons. 'These are so pretty.'

Marianne nodded her approval. 'After this evening, I am sure you will have many tributes sent to you, Lucy, but Drew wanted you to have something for your first evening.'

The two sisters went downstairs together. Marianne was dressed in green silk and carried a stole of silver spangles over her arm. She was wearing a magnificent necklace of emeralds and diamonds, and matching drops hung from her ears. She made a perfect foil for her sister's ethereal looks, being a warm, vibrant woman who was universally admired in society.

Drew's eyes lit up as he saw his wife and he greeted her with a kiss on the cheek before turning his gaze on Lucy. He nodded his head in approval. 'She is a sprite, an angel…' He took her hand, raising it to his lips to kiss the back. 'You look heavenly, Lucy. As I stand in place of a father to you, I think I shall have my work cut out this evening, defending you from the wolves.'

'Oh, Drew!' Lucy's laughter was warm and delightful.

'You do say such foolish things sometimes! You are not old enough to be my papa.'

'But since you have none, I shall stand your guardian,' Drew told her, a sparkle in his eyes. 'If anyone asks you to marry him, you must direct him to speak to me first. I shall make sure that you do not fall prey to a rake or worse.'

Lucy giggled, for she believed that he was teasing her. Surely he did not imagine that she would receive a proposal of marriage that evening!

The ballroom was crowded as Jack Harcourt entered that night. He was feeling pleased with himself, because he had discovered that Sir Frederick Collingwood was truly a cheat. He might have exposed him the previous evening had he chosen to do so, for the man was clumsy and careless, but he had allowed himself to be cheated of two thousand guineas—a small price to pay for what he had learned. At least the writer of the mystery letter had not lied about that, which meant that the rest of it was quite possibly true.

As the evening progressed, Collingwood had become careless and drunk more than he ought and, from a few unguarded comments, Jack had discovered that his information was correct. David Middleton had gone down heavily to Collingwood that last night—and he had said something about cheating. It was not very much, but it was enough to confirm Jack's suspicions. He had no proof, but he was almost certain that he knew what had happened. However, he still had no idea what the underlying reason for the quarrel was about. He had asked, but received no answers, though the closed expressions on some of the gentlemen's faces made him certain that it involved something more than merely gambling—or perhaps someone who had been dear to David?

He had now learned from other sources besides the letter

that David had left the gambling club with Collingwood late that night, and that they had been arguing fiercely about something—but what? Collingwood might have become enraged. It was likely that he had produced a pistol and shot David, somehow managing to move his body to that lonely road by the Heath where it was eventually found. Had the author of that mystery letter not decided to write to him, Jack might well have still believed that his death had been at the hands of a highwayman.

Jack was sure in his own mind that the letter he had been sent was genuine, though proving the identity of David's murderer was another thing entirely. However, he was working on a plan to draw Collingwood into a trap, and for the moment must put his personal concerns aside.

'Good evening, Harcourt,' a voice said from behind him. 'I wasn't sure whether you were in town or not.'

Jack turned to find himself facing Drew Marlbeck. 'Yes, I have some business I must sort out before I go down to the country. I am sorry that I have not called on you and Marianne before this, but I have been busy.'

'Come to dinner next week,' Drew invited. 'We are giving a small affair—nothing major. Marianne plans a rout for next month, I believe.'

'Thank you, I shall,' Jack said. His eyes travelled round the large room, coming to rest on a striking girl who was surrounded by gentlemen, all of them vying for her favours. He did not know her until she glanced his way, and even then he was not certain. 'Good lord! Is that Miss Horne?'

'Yes, she is rather stunning, isn't she?' Drew grinned. 'Marianne and her dressmaker had a great deal to do with the transformation, because her mama still sees her as her little girl—but the beautiful butterfly was always there, waiting to come out of her chrysalis.'

'She is beautiful,' Jack said, feeling a catch at his throat as he saw the way Lucy was teasing her admirers. She was still a little shy but it made her all the more charming, and her laughter was intoxicating. 'I can hardly believe the change.'

'As I said, Marianne has taken her in hand these past few days. It was just lack of confidence and her clothes, which were too young for her. She is eighteen—a woman, and a very lovely one. The man who captures her heart will be fortunate. Lucy has the sweetest nature, though she can stick up for herself if need be.'

'I am glad to hear it,' Jack said. He could hardly take his eyes from Lucy. He had thought her enchanting the last time they met, but now there was something more. Perhaps it was confidence or the clothes, but he certainly found it very appealing. 'Thank you, Marlbeck. I shall be pleased to dine with you next week. I may even stay in town a little longer than I had planned.'

'I shall tell Marianne to add you to her list for the rout,' Drew said, hiding his grin. He had not missed his sister-in-law's partiality for Harcourt, and he felt it would do very well. He knew of the rumours, of course, but considered it a minor thing. Even if his friend did have a bastard child somewhere, it had happened in the past, and it was often said that reformed rakes made the best husbands. Mrs Horne might not agree, but she could probably be persuaded.

As Drew moved off, Jack progressed slowly through the room. He was stopped several times by friends and acquaintances, because, despite the rumours, his credit was good enough to make him the target of the more ambitious mothers. He had a title and a fortune, and if he had transgressed in the past, that could be forgiven in the right circumstances.

Jack was a little disturbed to see that Sir Frederick Collingwood had joined the little group of admirers around Lucy. He frowned, because it angered him that the man was still at liberty to enter society at will. Collingwood was a cheat, a rake of the worst kind—and, in his mind, a murderer. He would not want Lucy Horne to be caught in his toils! However, he continued to be invited to many society affairs, and until Jack could prove what he suspected, Lucy and other young ladies would be exposed to his company. The sooner he found some way of exposing him, the better!

'Miss Horne,' he said, making his way to her side and cutting out several of the young bucks around her. 'I believe this is our dance.' He took her hand before Lucy could protest, sweeping her along until they reached the dance floor just as a waltz struck up.

Lucy looked up at him, her eyes wide as she said, 'I had promised this to Mr Bates, sir. I think you must have made a mistake.'

'Oh, no, I am quite sure it was promised to me,' Jack said, his mouth quirking at the corners. 'If I am wrong, I shall apologise, of course.'

'I think you have been very wicked to steal another gentleman's dance, sir.' Lucy's eyes sparkled at him. She feigned annoyance, but she could not prevent a little smile tugging at her mouth. 'However, I shall forgive you, because you dance the waltz divinely.'

'Thank you, Miss Lucy,' he said. 'I believe we are sufficiently acquainted for me to use your first name? After all, I can claim a prior friendship, can I not?'

Lucy shook her head at him. He was not the first gentleman to tease her that evening, and she was discovering that it was amusing to be teased and to tease in return.

'I am not sure it was friendship, sir, for you left Marlbeck without saying goodbye to me.'

'That was remiss of me,' Jack said. 'However, I shall do my best to make up for it. Will you allow me to take you driving in the park tomorrow afternoon?'

'I have an appointment for the afternoon,' Lucy told him. 'But I shall be pleased to accompany you in the morning—at eleven, if you wish?'

'Will you not be too tired after an evening such as this?'

'Not at all,' Lucy assured him. 'I like to go out early and it is better to be taken for a drive in town, because I cannot venture out alone and Mama does not rise early.'

'Then I shall be delighted to call for you at eleven o'clock precisely,' Jack said, smiling down at her. He looked rueful as the music ended. 'I think I must return you to your friends—but may I ask if there is another dance available later?'

'I have only one,' Lucy told him, 'and I think I must give that to Mr Bates. It is only fair that he should have it.'

'Then perhaps you will allow me to take you into supper?'

'Yes, thank you,' Lucy said. 'You are very kind, sir. I shall look forward to your company.'

Lucy was duly returned to her court, where another gentleman immediately claimed her. A smile and the promise of the waltz before supper pacified Mr Bates, and Lucy was led back to the dance floor. Jack Harcourt stood watching for a moment before moving away. Some of the older gentlemen had found themselves a niche in the card room, and it was there that he saw Sir Frederick Collingwood. However, Collingwood shook his head as he lifted an eyebrow.

'I do not play this evening, Harcourt. However, I shall give you your chance to recover—tomorrow, if you wish?'

'I have an engagement tomorrow,' Jack said. 'Shall we say next Tuesday?'

'Yes, that will suit me well,' Collingwood said, a sneer on his lips. 'What do you think of the latest rage? They are calling her a sylph and an enchantress. She is a pretty little thing—do you think she has much of a fortune?'

'I think she has something,' Jack replied, looking grim. 'But I doubt it would be enough to interest you, Collingwood.'

'No, I thought not,' Collingwood said. 'A pity, because she is a tempting little morsel. I should enjoy gobbling her up—but I dare say she cannot be had without marriage, and I need an heiress of some substance.'

Jack swallowed his anger with difficulty. The idea of Lucy Horne at this devil's mercy was enough to make his stomach turn, but he could not afford to offend him…yet. Given a free hand, he might have called him out on the spot, but he held his tongue. The time would come…

'I dare say her mother has other ideas,' he drawled, a hint of insolence in his voice. 'You would not stand a chance, my dear fellow.'

'Neither would you,' Collingwood retorted, stung by his tone. 'If what I hear is true, you are not one to call others black.'

'But is it?' Jack replied still in that insolent drawl. 'The trouble with whispers and rumours is that one never knows quite what to believe—and yet sometimes it is as well to heed them.'

He turned away, leaving Collingwood to his contemplation of the gaming. No doubt he was watching in the hope of picking a pigeon ripe for plucking on another occasion. Returning to the ballroom, he stood and watched Lucy dancing for a few minutes, before approaching a widow he knew quite well.

'Good evening, Lady West,' he said. 'How pleasant to see you here. Do you dance?'

'Why, yes, sir,' she said and smiled at him. 'As you see, I am out of mourning and life goes on, does it not?'

'Yes, indeed,' he said and offered her his hand. It would not do to let others think that he wished to dance only with Lucy Horne. Especially when someone like Sir Frederick Collingwood was present. He was not sure how he felt about anything just yet and for the moment he would play his cards close to his chest.

For Lucy the evening melted away in a whirl of pleasure and excitement. She had never dreamed that she would be such a success, and, had she been a less sensible girl, all the compliments she was receiving must have gone to her head. Contrary to her thoughts earlier, she did receive three offers of marriage, though she was sure that the gentlemen were merely jesting, vying for her smiles against their friends. However, there were others who were more serious in their attentions, and she was not alone for more than a few seconds together.

When Jack Harcourt claimed her for supper there were groans and protests, but no one actually tried to cut him out. Jack was known to be an excellent shot and well able to floor any opponent in a fist fight.

Jack found her a table by the open window and promised to return with some tempting trifles in a moment or two, but, feeling the cool air coming in from outside, Lucy went out onto the terrace for a few minutes.

'Miss Lucy—' a voice made her turn from her contemplation of the moon to see one of the young gentlemen she had danced with earlier '—how fortunate to find you alone.'

'Mr Lawrence,' Lucy said, startled to find that he was standing very close, because she had not heard him come out. 'I just wanted a breath of air. I must go back, for Lord Harcourt will have brought my supper.'

'Who needs food when we may taste the nectar of the gods?' he asked in a thick voice that made her realise he must be a little drunk. 'It drives me wild just to look at you. You are an angel…a goddess meant for love…'

'Forgive me, sir, but I do not think you are quite yourself,' Lucy said and attempted to go past him. He grabbed her arm, swinging her round to face him. She gasped and tried to pull away as she sensed the wildness in him. 'Let me go!'

'Not before I have tasted the sweet honey of your lips—'

'No! I do not want you to kiss me. Please take your hand from my arm and allow me to return to the ballroom.'

'I suggest that you do as she says, Lawrence,' a harsh voice drawled. 'Otherwise, you may find yourself in some trouble.'

The menace in Jack Harcourt's voice was clear. The young buck turned to look at him and what he saw caused the colour to drain from his face. He let go of Lucy's arm and stepped away from her, lurching into the garden.

'Perhaps that will teach you not to venture outside alone at an affair like this,' Jack said in a tone that cut Lucy like the lash of a whip. 'I would have thought you had learned your lesson on the island.'

'It was foolish of me,' Lucy said, her cheeks warm. 'I needed a little air and thought there could be no harm…'

Jack's eyes honed in on her face. 'When a girl looks as lovely as you do, Miss Horne, there will always be predators waiting to snap her up. Learn your lesson now and trust only those who treat you with the respect you deserve.'

'Yes, thank you. I shall be more careful,' Lucy said, feeling too embarrassed to meet his stern gaze. 'Please excuse me now. I think I shall go to the… I need to tidy myself.' She went past him swiftly. All thought of food had left her mind. She would not be able to eat a thing in his company!

Jack watched her go, feeling a stab of regret. He had been angry and he had upset her, making her feel embarrassed. He had not intended that, but his memories had made him too harsh. He was blaming her for another's foolishness and that was wrong. He must hope that she did not cancel their appointment to go driving, and apologise as best he could in the morning.

Lucy returned to the ballroom some minutes after she had fled from Lord Harcourt's presence. She had been foolish to run away and it would not be surprising if he continued to think of her as a child, because she ought to have stood her ground and defended herself. She had done nothing wrong. Mr Lawrence had been intoxicated and the incident might have happened to any lady he came across. It had not been wise to go outside alone, but at a respectable affair like this one she had been entitled to think herself safe from such an attack. Lord Harcourt had been unnecessarily harsh.

She glanced round the ballroom, but could see no sign of him. He did not reappear that evening and she realised that he must have left the house after she ran away from him. She wondered if he would call for her in the morning as he had promised, and decided that he would. No gentleman would default on an engagement with a lady, even if they had had a slight disagreement—and that was all it was, of course. Indeed, they had both overreacted, but Lucy was grateful for his help in rescuing her from Mr Lawrence and she would tell him so the next morning.

However, the magic of the evening had dimmed a little and she was glad when Marianne suggested that they should leave. She was thoughtful in the carriage, though she responded to her sister's questions, assuring her that she had had a wonderful time.

'It was very exciting,' she told Marianne. 'I had not

expected to be so successful. You must tell Drew that I did receive three proposals of marriage, but as I did not believe any of the gentlemen to be serious I did not refer them to him.'

'Oh, Lucy,' Marianne said and laughed. 'How amusing for you! It is all exciting and fun—but you must be careful that you choose carefully. I think you will have more serious proposals than you expect.'

'I think it was all just teasing,' Lucy told her. 'How could anyone be serious when they do not know me? Compliments of that kind are all very well, Marianne, but Drew did not behave thus with you—did he?'

A little smile touched Marianne's mouth. 'He said some wicked things to me, Lucy—but he did not ask me to marry him for a long time.'

'Exactly. He proposed when he was sure of his feelings and yours,' Lucy said, 'and that is how it should be. I shall not listen to anyone who speaks impulsively, for I cannot think it a considered decision.'

Marianne was surprised that her dreamy sister should be so serious about the subject of marriage; she would have expected her to be carried away by all the attention that had been lavished on her that evening. It made her thoughtful. Perhaps Drew was right after all…

Lucy fell asleep easily, though she dreamed of dancing in the clouds with a man whose face she could not see. When she woke it was early and still dark outside. She rose and went over to the window, drawing her curtains a little so that she could look out at the street. It had rained overnight and was cooler than it had been. She could hear the clip-clop of a horse's hooves somewhere and a young lad was crying out that he had fresh eggs for sale. As she watched, one of the maids left the house and went to buy from him.

Lucy returned to bed, but did not feel like sleeping. She picked up a copy of Lord Byron's latest poem that Marianne had subscribed and began to read it. In half an hour she would ring for her maid, because she wanted to be ready when Lord Harcourt arrived.

She was in fact ready half an hour too soon and the minutes dragged by very slowly—she was afraid that Lord Harcourt would not come after all. However, at five minutes to the appointed hour she heard him being admitted to the house and went downstairs to greet him.

She was wearing a dark blue carriage gown and a straw bonnet tied with blue ribbons. Her gloves were of York tan leather, her shoes black with a small heel and silver buckles. She had white silk stockings that just showed beneath her gown, and she carried a little lace parasol, which matched the blue of her gown.

'You are very punctual,' Lord Harcourt said, smiling at her in approval. Her hair was loose on her shoulders and she presented as an elegant and beautiful young lady. 'May I say how very charming you look, Miss Lucy.'

'Thank you,' she said, giving him an enchanting smile. 'You are very kind to say so—especially as I fear I did not thank you adequately for your help last night.'

'You are too generous,' Jack said as they went outside. His groom stood holding a pair of magnificent black horses, his phaeton one of the smartest that Lucy had seen about town. 'I believe I was hasty. I must apologise, but that young man is fast gathering a reputation and I was disturbed to see him accost you in that way. However, that was no reason to be sharp with you.'

'It did not occur to me that I would be in any danger at such an affair,' Lucy told him honestly. 'However, I shall be more careful in future.'

Jack gave her his hand to help her into the carriage, and took his seat beside her, nodding to the groom to stand back. 'I shall not need you again this morning, Ned.'

'Right you are, sir,' the man said and grinned as he watched his master drive off. It was a long time since his lordship had taken a young lady driving, and there were already bets being laid by his people as to how long it would take him to come up to scratch. Having seen her, Ned thought that he would lay his bet that it would be sooner rather than later.

Lucy was happily unaware of the speculation she had so innocently aroused in the minds of Lord Harcourt's servants. It was the first time that she had been taken for a drive by any gentleman other than her brothers-in-law, and she felt very pleased to be bowling along in such a smart equipage.

'Your horses are beautiful,' she said, admiring the way they stepped out, their heads up. 'You must be very proud of them, I think.'

'Yes, I am,' Jack replied, smiling. He was considered by many to be the best judge of horseflesh in London, and had many other equally magnificent horses in his stables. 'I have a breeding stables at home and I sometimes race the best of my stock at Newmarket.'

'Oh, how exciting,' Lucy said, giving him a sparkling look. 'Do they ever win?'

'Yes, quite often,' he said. 'Are you fond of horses, Lucy?'

'I like them,' she replied. 'I have not had much chance to ride, though Drew told me I could when I stay with him—but I am not sure I should know how. Aunt Bertha does not keep a riding stable. Papa put me up on his horse when I was younger, but I have not ridden since he died.'

'That is a pity,' Jack told her. 'Riding is an excellent pastime, Miss Lucy. It is good for health and for pleasure. You should certainly make an effort to learn.'

'Yes, perhaps I shall,' Lucy said. 'Not while we are in town—but later...' She hesitated, for in truth the future was uncertain. As yet she had not met anyone she would care to marry amongst her new acquaintances, but of course she had only attended one ball. 'I imagine it must be very pleasant to ride in the country.'

'In the country you ought either to ride or to drive your own pair,' Jack said, giving her a speculative glance. 'I think driving might suit you more than riding, Miss Lucy. Indeed, yes, I believe I could see you driving a smart rig of your own.'

Lucy tipped her head to one side, gazing up at him. 'Are you teasing me, sir? I did not know that it was proper for a lady to drive herself.'

'Oh, yes, I think it is acceptable in the country,' Jack replied, 'though only ladies with the consequence to carry it off dare do so in town, of course.'

'Oh...' Lucy looked at him consideringly. 'I wonder if Drew would teach me. I think he might if I asked nicely.'

'You are a minx, Miss Lucy,' Jack said, laughing huskily. 'I should be happy to let you drive my rig—but not this one. These particular cattle are too temperamental, but there are others with gentle mouths that would not take unkindly to a stranger's hand. Perhaps a turn around the park one morning—if you dare?'

'Oh, yes,' Lucy agreed instantly, her eyes alight with mischief. 'If you could bear to give your horses into my hands, I should like it of all things.'

'Then shall we make another appointment—for the day after tomorrow in the morning? I suggest the hour of ten—there will be less traffic in the park at that time.'

'Yes, please,' Lucy responded eagerly. 'I shall look forward to it very much, sir.'

'Likewise,' he replied, a smile playing about his lips. 'It should be quite an experience.'

Lucy looked at him curiously, wondering about the odd note in his voice. She could not know that Jack had never let a woman drive his horses or yet another man. He was known for driving only high-spirited beasts, and owned nothing that would be in the least suitable for a lady to drive. However, he knew someone who did, and he was sure that a few hundred guineas would secure the purchase of a rig and horses that his companion might manage easily—though whether his own reputation would survive being seen in such an equipage, he dare not think.

Marianne smiled as she saw Lucy come in later that morning. Her cheeks had delightful roses from the fresh air, and she was glowing, her eyes bright with excitement.

'I have no need to ask if you enjoyed your drive,' Marianne said. 'I am glad to see you enjoying yourself so much, dearest.'

'Yes, I am having fun,' Lucy agreed. She wondered whether to tell her sister that Lord Harcourt had offered to teach her to drive and decided that it might be best to keep the news to herself for the time being. 'What are we doing this afternoon, Marianne?'

'This is my at-home day. We shall have visitors to tea and this evening we are invited to a card party. I hope you have not forgotten that you have a fitting early this afternoon?'

'No, I had not forgotten,' Lucy said. 'It is for another ballgown. I had no idea that I should need so many dresses.'

'You have hardly begun,' Marianne said, looking at her indulgently. 'I was shocked when Drew brought me to town the first time, but there are so many engagements to attend, dearest. You cannot possibly wear the same dress more than twice or three times at most.'

'It seems such a waste,' Lucy said, wrinkling her brow as

she thought of how much money was being spent on her clothes. 'The cost of one ballgown could feed a family for some weeks, Marianne.'

'Yes, I know how you feel,' her sister said. 'But Drew supports several charities, Lucy. Even if you gave up all your pretty dresses you could not help every poor child. Drew and I both give time and money to help where we can—so do not feel guilty, my love. If you marry a gentleman with a substantial fortune, I dare say you will do what you can to help others.'

'Yes…' Lucy nodded. 'I had not thought of that, but it is a consideration for the future.'

Marianne saw the look in her eyes and raised her brows. 'Have you met anyone in particular that you like very much, Lucy?'

'No…' Lucy hesitated, and then said, 'Well, there might be someone, but I am not sure that he likes me well enough to ask me.'

'Well, there is no rush,' Marianne assured her. 'This is your first Season, dearest. If you do not meet someone you could be happy with, you have plenty of time. No one wishes to rush you into making a decision. Mama certainly does not, and I think you should be certain before you give your word to anyone. When you fall in love, you will know.'

'Yes, I am sure I shall,' Lucy agreed and smiled as she went upstairs to change into a more suitable dress for the afternoon. She believed that she had already given her heart irrevocably, but she did not think that Lord Harcourt was in love with her. He was very kind, and he liked to tease her at times—but he had given her no indication that he felt anything more than friendship towards her. She would be very foolish to hope for too much, even though he had promised to teach her to drive.

* * *

Jack was returning to his home that afternoon when he saw something that interested him. A young boy had just left his house, and, crossing the road, had gone up to a gentleman standing a short distance away. The gentleman asked him a question, which the boy answered and was rewarded with a coin. He ran off and the gentleman turned in Jack's direction. They recognised each other instantly, and the other man turned away at once, walking off at a smart pace.

What was George Garrick doing outside his home? And why had he paid the boy a gold coin for going to Jack's house? He thought that he might know, because suddenly things had begun to click into place. Someone who had once been proud to call him friend had written that mysterious letter—and that term applied very well to Garrick. They were no longer friends; indeed, Jack had once considered challenging him to a duel and they had fought—but with their fists. Jack blamed Garrick for Amelia's unhappiness. Had it not been for him…but it was madness to go down that road. Besides, it was not entirely Garrick's fault, though much blame must be laid at his door. Had it not been for one other person, Amelia might have married Garrick and would quite probably have been happy.

He brought his mind back to the present as a footman opened the front door for him and he went inside the house. His eye fell immediately on the letter lying on the hall table; as he picked it up and broke the seal, he knew that his intuition had served him well.

Further information has come to my attention. As yet I have no proof, but I believe I may soon know more about the murder of David Middleton. It concerns a gentleman that you know well—your sister's husband. If I am right, it explains much and is more sinister than you know. I shall write again when I have confirmed what I suspect. A friend who would be forgiven.

It would explain a great deal if Staunton were involved in this thing! But was it true? He knew Amelia's husband to be a bully, but would he have conspired with Collingwood to bring about the death of a man? Perhaps, if he had believed that Middleton might be a threat to him.

Jack frowned as he took the letter into his library, slipping it into the drawer of his desk. He was as certain as it was possible to be that both letters had come from George Garrick. Did that make them more reliable or less? He toyed with the idea of seeking his erstwhile friend and demanding that he speak plainly, and yet to do so would perhaps send Garrick into hiding. It might be better to play this little charade to the end and see where it led him. Besides, he had something that he needed to do first...

Lucy looked in vain for Lord Harcourt at the card party that evening. She could not know that he had made other arrangements, for he had not mentioned them to her. She had hoped that he would be one of the guests, but as the evening progressed she realised that it was not so. However, she found plenty to amuse her, gambling for small stakes at the loo table.

Several of the gentlemen with whom she had danced the previous evening were there, and they proved attentive, helping her to place her bets and encouraging her. She won twice and lost three times, but finished the evening only a few shillings out of pocket, for she had not gambled recklessly.

At supper she found that she was once more the centre of attention. Three gentlemen seemed to have formed a determined court and vied with each other for the honour of fetching her champagne and delicious trifles.

'Thank you, Mr Langham,' she said to the gentleman who procured her champagne. 'You are so kind.'

'It was a pleasure, Miss Lucy,' he replied. Of medium height, fair-haired and attractive, he was the heir to a fortune, though not a title. 'You must know that I would do anything to please you.'

Lucy flushed, because the look in his eyes was so sincere that she believed him. He had not yet said anything significant, but she believed that if he did propose he would mean it. Unlike Sir Hugh, a man of more mature years who had already proposed to her three times that evening, though in a joking manner that she did not believe sincere. Mr Peter Robinson had also given her hints that he found her very attractive, though he had said nothing to make her think he meant more than flirtation.

Because they were all so very kind, Lucy did not have a moment alone. However, she could not help wondering where Lord Harcourt was that evening and why he had not attended the party, for she believed that he had been invited. It was wrong of her to feel disappointed when she had so many kind friends, but she could not help it.

Returning home afterwards, Lucy was reflective. She had been met with nothing but kindness here in London, but the realisation that she did not respond wholeheartedly to any gentleman other than Lord Harcourt was growing on her. When he came into a room it was as if the sun had suddenly come out and everything seemed brighter, more exciting. She did not quite know what she would do if, at the end of the Season, he showed no interest in making her an offer.

Jack had his mind on other things that evening as he faced his opponent across the card table. Collingwood had lost the first hand, but since then he had won consistently. Jack had bet steadily though moderately, studying every move the other man made while appearing not to notice. He was not yet ready to strike, though he was almost certain now that he knew how Collingwood managed to cheat them all. It was sleight of hand and skilfully done, but as the evening wore on, once again Collingwood indulged in too much drink and made a careless slip.

Jack could have exposed him then, but he had held back. He was not certain why he was waiting. It had something to do with the second letter. If David's murder had been made to look as if it were merely over a card game to cover something more sinister, Jack wanted to know more about it. He had planned to bring things to a close this evening, but instead he went down to the tune of two thousand three hundred guineas before calling a halt. He needed to keep Collingwood on a string, until he was ready to strike.

'You are too good for me this evening, Collingwood,' he said carelessly and yawned. 'Perhaps another time?'

'Any time you wish,' Collingwood crowed. His sneer told Jack that he thought his opponent a fool and ripe for the plucking. 'I am always available to you, Harcourt.'

'Perhaps next week,' Jack suggested. 'I am engaged for most of this—shall we say a week today?'

'Yes, why not?' Collingwood agreed. 'If your purse will stand it—perhaps we should go for larger stakes next time, to give you a chance to recoup your losses?'

'Yes, why not?' Jack agreed, echoing his nonchalance. He rose from the table. 'I bid you goodnight.'

As he walked from the room, a gentleman came up to him. 'May I walk with you, Harcourt?'

'Yes, Greaves, if you wish; I shall be pleased with your company.'

He glanced at the gentleman as they went out of the club,

raising his brows at him. They knew each other sufficiently, although they were not close friends, but Jack trusted him for he had always thought Greaves to be honest. He was a gentleman of the old school, in his middle years, and a man of scrupulous honour.

'I wanted to warn you,' Greaves said. 'Collingwood is a cheat—and a dangerous fellow.'

'Thank you for the warning,' Jack said. 'I shall tell you that it was not necessary—but I ask you to keep that in confidence.'

'Ah...' Greaves nodded. 'I suspected as much. It is time Collingwood was taught a lesson. If you need a witness, I am your man—and there are others who have suffered at his hands.'

'I suggest you are here at the same time next week,' Jack said. 'I might have exposed him already, but I was waiting. Now I think I need wait no longer.'

'Good.' Greaves nodded his satisfaction. 'I shall make sure that when you make your move, your back is covered.'

Jack inclined his head. 'Thank you. I believe Collingwood is guilty of much more than cheating, but proving it may not be possible. However, it would be revenge enough to see him ruined and thrown out of decent society.'

'You are speaking of David Middleton, I know,' Greaves said, looking serious. 'I saw that game, Harcourt. Middleton left the table in anger, though I do not know what was said between them. Collingwood followed him out shortly after. They were heard arguing. I have wondered about it myself. There are others who might know—but I suspect it was not just over the cards.'

'I am certain that something happened between them,' Jack said, 'but proof is another matter.'

'Sometimes justice cannot be fully satisfied, but his ruin would be something.'

'Something,' Jack agreed. He knew it was not enough, could never be enough, but unless he could find the proof of Collingwood's guilt there was no more he could do.

He parted company with his companion and walked on, still deep in thought. At one time he had considered calling Collingwood out, perhaps provoking a quarrel, but of late he had felt less inclined. He knew that he was the far better shot and it would be little short of murder if his ball went home, as it undoubtedly would if he aimed for the heart. Two wrongs did not make something right, and he believed that he must settle for less than total satisfaction.

Yes, he must be satisfied to see Collingwood exposed as a cheat. He had, he realised, other priorities that might be jeopardised by risking a duel. A little smile played about his mouth. He was rather looking forward to taking Miss Lucy Horne for her first driving lesson—but first he must secure that rig! And for that he needed to take a trip out of town in the morning.

Chapter Four

The dance the following evening was smaller than the ball Lucy had attended earlier that week, but most of the gentlemen she had become acquainted with were there, which meant that she did not lack for partners. Unfortunately, Lord Harcourt did not appear and she felt a sharp pang of disappointment, because this was the second evening in a row that she had missed him.

However, she managed to enjoy herself, dancing with a string of young gentlemen, including Mr Tristram, who was very attentive, but she was careful not to venture out to the terrace alone, even though the ballroom was very warm. Mr Lawrence was present and she saw him watching her in a brooding manner several times, but he did not ask her to dance.

It was perhaps as well for her peace of mind that she was not present when he left the ballroom later that evening, joining his uncle in the back parlour, which had been set up with card tables for those gentlemen who did not care to dance.

'Why the long face?' Sir Frederick Collingwood asked as they went outside together to smoke a cigar. 'Are you in the dubs again? How much is it this time? I can spare a few hundred if you need it.'

'Thank you,' the younger man said. His uncle had paid his gambling debts before this, but usually requested a favour in return—and one of those favours was still haunting him. His had not been the finger on the trigger, but he had helped to cover up the evidence afterwards. 'As a matter of fact, I've been lucky at the tables. It isn't money.'

'A woman, then?' Collingwood's brows arched. 'Forget her, whoever she is. None of them are worth the bother. Find yourself a whore and get it out of your head, Lawrence.'

'She isn't easily forgotten, Uncle. I think I'm in love with her—but she dislikes me. I made a bit of a fool of myself... upset her.'

'In your cups, I suppose?' Collingwood sneered. 'Does she have a fortune worth bothering about? If she does, I suggest you abduct her. Show her that you mean business, Lawrence. After a night in your bed, she will come round fast enough, I'll warrant.'

'I couldn't do that,' his nephew said, frowning. 'She is an angel...a sweet innocent. I doubt she has a fortune, though someone said she would have ten thousand.'

'The Rainham chit has that much a year,' Collingwood said. 'Take the fortune and never mind that she has a face like a horse—you can find pretty whores to please you once you have the money safe. I would marry Rainham's girl like a shot, but he wouldn't have me. He has warned me off, told me that I won't get a penny if I try anything—but you might win her round.'

'Marry that dumpling?' Lawrence looked horrified. 'I would rather they threw me in the Fleet. It is her I want...Lucy Horne. She is everything I have ever dreamed of.'

'You've got it bad,' his uncle said, a mocking look in his

eyes. 'Well, I doubt she would look at you—but you could change her mind if you took my advice.'

'Thank you for the advice, but she would hate me,' Lawrence said. 'I might as well try for the Rainham girl. At least she has money.'

He went off gloomily, leaving his uncle in a thoughtful mood. If he was not mistaken, Harcourt was more than a little interested in the Horne chit. It might be amusing to have her snatched from beneath his nose. It was a pity Lawrence wasn't interested, but perhaps he could find a few young rakes that might think it a lark to snatch an innocent girl and have their pleasure with her. It was worth considering, but not for the moment...he wanted some more of Harcourt's money in his pocket before he stepped out of line.

Lucy was feeling nervous but excited as she dressed in a blue carriage gown the next morning. She had set a pretty hat at a rakish angle on her head, and was pleased with her appearance. She had begun to acquire the town gloss that she had wanted, and her confidence was growing all the time. Her popularity and the several offers of marriage she had now received had made her realise that she was attractive and sought after, and she could not help hoping that Lord Harcourt would become aware of it.

He was punctual as before, and she greeted him with a bright smile as they went outside to where the light curricle and horses were waiting. Lucy had no real knowledge of horses or carriages, but she knew at once that it was different from the rigs that most gentlemen drove. It was much lighter and smaller, and the horses looked more docile than those Lord Harcourt had driven on a previous occasion. She looked at him, her brows arched, and he nodded.

'Yes, it is a lady's rig, Miss Lucy, and the horses are well schooled to the touch of a young woman's hand.'

'Did you hire this just for me?' she asked, staring at him in wonder.

'Let us say that I have borrowed it from a friend,' Jack said. 'His wife used to drive it, but she is increasing and has given up driving for the time being. We came to an arrangement and you are at liberty to drive it as often as you please.'

'How generous you are to go to so much trouble for my sake,' Lucy exclaimed ingenuously. 'I did not expect it.'

'It would be too dangerous for an untried whip to drive my cattle,' Jack said. 'But these horses are gentle, obedient creatures and, providing you are careful with them, they will do exactly as you ask.'

'May I drive them now?' She was eager to begin, a gleam of excitement in her lovely eyes.

'Not until we reach the park,' Jack said. 'It would not do to begin your lesson in the street. No, you must allow me to drive you for the moment.' He could only hope that his credit would survive it if certain gentlemen he knew saw them in this! 'Come, let me help you.'

Lucy gave him her hand, sitting on the driving box beside him as they set out. She was very excited, though a little nervous. She glanced at his profile, thinking how attractive he was—and kind. She knew that Drew would have given her lessons at his estate had she ever asked, but this was exceptionally generous of Lord Harcourt—especially as she suspected that he received no pleasure from driving a rig of this style.

'I did not see you last evening, sir—or the previous evening.'

'No, I was otherwise engaged,' Jack told her. 'However, I shall attend Lady West's musical evening tonight—I believe you are engaged to her?'

'Yes, I am,' Lucy said. 'She is a great friend of Marianne's—and she has been very kind to me.'

'Lady West is also a friend of mine,' Jack said, a rather odd expression in his eyes. 'She told me that you would be attending. I shall be sure to see you there.'

Lucy's smile lit up her face. In her innocence, she could have no idea of how lovely she was or of the effect she was having on the gentleman beside her.

Jack visited a fencing club that afternoon. He was as skilled with the sword as he was with a pistol and he enjoyed matching his skill against the fencing master and any of his friends who happened to be there. He was not particularly pleased to see that Collingwood's nephew, Toby Lawrence, was already there with some of his cronies. However, he also found a friend and enjoyed a work out with him before going to the chamber set aside for patrons wishing to freshen up before leaving. It was as he was towelling himself down that he heard laughter coming from outside through an open window.

'It is a damned good notion, Lawrence,' a young man's voice said. 'Your uncle has the right of it. She is a flirt and deserves what is coming to her.'

'You shall not say a word against her,' Lawrence replied. 'She is divine—an angel…but why would she look at any of us? I have seen her driving with Harcourt. She was driving herself, though not in his rig. He must have got it for her. If he is interested, why would she take one of us?'

'Be damned to Harcourt,' one of the young rakes cried. 'I think we should make a plan to abduct her as your uncle suggested. Once we have her, we can make her choose between us.'

'Don't be a damned fool,' a new voice said. 'If Harcourt wants her, he would kill you!'

'He could try,' the young cockerel boasted. 'I know he is

skilled with the sword, but I am a match for any man with the pistols.'

'You haven't seen him at Manton's,' one of the others cautioned. 'I've seen him shoot the diamonds on a playing card and he's deadly accurate.'

'Well, how is he to know? Are you up for it, Lawrence?'

There was a slight hesitation, then, 'Yes, if you must—but she's mine first. I get the first chance to persuade her.'

'All right, but I'll have her if she refuses you. She won't refuse me.'

'When shall we do it?' another voice asked a trifle dubiously.

'There's a masked ball on Friday night. She is sure to be there. We'll entice her outside and then we'll grab her.'

The voices were moving away, becoming fainter. Jack was tight with anger. He could hardly believe that men who considered themselves gentlemen could speak of abducting a young woman of good family, and yet he knew that it had happened in the past. It would not happen to Lucy Horne, for he knew with absolute certainty that it was she they had been speaking of. He would be at the masked ball on Friday night and he would make sure that those young hellions did not get a chance to carry out their plan! If they dared to actually try to carry it out, they would come unstuck. In the meantime, he would speak to Drew Marlbeck about what he had overheard. It would be better if the two of them were alert and aware of what was going on, and made their plans accordingly.

He would say nothing to Lucy, for it would merely distress her, perhaps make her afraid to venture out into society at all, and he did not wish to damage her confidence. He could only hope that she would resist any attempt to lure her outside at the functions she attended in the meantime.

* * *

Lucy was happily unaware of the speculation and bets going on amongst certain young gentlemen. She was engaged for every evening that week and went from one glittering affair to the next, thoroughly enjoying being the centre of attention. She received five more proposals from young gentlemen that she hardly knew. But as all of them seemed either to be teasing her or slightly intoxicated, she merely laughed and shook her head at them.

Lucy could not know, but two of the gentlemen had been in deadly earnest and hoping to steal a march on Toby Lawrence. Annoyed that she had refused them, they added their voices to the growing speculation that she would take Lord Harcourt, who seemed to be paying court to her since he had been seen driving with her in the park three times. The fact that she had actually held the reins of an equipage in which Harcourt would not normally have been seen dead fuelled the flames of speculation and rumour.

Toby Lawrence had regretted telling his friends of his uncle's suggestion that he abduct Lucy Horne and force her to marry him by ruining her reputation. He was genuinely in love with her, and knew that such a course could only lead to Lucy hating him for ever. Even if he managed to compromise her and bring about the marriage he desired, she would despise him.

If he could he would have drawn back, but the speculation about Lord Harcourt's interest had piqued his pride, and his friends were keen for what they saw as a lark. They had decided that they would all go to the masked ball dressed in the same costume, as sixteenth-century pirates, and only the colour of their masks would be different.

'She would never go outside with you,' Philip Markham said. 'But she is quite willing to dance with me, and if she thought it was me she might trust me enough.'

'She does not go outside with anyone,' Toby Lawrence said gloomily. 'I upset her when she went out for some air once and Harcourt must have warned her against it.'

'Then we shall have to think of some ruse to lure her into the gardens,' Markham said. 'But if I dance with her earlier wearing a red mask and then we change, you can lure her outside. Once we have her in the garden, you can unmask and tell her that you adore her and wish to marry her. If she refuses, we will come out of hiding and pounce on her—carry her off and teach her a lesson.'

'Could I not just rescue her from you and earn her goodwill?' Lawrence said reluctantly. 'She will hate me for this.'

'If you're too squeamish, I'll do it,' Markham said, 'but then I get the first chance with her. She won't refuse after I've had her.'

'No! Damn you,' Lawrence said, furious that his friend should speak of her with disrespect. 'It was my idea and I want her. You don't care about her, Markham. I love her.'

His friends laughed jeeringly. He flushed and turned away, angry and frustrated. He knew it would be easy to stop this thing, because if he went to the Marquis of Marlbeck he would have a word with Markham's father and that would finish it—and yet if he did nothing, he was certain that she would marry Harcourt. He was torn between taking what he wanted and the fear that, by doing so, he would lose what he truly desired.

'May I ask what you will be wearing this evening?' Jack asked when he called for Lucy to take her driving that Friday morning. 'Or is it a big secret?'

'Oh, I shall be dressed as Marie Antoinette,' Lucy said. 'I know that some people are keeping their costumes a secret, but I do not mind you knowing, Lord Harcourt.'

'Do you think you could call me Harcourt?' Jack asked with a lift of his right eyebrow. 'I believe we can claim to be more than mere acquaintances now, Miss Lucy?'

'Yes, perhaps,' she said and gave him a shy glance. 'I have thought of you as a friend for years…since my sister's wedding.'

'Have you? How kind,' Jack said, glancing at her sideways. He saw the faint flush in her cheeks and wondered. Had he perhaps encouraged her to expect an offer by offering to teach her to drive? It had been an impulse, but not one he had regretted, for she had surprised him by mastering the whip from the start. He had no hesitation in handing her the reins when they entered the park, giving himself time to think and observe.

Lucy had the makings of a fine whip. For a girl who looked as fragile and delicate as she did, it was surprising how easily she controlled her horses. They were, of course, well schooled to a lady's hand on the reins, but even so she had done very well. He felt a sense of pride as he saw how others turned their heads to watch as they drove by, for Lucy made a charming picture. He knew that tales of her driving would even now be circulating in the clubs and drawing rooms of London, and felt a slight unease. Had this little escapade influenced those young rakehells—or would the attempt at abduction have been planned anyway?

He had communicated his information concerning it to Drew and they had made their plans. It would be impossible for the abduction to be carried out, but they had decided to let it go ahead so that the culprits could be caught in the act and taught a lesson.

As Drew had said, 'We cannot allow this kind of thing, Jack. Young girls of good family would go in fear if they were to succeed.'

'They shall not succeed,' Jack had promised. 'I know them

all, and I shall be on my guard—but two heads are better than one and I wanted you on board.'

'I am grateful for your confidence,' Drew told him grimly. 'But the fact remains that we learned of this by chance. Had you not overheard them plotting…' He shook his head. 'Their fathers will receive a visit from me when this is all over!'

'You must do as you please in that regard,' Jack said. 'I have my own ideas—but what matters is that Lucy remains safe.'

They had parted on a note of mutual agreement and Jack was satisfied that they had covered every eventuality, other than a possible change of venue. However, since the plotters could have no idea they had been overheard, it was unlikely they would alter their arrangements.

'Drew told me that he has horses in his stables at Marlbeck that I may drive whenever I wish,' Lucy said, breaking into his musings at that moment. 'If you had not been so kind as to teach me, I might never have thought of it, sir. I am so grateful to you, for it is something I believe I shall always enjoy.'

Jack turned his head to look at her. Her cheeks were glowing from the fresh air and her eyes bright with mischief. She looked extremely beautiful and he felt a surge of burning desire. How foolish he had been to see her as a child. She was a lovely, warm and desirable woman—young and still innocent, but quite definitely a woman.

'I am glad to have been of service to you, Lucy,' he said, forgetting the formal usage of her name in his sudden overwhelming passion. 'I hope you will save at least three dances for me this evening?'

'Yes, of course, if you wish it,' she replied and her heart raced for she had never seen him look at her in quite that way. 'I think it will be great fun—don't you?'

'Yes, I think it will,' Jack agreed with a smile. She was

beautiful, poised on the edge of her womanhood, ready for love—and he knew that his body had responded to her in a quite unexpected way. However, he believed himself too old for her, both in years and experience. Life had taught him bitter lessons, which he had taken on the chin, retaining his sense of balance—but she was untainted, perfect. He sensed that she might accept him if he proposed to her—but did he have the right? Surely she deserved a younger man—someone who had not tasted so deeply of the bitter cup of life?

Lucy was unaware of Jack's thoughts, though she had sensed a change in him. She concentrated on her driving until it was time to turn for home, when Jack took control once more, because he did not wish to expose her to the dangers of driving through the streets just yet. She was learning fast, but there were too many accidents in the crowded London streets, and she might not be able to handle her horses if a wagon should shed its load ahead of them or a stray dog dash into the road barking, a child at its heels.

When they arrived back at the Marlbecks' house, Jack gave the reins to his stablehand and got down, offering his hand to Lucy. Her heel caught in the hem of her gown as she descended and she pitched forward into his arms, saved from a fall only because he held her tightly against his chest. Lucy was a little shocked—she had not expected it and the overwhelming rush of emotion made her cry out. She looked up at him, eyes wide, heart racing wildly as she gazed into his eyes and saw the smouldering passion there. Had they not been in public view, she was sure that he would have kissed her.

'Forgive me,' she said breathlessly as he set her on her feet and then released her. 'That was foolish of me. I do not know how I came to trip.'

'It is easily done,' Jack said, resisting the urge to kiss those soft lips that suddenly seemed all too enticing. 'Forgive me, I have another appointment. I shall see you this evening, Lucy.'

'Yes, Harcourt,' Lucy said. 'Thank you...for everything.' The smile she gave him was shy, questioning. Almost against his will, Jack took her hand and kissed it.

'Until this evening.'

'Yes...' Lucy was breathless as she watched him return to the rig and take the reins. 'This evening...'

Her heart seemed to beat at twice its usual rate as she went into the house. Surely she could not be mistaken—he *had* looked at her as if he wanted to kiss her, hadn't he? The back of her hand still tingled where his lips had touched it, and she had wished that it was her lips he had kissed.

Lucy had tried to control her feelings for Lord Harcourt, because she had not thought he saw her as a woman—but this morning something had changed. She was certain that she had seen passion in his eyes as he looked at her, and she could not help a little surge of hope. If he cared for her, there was nothing to stand in their way, because her family surely could not refuse him or think him unsuitable.

'Lucy, I wanted a word with you, dearest,' Mrs Horne said as her daughter came downstairs after changing from her carriage gown. 'Please come into the back parlour. We may be alone there, for Marianne has gone out this morning.'

'Is something the matter, Mama?' Lucy asked, because her mother looked serious. 'You are not ill, I hope?'

'No, Lucy, I am quite well,' Mrs Horne told her. 'Your Aunt Bertha has written to me, because she is not feeling quite the thing. I think I should go home, Lucy. I do not wish to neglect her after all that she has done for us. However, there is no need for you to accompany me. Your sister and Drew are chaperons enough, my love. I know that I leave you in safe hands.'

'Thank you, Mama,' Lucy said for she would not have wished to return home so soon, especially as she had seen something in Harcourt's eyes that made her think he was at last beginning to notice her. 'I am very sorry Aunt Bertha is unwell.'

'Yes, so am I,' Mrs Horne said, 'because she has been exceptionally good to us as a family, Lucy. Therefore I shall go to her at once. I know you will be a good girl and give no trouble to your sister. However, there is something I must say to you before I leave.'

'Yes, Mama?' Lucy looked at her uncertainly.

'It concerns Lord Harcourt,' Mrs Horne told her. 'I do not doubt he is a gentleman and that you are safe in his company, otherwise I should not have allowed you to go driving with him. However, I have heard a disturbing rumour, dearest. It is something I should not normally discuss with you, but I feel that you should know…' She hesitated, because she would not have dreamed of mentioning such a subject to her daughter had she not been forced to leave town.

'Something about Lord Harcourt?' Lucy stared at her, a cold shiver running down her spine. Miss Tremaine had told her that he was a rake, but she knew that that lady had been disappointed because he did not offer for her. 'What has he done to make you look like that, Mama?'

'I have heard that he has a bastard child,' her mother said and Lucy gasped—she had not expected this. 'I do not know if it is true—and in itself it is not so very terrible, for I dare say other gentlemen have similar secrets. However, I have heard that he retains a friendship with the woman believed to be the child's mother—a woman of the lower orders, I understand.'

'I do not quite understand you, Mama.' Lucy was too stunned to take it in immediately.

'I am saying that he has a mistress, Lucy. It might be that he would give her up when he married...but it seems he has something of a reputation and it might be that he would continue to visit her after marriage.'

'Oh, I see.' Lucy flushed beneath her mother's gaze. 'Surely he would not—if he truly loved his wife?'

'I cannot say, Lucy,' Mrs Horne said, looking serious. 'I do not say that I would necessarily forbid such an eventuality if he were to ask for your hand, but I would insist on a long engagement, my dearest.'

'He...has not asked me, Mama.' Lucy's cheeks were bright red.

'No, I did not think he had, for he would probably have come to me or Drew before he spoke,' Mrs Horne said. 'However, should he speak after I have gone home, remember that I would not give my permission until you had been given a chance to know him very much better.'

'Yes, Mama, of course,' Lucy said. 'But perhaps the rumours are not true—it may all be just a silly tale. Besides, even if there was such a child, it does not mean that he is still...with its mother...'

'No, of course not,' Mrs Horne agreed, for she was a fair-minded woman and did not wish to distress her daughter. It was only her suspicion that Lucy was very attracted to Lord Harcourt that had made her speak out now. 'I am not forbidding you to see him—nor have I set my mind against a marriage between you, my love. I just wished you to be aware of the situation.'

'Thank you, Mama. You are very good to speak to me this way,' Lucy said, because she understood that her mother was being extremely fair in this matter. Some mothers might have forbidden their daughters to go driving with a man after hearing such rumours, but of course Lord Harcourt had been of great help to their family some years earlier and therefore Mrs Horne was inclined to trust him despite the scurrilous tales. 'You are right to trust Lord Harcourt, for I know him to be a perfect gentleman—and he has said nothing to me that you would censure.'

'I did not think it,' her mother assured her. 'But my concern is for you, Lucy. I know your tender heart and I do not wish you to be hurt in the future, my dearest.'

'I am sure that I shall not be,' Lucy said. 'I will not pretend that I am not attracted to Lord Harcourt, for I am—but I know that your advice is sound and I should wish to know him better before I married. I should not wish to marry any gentleman without knowing him well, Mama.'

'Then we need say no more about it,' Mrs Horne told her with a smile of relief. 'I can leave you in your sister's care with a light heart. I am leaving almost immediately so I shall not be attending the masked ball this evening, but I know that both Marianne and Drew will be there to look after you.'

Lucy embraced her mother. She was very thoughtful as she saw her off a little later that morning, for the story her mother had told her must have come from a reliable source or she would not have thought it necessary to mention it to Lucy.

It was very likely that Lord Harcourt had an illegitimate child, but that in itself was not so very dreadful. Lucy was sensible enough to know that these things happened and, considering everything, she did not think it would upset her so very much. However, a continuing liaison between the child's mother and Lord Harcourt was another matter. She was not sure that she could accept such a situation and knew that the thought would give her some uneasy moments in the future.

However, she decided that she would forget it for the time being. As yet Lord Harcourt had said nothing to indicate that he would make her a proposal of marriage, even though she did suspect that he had begun to see her as a woman and not a child. She would see him again this evening at the masked ball, and she would behave exactly as if she had heard nothing at all.

'You look lovely, my dearest,' Marianne said as she saw her sister dressed in her costume that evening. Lucy's dress was pale blue silk with voluminous skirts and panniers. Her hair was dressed high on her head in curls, with one ringlet allowed to fall on her left shoulder, and she wore a black mask trimmed with silver over the top half of her face. 'Somehow that costume makes you look older...more sophisticated. I think it is as well that Mama is not here for she might have thought it too daring for you, my love.'

Lucy glanced at herself in the long cheval mirror, feeling a little surprised as she saw her reflection. Marianne was quite right, for the dress was low cut across her breasts, showing more of the pearly soft flesh than she would normally have revealed. However, it was the hairstyle and the mask that had given her a rather wicked look; she might have been a courtesan from the court of the French King instead of pretty, innocent, Lucy Horne!

'Do you think I should wear some lace at the neck?' she asked her sister. 'I should not want to appear fast, Marianne.'

'No, my love, I do not,' Marianne said, surprising her. 'You are not a child, though Mama would keep you one if she could. If you behave with modesty, as you always do, even the strictest chaperon could not fault you for wearing that gown. Many ladies will be wearing far more daring costumes.'

'Yes, I expect so,' Lucy agreed and giggled as she picked

up her fan. 'It is so exciting. I am not sure I shall be able to guess who everyone is—shall you?'

'Oh, I usually know people when they speak,' Marianne said. 'But the fun is in guessing who everyone is when you first get there.' She smiled at her sister. Both she and Jo had always said that they thought Lucy would be the most beautiful of them all when she grew up, and that night she had proved them right. 'I think you will have to fight the gentlemen off this evening, Lucy—but don't worry, dearest. Drew and I will be there to see fair play.'

Marianne might not have felt so pleased about things had she known what her husband and Jack Harcourt knew, but they had not confided in her. Drew had counted on Mrs Horne being one of their party—he knew that she always kept an eagle eye on her daughter—but her absence meant that he and Jack would have to be extra-vigilant.

Jack was one of the first guests to arrive that evening. As luck would have it, the costume he had ordered was for a gentleman of the seventeenth century and, as the coat was dark blue velvet, the petticoat breeches of a paler blue silk, he was a perfect foil for Lucy when she arrived. His first sight of her took his breath away, and he knew an overwhelming desire to kiss her and hold her in his arms. This was followed swiftly by an urgent need to protect her from all harm, even at the cost of his own life. He would thrash those young devils if they laid rough hands on her!

Lucy was immediately besieged by gentlemen wishing to be her partner, but, safe in the knowledge that she had promised to keep three dances for him, Jack took his time about approaching her. She looked at him uncertainly as he came up to her after the third dance, her soft mouth quivering.

'Is that you, Lord Harcourt?'

'Yes, Majesty,' he said and made an elegant leg as she offered her hand. 'Where is the King this evening?'

Lucy laughed huskily. 'Why, I think you may be him,' she replied, her eyes dancing with mischief. 'I have kept the dances you asked for, Sire.'

'Then shall we dance, Madame?'

Lucy gave him her hand, feeling a surge of what she believed must be desire as he took her into his arms and they began to waltz. She had never felt quite this way before and it both thrilled and frightened her. She gazed up at him, at his mouth, which, when relaxed, was so kissable, and his firm chin, which spoke volumes of determination. It felt so right to be here in his arms this way, and she wished the dance might go on for ever, but too soon the music was ending and she was claimed by her next partner.

All the young gentlemen pretended not to know who Lucy was, making outrageous guesses to tease her, though she suspected that they had guessed long ago, as she had most of them. She was given no rest, passing from one partner to the other as the evening wore on in a haze of laughter.

Lucy danced with Lord Harcourt again mid-evening, but this time it was a progressive and they had to part to dance with others. However, she had reserved the supper waltz for him, and once again it was a magical experience. By the time it ended, Lucy knew that her heart had been irrevocably given to him, and that if he did not ask her to marry him she would not wish to marry at all. It was foolish of her to feel this way, but she could not help it, and even the tale of his illegitimate child could not prevent her from feeling that he was the only man she would ever love.

After the dance was over, Jack looked down at her face, catching a hint of the way she was feeling. 'May I take you into supper?' he asked.

'I think I must take a few minutes to refresh myself,' Lucy told him, a hint of shyness in her now as she looked up at him. 'But if you reserve a table for us, I shall join you later. I am not very hungry...perhaps just a syllabub?'

'Your wish is my command, Majesty,' Jack said. 'I shall be waiting for you.'

He watched as she left the room. Glancing at Drew, he crossed over to where he was standing by the French windows.

'Lucy has gone to refresh herself,' he said. 'Have you seen anything suspicious yet?'

'Nothing... There they are, the three of them.' Drew's mouth tightened. 'By the look of it they are plotting something. Go out into the garden, Jack. I'll watch for Lucy to return and do what I can to head them off. If they mean to strike tonight, it must surely be soon.'

'Yes, I agree,' Jack said. 'I'll be on the terrace...'

He walked out of the ballroom, through to the supper room. There was a terrace outside, where ladies and gentlemen were parading to take the air before settling down to supper. Jack moved into the shadows, away from the lights and the buzz of voices. He hoped that their three plotters had not decided to put off their attempt at abduction, for they needed to be caught in the act.

Lucy returned to the ballroom a few minutes later. She had stopped to talk to her sister, who had also gone to the room reserved for ladies to refresh themselves. Marianne suggested that they should go into supper together, and Lucy agreed; she could see no sign of Lord Harcourt, and was a little puzzled. However, as she moved towards the buffet table, a young lady with whom she was slightly acquainted came up to her.

'Miss Horne,' Amy Robinson said. 'Someone gave me a

message for you. He asked if you would go out to the terrace. He said that he has your supper waiting for you.'

'Who gave you the message?' Lucy asked, for she thought it a little odd, though she knew that one or two tables had been set outside on the terrace.

'I did not ask his name—but he was dressed in a costume of your era.'

'Oh, I see, thank you,' Lucy said and smiled at her. 'That would be Lord Harcourt. I shall go out to him.'

She had been doubtful even though the message came from a lady she knew, but her doubts fled as she realised that Lord Harcourt was waiting for her. She supposed that he had found the supper room too crowded and preferred to eat outside in the coolness of the summer night. She left Miss Robinson and walked towards the open windows, a little smile on her lips—the idea of an open-air supper appealed to her.

Going out to the terrace, Lucy hesitated. She could see the little wrought-iron tables, which were all occupied, but there was still no sign of Lord Harcourt. She hesitated at the edge of the three steps leading down to the lawns, and then, lifting the hem of her dress, walked down them, away from the lights that spilled out from the windows of the house towards the shadows.

As she did so, two young men attempted to follow her from the same set of French windows. Drew moved to block their passage, removing the mask he had worn all evening as he confronted the pirates.

'Gentlemen,' he said pleasantly. 'I should like a word with you, if you please.'

'We have other business,' Philip Markham said, his mouth curling in a sneer. 'Perhaps another time.'

'No, I do not think my business will wait,' Drew told him. 'Unless of course you would prefer that I took it up with your fathers?'

'He knows,' Peter Robinson said and took off his mask. Drew's threat had thrown him, because his father had already threatened to cut off his allowance if he did not behave himself, and he had never been that keen on the plot to abduct Lucy. 'Give it up, Markham. It was a damned stupid idea in the first place.'

'Shut up, you fool,' Markham said. 'You are a coward and a blabbermouth.' He took off his mask. 'It was Lawrence's idea in the first place. I wash my hands of it.'

'Very sensible,' Drew said, still in that pleasant tone, but with a look that sent chills down the spines of the two young rakehells. 'Otherwise, your fathers' censure may be the least of your troubles. Believe me, gentlemen, you would not like to know me when I am angry.'

'It was just a lark,' Peter Robinson protested and quailed as he saw the look on Drew's face. 'Listen, Marlbeck, I'm sorry. I didn't want to go along with it in the first place.'

'Coward,' Markham said. 'I'm not afraid of you, Marlbeck, but it was Lawrence's uncle who came up with it—and we thought it was a bit of fun. I dare say we should never have carried it through.'

'Rest assured that you would not have been allowed to carry it through,' Drew said. 'And if anything should happen to Miss Horne in the future, I shall know where to come.' He inclined his head as he heard something outside, which sounded like a startled cry. 'Now, if you will excuse me…'

Drew turned his back on them and went out to the terrace. He was just in time to see a scuffle between two men taking place near a fountain deep in the shadows, and realised that Toby Lawrence had indeed attempted something, even though his friends had not been there to help him. Jack was struggling with him, and, as Drew watched, he landed a punch on his jaw, knocking him to the ground. Lucy came running towards him at that moment, her face pale.

'Drew!' she cried. 'I came out to find Lord Harcourt and... someone tried to grab me. He was trying to drag me into the bushes when Lord Harcourt came and stopped him.'

'Are you all right, Lucy?'

'Yes. I was startled for a moment, but nothing happened. It was all so quick. He had only just laid hands on me when Lord Harcourt sprang on him.'

'We made sure of that,' Drew told her. 'Three young idiots had it in mind to kidnap you and force you to marry one of them, Lucy. Jack got wind of it and we set this up, made it easy for Lawrence to make the attempt, while I headed off the other two. We had to make certain that they tried it or we should never have been certain you were safe, but it is all over now. I have dealt with two of them, and Jack is more than capable of sorting young Lawrence out.'

'You meant it to happen?' Lucy stared at him incredulously. The incident had been over so quickly that she had hardly had the time to be frightened, but now she was angry. 'And you did not think it necessary to tell me?' She threw him a look that spoke volumes of her disgust and went into the supper room, making her way to Marianne.

'What is it, dearest?' Marianne asked, seeing her face. She had also noticed that Lucy's gown had a slight tear at the waist. 'Did someone try to harm you?'

'It was merely some kind of jest,' Lucy said. 'Apparently Drew and Lord Harcourt knew all about it. They are dealing with the culprit now.'

'Oh, Lucy,' Marianne said, sensing that her sister was more upset than she was prepared to reveal in public. 'Would you like to go home?'

'Yes, I should,' Lucy said. She was feeling so angry with Drew and Lord Harcourt that she did not think that she could bear to meet them in public just yet. 'If you do not mind?'

'No, of course not,' Marianne said. 'Go up and get your cloak, dearest, and bring mine. I shall tell Drew that we are leaving at once.'

Lucy nodded and left her. She did not look at anyone as she went upstairs. She felt very angry, for she believed she had been made to look foolish. She had trusted Miss Robinson when she had spoken of a man in seventeenth-century costume, because she believed the message came from Lord Harcourt. Indeed, it might well have been so, she realised, since he had wanted her to walk into the trap set for her—so that he could catch Mr Lawrence trying to abduct her!

Lucy knew that Drew and Lord Harcourt had been acting in her best interests, for had they not controlled the little plot it might have gone awry and she could have found herself at the mercy of three ruthless young devils, forced to accept one of them as her husband to save her reputation. However, perhaps because it had all gone so smoothly, with hardly a ruffle to her peace of mind, she felt humiliated and annoyed that she had been used as a pawn. If they had simply told her the names of the gentlemen involved, she would have given them all a wide berth.

She thought she knew who it would have been, for she had noticed them all huddling together earlier in the evening, and she had seen the way they had all dressed alike, the only difference the colour of the masks they wore. Lord Harcourt might have given her the credit for having the sense never to accept any invitation to meet one of them on the terrace or to take the air with any gentleman she did not absolutely trust, but perhaps he did not understand that she had learned her lesson?

She would not have gone out to meet anyone but him—and had he been in the supper room as they had arranged, it need not have happened at all. She knew that her friends had been trying to protect her, but she could not feel grateful or pleased by their efforts. She was not a child and she did not wish to be treated as one!

Lucy's anger had not abated by the time she came down, though she was able to greet Drew with a polite smile when he asked her if she felt unwell.

'I am perfectly well, thank you,' she replied. 'But I think I should prefer to go home. Please thank Lord Harcourt for...what he did, though had I been told what was expected it would not have been necessary.'

'But they might have tried another time and we might not have been there,' Drew said, for he sensed that her feelings had been hurt. 'We did not do this lightly, Lucy, believe me.'

Lucy looked at him hard. She had always liked and trusted her sister's husband, and she began to realise that perhaps the small incident had been easily brushed over only because of what they had done.

'Yes, I see...but I ought to have been told, Drew. I am not a child, though some people may think it.'

She walked away from him with dignity. Drew met his wife's eyes.

'I fear we have upset Lucy, my love. She does not realise the consequences of what might have happened. That fool Lawrence has challenged Jack to a duel.'

'Oh, Drew!' Marianne stared at him in horror. 'That is awful. I am so glad Mama is not here, because she would have been very distressed by all of this.'

'I dare say we shall manage to brush it under the carpet,' Drew said. 'Jack will fire in the air and we shall keep the reason for their quarrel as quiet as we can.'

'I do hope so, for Lucy's sake, because I would not like her name to be dragged through the mud,' Marianne said as she prepared to follow her sister. 'She is waiting for me. We shall discuss this further when you come home, dearest.'

'I must stay with Jack for now. Naturally, he named me as his second.'

'Must he really fight a duel?'

'I fear there is no getting out of it,' Drew said. 'Jack knocked him down, but it was Lawrence who issued the challenge. You could not expect him to refuse?'

'No, I suppose not,' Marianne said and sighed. 'You will tell me what happens?'

'Of course.' Drew smiled at her. 'Do not worry, Marianne, this will all be forgotten in a few days.'

'I pray that you are right,' Marianne said, 'for otherwise Mama will never forgive us!'

Lucy felt calmer by the time they had reached Marlbeck House. She kissed her sister when Marianne asked if she needed anything, telling her that she was perfectly well and did not need a tisane to make her sleep. Indeed, she did not wish for it, because she wanted time alone to consider what had happened.

Once she was alone in her room, having dismissed her maid after she had been helped out of her costume, Lucy sat staring at herself in the dressing mirror. She knew that the gown she had worn that evening had been a little more daring than usual and it had crossed her mind that perhaps she had brought the attack on herself. However, if Drew and Lord Harcourt had planned their response to the kidnap attempt, it meant that it had nothing to do with the way she had looked that evening. And she was certain that she had done nothing immodest to make any gentleman believe she would welcome such an attempt. She had smiled at their jests, refused their offers of marriage kindly, but never flirted as some of the older ladies did—so why had she been chosen as their victim?

Had it been some kind of a jest? Lucy could not help feeling uncomfortable, because she must surely have done something to make the three gentlemen choose her as their victim. Had she laughed too freely or done anything to make them think that she was fast? Try as she might, Lucy could think of no reason why they would have supposed her to be a willing victim—and that made her realise that they must have been ruthless to plan it. She felt coldness at the base of her spine as it dawned on her that she had been in far more danger than she had supposed. In the heat of the moment it had seemed just the foolishness of a young man who was probably intoxicated, but seen now from a distance she perceived it was much more.

Instead of being safe in her own bedroom this evening, she might have been a prisoner somewhere and... Lucy shuddered as she finally understood what had been intended for her. She would have been seduced, perhaps raped, for she would never have agreed to their suggestion that she choose one of them for her husband—and she would most certainly have been ruined. It was such a horrible prospect that she was suddenly overcome by tears and ran for the bed, pulling the covers up tightly about her, as if to protect herself.

In the morning she would thank Drew properly, and, when she saw Lord Harcourt, she must thank him, though at the moment she felt so embarrassed that she hoped he would not call for a while.

Jack looked at his opponent in the grey light of dawn. They had both chosen their seconds and met at the appointed place and time. He saw that Toby Lawrence looked sick, frightened even, and if it had not been for the seriousness of what he had planned, Jack would have let him off with a warning. However, the young cub must be taught a lesson, though he had no intention of killing him or even wounding him. He would fire in the air, but he would make Lawrence come up to scratch so that he learned a valuable lesson.

'You will walk for ten paces and then turn on the command. When I say fire, you are free to fire one shot at will…' Drew's voice echoed on the still air.

Lawrence had chosen a dark coat; done up to the throat, it covered his shirt and gave less of a target. Jack had no doubt that he had been schooled by his uncle, for Collingwood had witnessed enough duels when he was younger. He might even have been a fair shot once. Jack himself was a crack shot, having learned his skill under enemy fire, but he meant to make no use of it here. He had removed his own coat and was wearing only his shirt and a dark waistcoat and breeches, his long boots as immaculate as always. The difference in their manner was noticeable, for Jack was calm, unruffled, his face giving no sign of his feelings, whilst Lawrence looked like a scared rabbit.

They stood back to back, then took the ten paces and turned. Lawrence jerked his arm up, firing immediately without waiting for the command. His shot nicked Jack's left arm, burning the fine white linen and causing a trickle of crimson to stain its crisp perfection. Jack held his stance without flinching. He gave no sign that he had even felt the shot as he levelled the pistol at his opponent's chest, his finger on the hammer. Lawrence gave a cry of fear, his courage fleeing as he saw what he thought was his death sentence in Jack's eyes.

'I didn't mean to hurt her,' he blurted out. 'I swear it wasn't my idea. I love her. I wanted to marry her, but she didn't like me.'

'You will never touch her again,' Jack said and fired in the air. Lawrence gave a little scream and fell to his knees. He was trembling, feeling the hot sting of urine as he wet his breeches, tears running down his cheeks as Jack walked up to him, standing over him, cold, angry, relentless. 'Let that be a lesson to you. Do not listen to bad advice, sir. I have let you live this time—but if I hear that anything has happened to Miss Horne in the future, I shall kill you.'

Lawrence shook his head, too ashamed to meet the other man's gaze. 'I swear it won't—by my hand. I loved her. It was my uncle's idea and then Markham…he goaded me into it.'

'He has been dealt with. Sir Frederick has yet to pay his dues, but the time is coming, believe me.'

Toby Lawrence looked up at him. What he saw in Jack Harcourt's eyes at that moment made him shiver. He knew that his uncle thought of this man as a pigeon to be plucked, but he was so very wrong. If he had been braver, he might have warned him, but he knew that he would not do so. He meant to leave London for the country in the morning. It would be many months before he would dare to show his face in town again.

'Let me look at your wound,' Drew said, coming up to Jack at that moment. 'The young idiot fired too soon. He should find himself before the magistrates for that.'

'It is nothing,' Jack replied. 'A scratch, no more. He was too terrified to wait and I think he has been punished enough. It is the man who pushed him into this that I want, Drew—and believe me, when I have finished with him he will be sorry.'

Chapter Five

'Are you feeling more the thing now?' Drew asked Lucy later that day. She had just come in from a shopping expedition with two friends and she seemed happy enough, her cheeks pink from the fresh air.

'Yes, very much better,' she told him with a smile. Neither of her friends had mentioned the incident of the previous evening and she did not think that they had heard of it. 'I am sorry if I was abrupt last night. I know that what you did was for my sake, but...' She drew a deep breath and shook her head.

'I understand,' Drew told her with a smile. 'There is nothing to apologise for, Lucy. I hope this has not spoiled your visit or made you wish to return home—though if it has, you have only to say.'

'No, I shall not run away,' Lucy said, raising her head proudly. 'Last night I was too upset to stay at the ball, but I am calmer now I have thought it over. I did nothing to invite what happened, therefore I have no need of shame.'

'Certainly not,' Drew said. 'You must not even think it, Lucy. It was just some young hotheads who had gone beyond the bounds of what is allowable. They have been punished for it. They have learned their lesson and I do not think that any of them will bother you again.'

'Thank you...' Lucy blushed. 'I did not thank Lord Harcourt, because I was too...upset to think of it last evening.'

'I believe he understands,' Drew said. 'I am sure he needs no thanks for what he did.'

'Will he be at Marianne's party this evening?'

'No, I do not think so,' Drew said. 'I believe he may be detained elsewhere.'

Jack's wound had not been serious, but it had been deeper than he would allow and it must be sore. It would probably be a day or so before he could bear to wear his tight-fitting coats again, and he would not venture into society until he felt ready.

'Oh...' Lucy looked at him thoughtfully. She was not sure how she felt about that. A part of her wanted to see Jack Harcourt very much and yet another did not. She was still afraid that he would censure her for falling into the trap—and she was a little angry. He might have given her some hint so that she knew what to expect. If he could keep secrets from her over such a thing, what else might he keep secret in the future? Perhaps she did not know him quite as well as she had thought? 'Well, I dare say it does not matter. I shall see him one of these times.'

'I have no doubt of that,' Drew replied. He was certain that his friend had strong feelings for her, and he wondered what was holding him back. He had expected Jack to speak to him before this.

'People are talking,' Marianne said to her husband two days later. 'News of the duel has got out, and people are speculating about the reasons behind it. Lucy's name has been linked with Jack Harcourt's—I have heard that they are laying bets in the gentlemen's clubs on him making her an offer. Is that true?'

'Yes, I rather think it may be,' Drew admitted and frowned. 'We did our best to scotch it, Marianne, but you know how these things get out. There were already rumours before the duel, but now they are keeping a book on it at White's. I think the marriage is expected and only the timing is a source of speculation.'

'That is terrible,' Marianne said, looking upset. 'Why will gentlemen do such things? If he does not ask her, it is bound to make people think the worst. Lucy's reputation will suffer and that is not fair.'

'I agree, but there is very little we can do about it for the moment, my love. Lucy is blameless, of course, but tongues will wag. I think Harcourt cares for her, but perhaps I should give him a hint?'

'If he needs a hint, he does not truly care for her,' Marianne said. 'I do not wish her to be pushed into something that may turn out badly. Those stories…if he truly has a mistress and they have a child…I do not want Lucy to be made unhappy.'

'I am sure Jack would not continue to keep a mistress once he married,' Drew said. 'If he loves Lucy, and I believe he does, he would not do anything to hurt her.'

'I wish I could be sure,' Marianne said. 'I understand that he is your friend, and he has helped Jo and us in the past—but Lucy is my little sister. I know she is grown up now, and seems well able to fend for herself, but—'

'I agree,' Drew said and hushed her with a kiss. 'If these rumours continue, I'll have a word to him. I know Jack has something else on his mind at the moment, but once that is over I am sure he will know what he ought to do concerning Lucy.'

'She would not wish him to ask merely because of gossip,' Marianne said. 'I think she is very much in love with him.'

'I believe Jack loves her, but as I said, he has something he has to do before he can think of marriage...' Marianne raised her fine eyebrows, but he shook his head. 'It is Jack's business, my love. I dare say you will hear about it soon enough.'

Jack entered the club that evening, his eyes searching for and finding both his quarry and the men he had hoped to see here—the witnesses to what he hoped would be his final meeting with Sir Frederick Collingwood. He had allowed the man to think him easy pickings, but tonight he would show him that he was alert to all his tricks and he would beat him at his own game, though without the use of marked cards.

Collingwood had seen him. His first glance was speculative, for he had heard of the duel between Harcourt and his nephew, though Lawrence had made a bolt for it afterwards without coming to tell him what had happened. He stood up, raising one eyebrow as Jack approached his table.

'Does our challenge still stand, Harcourt?'

'Of course,' Jack replied, face and tone expressionless, though the keener eyes amongst them might have noticed a gleam in his blue orbs. 'It was a mere squabble, Collingwood. I do not hold that insolent pup's misdemeanours against you—why should I?' He flicked his fingers in a careless manner that did not quite hide his anger.

Collingwood felt a sliver of ice at the nape of his neck. He had no way of knowing if Harcourt was aware that he had put the notion of abduction into his nephew's head, but he sensed something that made him uneasy. However, he gave no sign as he sat down, and Harcourt joined him. He was in need of money as always, for he had lost heavily on the horses that week and hoped to recoup that evening, at least enough to tide him over until he found another rich pigeon ripe for the plucking.

'Shall we say the same stakes as before—or would you care to play for something more?'

'Shall we say double—or treble?' Jack shrugged carelessly. 'It hardly matters—it is but a game of chance, is it not?'

'I would say skill comes into it,' Collingwood sneered, but Jack merely stared at him, not a flicker in his eyes, no sign that he had even realised it was meant as an insult.

They sat down at the table and cut for who should deal, the luck falling to Collingwood. Jack accepted it, though he knew that the cards had been marked. He smoothed his finger over his card, for it was only the high cards that had been marked. He was well aware that it was one of the ways Collingwood managed to cheat his victims. He raised his brows, glancing towards Sir Richard Greaves, who was standing a little distance away with two other gentlemen. Sir Richard took the hint and the three strolled over to the table.

'May we join you?' Greaves asked pleasantly.

'This is a private affair between Harcourt and me,' Collingwood said, a hint of annoyance in his tone.

'Why not?' Jack said. 'Pull up your chairs, gentlemen.' A flicker of something showed in his eyes as he saw Collingwood's chagrin. 'We were to play piquet, but I think single whisk would be better for the five of us. What do you say, Collingwood?'

'I suppose it does not matter,' Collingwood muttered unwillingly. It was clear to all of them that he was seething inside, but no one moved an eyelid, giving him nothing. 'As you wish, Harcourt. Our private challenge may wait for another time, I dare say.' His mood brightened as he realised it would give him yet another chance to fleece his victim.

'I suggest a fresh pack of cards,' Greaves said. 'Since it is to be a new game—perhaps I may supply them?'

'As you wish,' Collingwood said and shrugged. He handed the old pack to Greaves and took the new one, which one of the waiters supplied from the stock kept at the club, breaking it open. 'Shall we cut again?'

'Oh, I think we may accept that you shall deal first,' Jack said. 'Gentlemen, are you agreed?'

There was general assent, for the newcomers were following his lead. All of them had lost heavily to Collingwood at one time or another, but none of them had been brave enough to accuse him of cheating.

The first few hands were unremarkable. Harris won the first, Collingwood the second, and Saunders the third; Collingwood took the fourth. Jack yawned and suggested that the stakes be doubled. This was the signal for Saunders, Greaves and Harris to withdraw, which they did with a rueful excuse that they were temporarily short of funds.

'I'll take you,' Collingwood said, for this was what he had been waiting for—his chance to fleece his victim. 'Shall we say one hundred guineas a trick?'

'That should make it more interesting,' Jack agreed and pushed a small pile of gold into the middle of the table.

Collingwood won the first trick and Jack pushed more money into the pot, but he won the second, third and fourth, watching Collingwood push his money forward. Collingwood won the next two and Jack moved his money into the middle of the table. For the last trick, Collingwood laid the Queen of Hearts, which were trumps for that hand, a grin spreading over his face as he saw Jack's hesitation.

'My game, I think,' he said and reached for the money. As he did so, Jack reached out and caught his hand.

'Not so fast, my friend,' he said in a voice of ice. 'I think we have two issues here—the first being that I have the King of Hearts, and the second that you are wearing a ring once given to David Middleton by someone he loved…'

Collingwood shot a startled glance at him. The colour washed from his face as he looked into Jack's eyes.

'I won it from him in a card game,' he blustered, trying to withdraw his arm. 'Let's see your King…I don't believe you have it…'

'Oh, yes, I do,' Jack said and, still holding his opponent's arm in a tight grip, he flicked back Collingwood's wide cuffs and extracted the King of Hearts. 'There it is—exactly where I knew it would be, in your sleeve. Once Greaves relieved you of your marked cards, it wasn't quite so easy for you to cheat us—but you managed to secrete the King of Hearts two games ago, and you waited your chance.' He caught hold of David's ring and pulled it from Collingwood's finger. 'I'll have this, if you don't mind.'

'Damn you!' Collingwood blustered, snatching his arm back. 'Where did that come from? You must have had it in your hand all the time. How dare you accuse me of cheating? I demand that you retract at once!'

'Or you will challenge me to a duel as your foolish nephew did?' Jack asked, arching his left eyebrow. 'Do not imagine that I would fire in the air as I did for him. No, it would give me great pleasure to shoot you—as you shot David Middleton. Except that you never gave him a chance to fire back, did you?'

'What are you talking about?' Collingwood pushed his chair back, looking about him wildly. 'I had nothing to do with his murder. Everyone knows it was a robbery.'

'The robbery took place at the card table earlier,' Jack said in a cold hard tone that sent shivers down the spine of more than one man present. 'First you cheated him, as you tried to cheat me this evening—as you have cheated all of us one way or another. When David threatened to expose you, have you drummed out of society, you killed him.'

'No, damn you! This is all a pack of lies. No one will believe you. You had the King in your hand…'

'No, you had it in your sleeve,' Greaves said. 'I have been watching the whole time and I saw you slip it into your sleeve. You are a liar—and anyone who knew David Middleton would know that he would never gamble away a ring that was precious to him. You are a cheat, Collingwood, and very likely a murderer. Once word of this gets out, you will not be welcome in this club again—or anywhere in decent society, for that matter.'

'Gentlemen, take what he owes you,' Jack said getting up. 'The pot would have been his for he held the King and the Ace, which you may find in his pocket. I am content to have this…' He showed them David's ring before slipping it into his own coat pocket. 'Collingwood, I have nothing more to say to you. Let these gentlemen deal with you as they will…' He inclined his head to the others. 'Goodnight, gentlemen.'

'Damn you, Harcourt! You have no idea what you do… you'll be sorry for this.'

As Jack turned away, Collingwood jumped to his feet. He pulled a pistol from his coat pocket, aiming it at Jack's back. Before he could fire, Greaves struck him from behind with a heavy silver-headed cane, sending him crashing to the floor. The pistol fired as he fell, the ball striking the leg of a large gaming table and splintering it. Jack glanced back, but saw that the situation was under control and continued to walk from the room.

'Send for the watch,' Greaves told one of the waiters, who had come rushing towards them at the first sign of trouble. 'This man is a cheat and may already have killed. He just tried to shoot Lord Harcourt in the back.'

'Leave him to us, sir,' the man said and signalled to his companions. Three burly men dragged Collingwood off as he began to stir. 'We'll keep him safe until they come for him.'

'Harcourt!' Greaves cried, and followed Jack from the room. He caught up with him as Jack stopped to exchange a few words with the attendant who had brought him his hat and cloak. 'Wait a moment. You took a damned risk just now. He would have killed you.'

'I had every confidence in you,' Jack replied with a smile. 'It was my hope that he would do precisely as he did—try to shoot me in the back before witnesses. He might have brushed through a charge of cheating—he will not escape this. He is finished in society and may well stand trial for attempted murder. I ask no more.'

'He is undoubtedly guilty of murder. It was in his eyes when you accused him,' Greaves said. 'We all witnessed his attempt to shoot you in the back. You have done us all a service, Harcourt—but you took a terrible risk all the same.'

'A calculated one,' Jack replied. 'I knew that you would be watching him and I believed you a resourceful man. I am very glad to know that my judgement was not wrong. I must thank you for saving my life, Greaves. If ever I may be of service to you, please do not hesitate to ask.'

'You are a cool one, Harcourt,' Greaves said and gave a harsh laugh. 'I swear I would rather have you as a friend than an enemy.'

'Believe me, I am usually the easiest of fellows,' Jack told him with a wry look. 'David was my best friend. There was something that bound us...but it is enough. I am satisfied that his spirit is at rest at last.'

'Well, he has been revenged,' Greaves said. 'Put it behind you now, Harcourt. It does no good to brood on these things. Nothing more you can do now.'

'Very true,' Jack agreed. 'Yes, I shall forget it now, for there is no more to be done. Justice has been served this night.' He offered his hand. 'Accept my sincere thanks for your part, sir.'

'Glad to do it,' Greaves said gruffly. 'I had better go back and make sure they don't let that rogue escape when he comes to his senses.' He frowned. 'I have been hearing tales, Harcourt. May I wish you happy—or is it merely a rumour?'

'As yet it is no more than that,' Jack said. 'But if the lady in question will have me, I think you may soon be able to offer your congratulations.'

'Ah, I thought you would not play fast and loose with a young lady's reputation,' Greaves said, nodding his satisfaction. 'I hope you will invite me to the wedding?'

'If she accepts, I shall certainly do so,' Jack said and clapped his hat on. He inclined his head and walked from the club as Greaves went back into the card room.

Jack saw a hansom cab waiting outside and signalled to it. He was not in the mood for walking, because there was a hint of rain in the air. Besides, to walk through the streets of London at night one must be prepared and Jack was unarmed. He had purposely left his pistol at home, because he had wanted to make sure that he had no weapon if Collingwood had shot him in the back. He had wanted to make sure that his enemy would hang this time.

Jack knew that he had taken a risk. If Greaves had not been alert, he would almost certainly have been killed, but he had been pretty sure that he could trust the man he had chosen to be his witness. Besides, he had known that he had no choice but to take that chance if he wanted to bring David Middleton's murderer down. Only a public denunciation would have made Collingwood lose his head, and the risk was always there that he would succeed in getting his shot off. It was for this reason that Jack had held back with regard to his courtship of Lucy Horne. His first duty had been to David, but it was done and he was free to carry on with his own life.

Jack was aware of a feeling of lightness. He had carried the burden of his friend's murder for a long time, and he was relieved that the business was finally over. There might be something he was missing—something that concerned Staunton—but he would continue to investigate the matter in a discreet manner. Collingwood was finished in society, but his sister's husband would be far more difficult to bring down, even if it were possible—and as yet he only had Garrick's letter to suggest it had been more than a quarrel over cards. It might be as well to try to contact him, but for the moment he had personal business.

At first, he had not been certain that it would be fair to Lucy to ask her to be his wife, because he was several years older—and he had seen and done things in the course of his duty as a soldier and an agent for the government that were best forgotten. However, since the duel with that young idiot Lawrence, Jack had realised that the gossips had had a field day. The situation was reversed and it would now be unfair to Lucy not to ask her, regardless of his own feelings. Even if he had not found her totally fascinating, he would still have felt it his duty to ask her. Fortunately, he had known for some time that it was what he wanted most in the world. Perhaps the age difference need not matter for he was a strong, fit man and in the prime of his life.

He smiled as he settled back against the squabs of the hansom cab, thinking of how and when best to propose to her. He had seen a ring that he thought she might like, and he would buy it first thing in the morning. Of course she would have the pick of the Harcourt jewels once they were married, but he thought he would give her a new ring for their engagement. Lucy should have something uniquely for her.

Of course, she might turn him down...but why should she? Jack was fairly sure that Lucy liked him rather a lot. He had seen a look in her eyes once or twice, but there was always the chance that he had been mistaken. Jack knew a moment's unease. He had never been in love before and women had come easily to him, though he had chosen carefully—usually a widow in need of comfort. Supposing Lucy decided that he wouldn't do for her?

Lucy was conscious that people were watching her as she moved through the ballroom with her sister. It was not unusual, for she had often been the centre of attention since her first dance. However, she sensed that this evening there was something different and she thought she caught a hint of censure in the eyes of one or two of the older ladies. She did not know what she could have done to deserve it—unless people were talking about the duel?

Lucy was asked to dance almost at once and her card was soon filled, apart from the three spaces she had deliberately kept free. However, she thought that she had not been asked by quite as many gentlemen as usual, though of course Mr Lawrence and Mr Markham were not present. Mr Tristram was there, but he had sent her a reproachful look and was not amongst the gentlemen vying for her dances. She suspected that she might have hurt his feelings in some way, but was not sure how. It was not until after the fourth dance that Lucy learned what people were saying.

Amy Robinson came up to her during the interval, a shame-faced brother in tow.

'Miss Horne, I wish to apologise to you,' Amy said. 'I had no idea what my foolish brother had got himself into and my message to you was quite genuine.'

'Yes, I realised that,' Lucy said. 'I attach no blame to you, Amy.'

'Thank you.' Amy fixed her brother with a hard stare. 'Well?'

Peter Robinson blushed bright red. It was obvious that he had been dragooned by his sister and was feeling uncomfortable. 'I am very sorry for my part in that affair, Miss Horne. I never thought it was a good idea, but I should have tried harder to stop them. I am so sorry—I know all this gossip must upset you. I would not have hurt you for the world.'

'Thank you,' Lucy said. 'But what exactly are you speaking of? I have heard nothing.'

Amy threw an awful look at her brother. 'Some people are saying that Lord Harcourt hasn't come up to scratch, because of what happened.'

'Oh, I see...' It was Lucy's turn to blush. 'That is all nonsense, of course. I do not know why anyone should even think that he—' Amy was looking at someone behind her, her expression puzzling. Lucy turned and swallowed hard as she understood the reason for Amy's embarrassment. 'Lord Harcourt...good evening.'

'My dear Miss Lucy,' Jack said. 'They are about to play a waltz—my dance, I believe?'

'Well, yes...' Lucy said, for she had kept it just in case he arrived. 'I believe it is, sir.' She gave him her hand, her heart beating rapidly. 'Thank you.'

'It is my pleasure,' Jack told her and smiled down at her. 'I have been waiting for this, Lucy.'

As he placed his hand at the small of her back, Lucy felt a shiver of desire run through her, for the way he was looking at her told her that he meant what he said, and that what he felt for her was no light thing. She relaxed into his arms as he began to whirl her round and round, their feet covering the floor so swiftly and lightly that she felt as if she were dancing on air.

'I have missed you,' she said, gazing up at him, her face

more eloquent than any words. 'Drew told me that you had business elsewhere. Is your business done, sir?'

'Please, do not call me sir—unless I have displeased you. I am Harcourt—and perhaps in time you may wish to call me Jack, as my closest friends do?'

'Am I a close friend, Harcourt?' Lucy's eyes held a challenge.

'I think perhaps you know what I mean, Miss Mischief,' Jack said, teasing her. 'However, a dance floor is not the proper place to say what I feel—so perhaps I may call tomorrow?'

'To take me driving?' Lucy asked, deliberately misunderstanding him. 'Yes, I should like that very well, Harcourt.'

'If you wish, we may go driving,' Jack replied. 'I think you are a minx, Lucy. And I am well served for believing you still very young and innocent, am I not? It is quite obvious that you are not in the least childish!'

Lucy arched her brows at him, but did not rise to the bait. She was certain of what her answer would be, if he should ask her to be his wife—but she did not see why she should let him off lightly. He had teased her for a long time and deserved a little teasing in return.

'Oh, yes, I love to drive of all things,' Lucy said. 'I shall look forward to the expedition, Harcourt.'

Jack gave a husky chuckle—she had neatly reversed the situation on him. Until this moment he had been in control of the situation, but now she held the reins very firmly in her dainty hands, and he must dance attendance to her tune. He was amused, for he had never been caught in a woman's toils before—never felt such an urgent need to kiss someone until she melted into his body and became a part of him. Passion, lust, affection—he had known them all in varying degrees, but he was beginning to realise that love was a very different thing. Lucy might appear to be a playful kitten, but a kitten's claws could be sharp.

Their dance ended and Jack returned Lucy to her sister's side, where she was soon claimed by another partner. Instead of retiring from the ballroom as he usually did between dances, he asked Marianne to partner him and afterwards stood talking to her, his eyes hardly leaving Lucy as she flitted about the room like a jewelled butterfly.

He danced with her again before supper and took her into supper, making sure that this time she ate her syllabub and sipped her champagne in comfort. After supper he danced with her again. All three dances had been waltzes. His attentions could not go unnoticed, and by the end of the evening it was impossible to lay odds on him making an offer, which did not please a certain lady who had hoped that he might make her an offer.

It was as Lucy was leaving the ballroom to fetch her cloak that Lady West came up to her. Lucy smiled—the widow was a friend of her sister's and she had no reason not to like her. However, her smile faded as she saw a look of hostility in the lady's eyes.

'I have heard that you are to marry Lord Harcourt,' she said coldly. 'My advice to you would be to think carefully, Miss Horne. I do not know if you have heard about his bastard child? You may think it only a story, but I can tell you that it is quite true. He supports it and the mother…with whom he has an unshakeable relationship.'

'I beg your pardon?' Lucy was shocked, as much by the venom in the other lady's tone as her words. 'Surely this is not a subject for discussion here, Lady West?'

'I was his mistress for almost a year,' Lady West went on regardless. 'He broke it off because I asked him not to see her...I do not imagine you will fare any better once the first flush of passion has gone. Be careful, Miss Horne. Harcourt is a rake and will break your heart if you let him.'

She walked away, leaving Lucy to stare after her in dismay. Her mother had broken the tale to her gently so it had not come as a great surprise—but the tone in which Lady West's revelations had been made, and her own affair with Harcourt, was disturbing. Lucy was not a naïve child; she understood that liaisons went on, and she knew that Lady West's husband had been more than twice her age, and sickly for some years before he died. She did not condemn the lady or Harcourt, for it was not her place to do so, but it made her wonder if his reputation as a rake was well deserved.

It was a very thoughtful Lucy who went to bed that evening. Her heart told her that Harcourt loved her and she knew that she loved him—but was that enough? Lucy suspected that for a marriage to be happy ever after, as in her storybooks, it took respect and liking as well as passionate love. Otherwise, it could all fall apart once the first glow of desire had been satiated.

Marianne and Drew were very much in love after nearly three years of marriage, and Jo was a complete convert to the idea of romantic love despite her doubts before she met Hal Beverley. Lucy very much wanted to believe that she would be as happy with Jack Harcourt—but she could not forget her mother's gentle warning.

She must give some thought to her answer—and, even if she said yes, she would ask for an engagement of some months. It would not hurt them to wait, for she was only eighteen and they had their lives before them.

Lucy had not slept as peacefully as usual that night. A part of her had longed for the morning and the moment when Jack asked her to marry him—and yet she was unsure of her answer. She wanted to trust him completely, to give herself with a whole heart, but between them her mama and Lady West had sown the seeds of doubt.

She had dressed very carefully in a new carriage gown of pale blue silk. Her bonnet was of chip straw with matching ribbons, her gloves a pale tan leather, her shoes black and shiny with a small heel. She had allowed her hair to fall softly on her shoulders at the back, a few pale wisps escaping to frame her lovely face. As she heard Jack's voice in the hall her heart started to pound madly, and for a moment she was almost too scared to go down, but then she conquered her fears, lifted her head and smiled as she walked down to greet him.

Jack gazed down at her, his heart jerking. She was young and lovely, and he had been fairly caught. He had never expected to feel this way about a woman, and it still surprised him every time he experienced a rush of overwhelming desire when he smelled her perfume or touched her hand.

'You look beautiful, as always, Lucy.'

'Thank you,' Lucy said. 'It is a lovely morning, Harcourt, just right for driving—do you not think so?'

Jack frowned—he had not seen this much reserve in her before, and he sensed that she was troubled. 'Yes, a beautiful morning,' he said. He had not been sure that she really meant to go driving, but it appeared that she did. 'Shall we go?'

'Yes, thank you,' Lucy said. 'We have only a few days left in town, Harcourt. Unless I stay with Marianne, it may be some time before I go driving again.'

Jack did not immediately reply. His intent had been to propose that morning, but suddenly he was uncertain. Lucy certainly wasn't encouraging him. He wondered if he had misjudged her feelings towards him, though he had been almost certain the previous evening.

Lucy smiled as he helped her into the curricle, but she did not look into his eyes. A restless night had not resolved her doubts. She knew that her feelings for Jack were strong, and she longed with all her heart to be his wife—but would she regret it if she said yes without knowing him better? She did not wish for a marriage of convenience, and it would not suit her to know that her husband continued to support a mistress.

She was glad that Jack's tiger accompanied them to the park for she knew that he would not speak in front of the lad. However, when they had been driving round the park for some twenty minutes or so, Jack suggested that they should get down and walk for a while.

Lucy agreed, giving him a slightly apprehensive glance as he helped her down. She took his arm and they strolled towards a pleasant spot beneath the trees, away from the bridle paths.

'Lucy,' Jack said after a moment, 'you must be aware that I have a high regard for you?'

Lucy turned to look at him, her clear gaze a little disconcerting. 'As I have for you, Harcourt. We are good friends, are we not?'

'I thought perhaps we might have something more than friendship?'

'Yes, we might,' Lucy said. 'I think we may like each other very much, Harcourt—but we do not know each other well, do we?'

'Ah…' Jack frowned, for her question was unexpected. He had supposed that she was waiting for him to make an offer. He arched his brows. 'If I were to propose marriage today, Lucy, what would your answer be?'

'I should ask you if I might have a little time to think,' Lucy said, giving him a shy glance. 'I do like you very well, Harcourt—but I should prefer to know you better. A few dances, some carriage drives…' Her cheeks were pink, for she could not say what was truly on her mind. 'Besides, Mama would insist on an engagement of some months—she has said as much.'

'Yes, I see,' Jack said, gazing intently at her face. It had begun to dawn on him that he hardly knew Miss Lucy Horne at all. She was lovely and her smile could light up a room, but what went on in her head? He would certainly not have expected her to answer him as she had. 'But you do not refuse me, so I believe that I may hope?'

'Oh, yes, of course,' Lucy replied. For a moment she wished that she had given him a different answer and yet she wanted to be sure. 'You may take it that we have an understanding, though no promise has been made on either side.' Her eyes came up to meet his directly. 'If you were to discover that your true happiness lay elsewhere, I should understand.'

'Would you?' Jack's eyes narrowed. He suddenly realised what all this was about. Someone had been telling Lucy tales, and the devil of it was that he could deny nothing. 'Believe me, Lucy, if I did not think that there was good reason to expect that we should be happy together, I should not consider marriage.'

'Oh…' Lucy blushed and looked away. Perhaps she had been foolish to allow others to affect her judgement. 'Are you offended, Harcourt? I should not wish to cause you any hurt or distress.'

She had in fact injured Jack's pride, but he was not prepared to admit it. 'You have not,' he said less than truthfully. 'I think your caution does you credit. I must see what I can do to earn your good opinion.' He smiled oddly. 'Perhaps we should return? I dare say we shall see each other again this evening.'

'And we are still friends?' Lucy asked anxiously, for she had sensed his withdrawal.

'Yes, certainly. We shall be friends for the moment, but I must be honest and tell you that I hope for more.'

'As I do,' Lucy replied in a small voice.

She felt a little subdued on the return journey, for she knew that, despite his denial, she had caused offence. She had begun to regret her answer, but it could hardly have been different in the circumstances. Besides, he hadn't actually proposed.

She was only fooling herself! They both knew that he had held back because she had requested time to think. Jack was too much the gentleman to press his claims on her against her will. He continued to make polite conversation, smiling as he handed her down outside Marlbeck House.

'Do not look so distressed, Lucy. I shall find some way for us to spend more time together.'

'I should like that,' she said shyly. 'Thank you for taking me driving. I shall look forward to this evening.'

'I may not be there,' Jack said. 'A thought has occurred to me and it may take me from town for a day or so. You will hear from me soon.'

Lucy felt her spirits sink as he got back into the curricle. Now that he was leaving she was afraid he would be angry and think better of continuing his courtship. Why should he bother when he must surely be able to take his pick of young ladies who would be only too delighted to accept his offer?

Going into the house, Lucy decided that she had been foolish to take notice of Lady West, who was almost certainly jealous. As for her mama—she knew that Mrs Horne would have accepted an engagement as long as Lucy was happy.

How could she have been so stupid? Lucy regretted the wasted chance. She might even now have been telling her sister that she was engaged to Lord Harcourt!

Chapter Six

Lucy did not see Jack that evening. It was merely a card party and she would not have spent much time in his company had he been there, but she missed him. The manner of their parting had thrown a cloud over her, for she could not help wondering what would happen now.

'Is something wrong?' Marianne asked as they were driven home. 'You seem a little quiet, dearest. You are not feeling unwell?''

'Oh, no,' Lucy told her, forcing herself to smile as if nothing troubled her. 'However, I am glad we are going home at the end of the week. I have enjoyed my visit very much, but I think I should like to be in the country again.'

'Yes, I feel much the same,' Marianne said. 'It is pleasant to meet one's friends and be entertained for a while, but my home is in the country. I am fortunate that Drew feels the same, for it is not always the case. Some husbands and wives live apart for much of the time. I should not wish for that, but Drew likes nothing better than to be with me. We shall go down to his estate in Hampshire later in the year. Perhaps you would like to come with us, Lucy?'

'Yes, I should if...' Lucy faltered and her sister looked at her.

'I have Drew and Andrea, of course,' she said thoughtfully. 'I had hoped...has no one spoken to you?'

Lucy did not meet her gaze. 'Several gentlemen have proposed, though most were in jest, I think. I did not care for any of them other than as acquaintances.'

'I meant someone you like very well?'

'Oh...' Lucy blushed. 'Yes, of course. I should have realised that you would have guessed. I do like Lord Harcourt very well, but we have decided that we ought to get to know one another better.'

'Ah, I see.' Marianne nodded. 'Did Mama make you promise that, dearest?'

'Mama said that she would insist on an engagement of some months. However, I felt that I should like to know Lord Harcourt better.'

Marianne studied her intently. 'Have you heard gossip that distressed you, Lucy?'

'Yes. Someone made a point of telling me that she had been his mistress in the past—and that he had an unshakeable attachment to the mother of his bastard child.'

'And that led you to wonder if he might be unfaithful once you were married?' Lucy nodded. 'If I were you, I should put it from your mind, dearest. I am perfectly certain that Jack Harcourt would never behave in such a way. I do not know the truth concerning the child—no one does, not even Drew. It is something that Jack will not speak of to anyone. However, I would not believe a woman who told you spiteful tales regarding its mother.'

'I should not have done so, had Mama not already warned me. I do not condemn him for the past, Marianne. He was free to do whatever he wished, for his actions harmed no one, as a single man. I simply wanted to be sure that we should suit.'

'Yes, I understand.' Marianne was surprised—her sister had always been such a dreamer as a child, but it was clear that she had grown into a sensible and thoughtful young woman. 'You know your own mind best, dearest—but if you love him, you should not hold back. Otherwise, you might come to regret it.'

Lucy was not sure that she did know her own mind, because she was torn two ways. Her heart told her that she loved Jack Harcourt no matter what, but her head warned her to be careful.

It was two days later that Lucy returned home from a shopping expedition. She had returned some books to the lending library and purchased a few items, which she intended as gifts. Her Aunt Bertha was partial to a certain type of almond sweets, and her mother always appreciated nice perfume or soap. She had bought small gifts for several friends, whom she would see for the last time for some months that afternoon, at a tea party.

As she entered the house, she saw a posy of flowers lying on the hall table and stopped to look at them. Seeing the card attached, she realised that Jack Harcourt had called and left them for her. She felt disappointed to have missed him, because they were not going out that evening, as Marianne wished to be up early for their journey.

She sniffed the intoxicating scent of the lilies as she carried them up to her room. There had been nothing but a brief greeting on the card and she wondered when she would see Harcourt again. However, as she began to walk along the landing she saw her sister coming from the nursery wing.

'Have you been visiting Andrea?' she asked. 'I have a present for her, Marianne. It is a little silver rattle with bells. Do you think that she will like it?'

'I am sure she will, dearest,' Marianne said. 'It is a pity you were not here earlier, because Jack Harcourt called. I see you have his flowers.'

'Yes, I do,' Lucy said. 'It was kind of him to call and bring them.'

'Jack brought us an invitation, Lucy. He has persuaded his sister to stay with him at his country home, and we are invited to join them for a few days. Mama is also to receive an invitation, though, as I told Jack, I am not sure she will be able to leave Aunt Bertha.'

'Jack's sister?' Lucy looked at her in surprise. 'I had no idea that he had a sister. Is she younger or older?'

'Lady Staunton is five years younger than Jack,' Marianne told her. 'Her first name is Amelia and she is very pretty—she has hair just a little darker than mine, Lucy. She was married three years ago and her husband is often away, for he is an ambassador. Amelia accompanies him when she can, but she has a son of two years and came home to be with him, because he had been ill. Jack says that she does not go out enough these days, and so he persuaded her to stay with him. It is not often that Amelia will visit him and so Drew says that we shall join them in Suffolk for a few days. If Mama can come to be with you, you may stay longer, Lucy.'

'Oh…' Lucy's heart gave a leap of excitement. The past two days had been uneasy ones, for she had wondered if she had spoiled everything by asking for time to get to know Jack, but now she saw that he had kept his word. By inviting his sister to stay with him, he had made it possible for her to visit him at home with Marianne and Drew—and her mama, if Aunt Bertha could spare her. 'That is wonderful, Marianne. I shall enjoy meeting Lady Staunton very much—and staying with Lord Harcourt, of course.'

'Yes, I rather thought you would,' Marianne said, a teasing

note in her voice. 'It was clever of Jack to arrange it, because it is the perfect way to get to know one another better.'

'Yes, it is,' Lucy said. 'Meeting someone in polite society is all very well, Marianne, but I think that people are not themselves until they are at home with those they care for.' She blushed. 'Do you think me too cautious or foolish?'

'No, indeed, I do not,' Marianne said. 'I am surprised at your maturity of thought, dearest, for I am sure that many young girls do not give as much consideration to such matters.' She had always thought of Lucy as a dreamy child, but now she realised that what she had taken for dreaminess might actually have been something else. 'So I may tell Drew that you are happy with the scheme?'

'Yes, very happy,' Lucy said and her eyes lit up with excitement. 'To tell you the truth, I have wished that I had given a different answer—but now everything is just as I should like it. Mama will be happy too.'

'You are a good girl to think of her,' Marianne said. 'But when it comes to your happiness, my love, you must follow your heart.'

'Yes, I shall,' Lucy told her, looking thoughtful. 'Now, I must go to my room and wrap my gifts, for I shall not see some of my friends again for a long time.'

Marianne watched her sister disappear into her bedroom, smiling because she had sensed the relief and pleasure Lucy had felt in the invitation. She was certain that Jack held very strong feelings for her beloved sister, because he had gone to some considerable trouble to persuade his sister to visit him. Lady Staunton hardly ever went near her family's estate in Suffolk, preferring to live quietly at home when she was not travelling with her husband. Jack's arguments must have been powerful, but what sister would not be curious about the girl her brother wished to marry?

* * *

Lucy had spent a pleasant afternoon with several of her friends, including Amy Robinson, who had become something of a confidante since the abduction attempt. They walked home together, for Amy's home was only one street away from Marlbeck House.

'I shall miss seeing you,' Amy said. 'We go down to Bath in three days and after that we shall return home. I would not tell everyone, Lucy, but I have received a very flattering offer from Lord South and we shall announce our engagement in *The Times* shortly. I hope you will come for my wedding?'

'I should like to very much if I can,' Lucy told her. 'We have been invited to Lord Harcourt's estate for a few days. Lady Staunton is to be a guest.'

'Lady Staunton?' Amy wrinkled her brow. 'I think Mama knows her. I remember she said something about her marrying a much older man. He is an important, wealthy man, I believe?'

'Yes, so I understand,' Lucy replied. 'I think—' She broke off as she saw a young child dash into the road in front of a wagon, which was bearing down on him fast. Even as she took a step into the road in pursuit, she saw a man snatch the child up just as the wagon lumbered by. 'Oh, how brave…' Her eyes were drawn to the man, because she had recognised him. 'Did you see that, Amy?'

'Yes, it was quick witted of him,' Amy said. 'You would have been too late, Lucy, and you might have been injured yourself—but then, it is no more than I would have expected of Lord Harcourt. He was commended for valour so many times when he served under Wellington, you know. My father was surprised that he did not give up the army when he inherited the title, but he continued with his duty, and it is only these past few months that he has begun to take over the management of his estate and use his title.'

'Oh...' Lucy was not truly attending, for she could not take her eyes from Jack Harcourt, who was still comforting the child, and its mother. She watched as he held the small boy in his arms, feeling the sting of tears as he returned him to the mother's arms. He was not even aware that his small act of bravery had been witnessed, and Lucy did not intend to draw his attention to herself. She walked on with Amy, glancing in a shop window until Jack had moved away. 'It is usual for gentlemen to sell out when they inherit. I wonder why he stayed on?'

'It may have had something to do with the war with France,' Amy said. 'I am not sure, but I know that Papa says we should all be grateful to men like Lord Harcourt.'

Lucy looked at her. She had sensed an air of mystery surrounding Jack Harcourt on more than one occasion. When he had helped Drew catch that French spy, and later, when Hal had his accident and went missing, he had searched for him...clearly he had more secrets than an illegitimate child.

The act of selfless bravery that she had witnessed that afternoon remained with her as she parted from her friend with promises to write and went inside the house. She had begun to realise that it would be exciting to know Jack very much better and felt a tingling sensation down her spine. Just what kind of a man was he really?

Jack found another letter waiting for him when he returned home later that day. This time it had been signed by George Garrick and requested a meeting at Jack's earliest convenience.

I have managed to confirm what I believed, and I think you would be very interested in my discovery, Jack. I know that what I did was unforgivable and I have regretted it more times than you can imagine. Perhaps it is too much to expect forgiveness—but I would like to make amends for my beha-

viour, and this concerns Amelia. Believe me, I never stopped loving her. If you care for her safety, you must trust me in this. George Garrick.

Jack frowned as he read the letter again. He was intending to go down to his estate later that day, but it might be as well if he heard Garrick out. A part of him was angry that he had dared to mention Amelia, and yet he too had suspected that there was more to this affair than met the eye. If he was right, David's quarrel over a card game with Collingwood might only be the start of a very murky affair.

Garrick stated that this business concerned Amelia. In Jack's eyes that could mean only one thing, in which case he must certainly see him before he set out for Suffolk…

Lucy sat before her dressing table, brushing her long pale hair. She had spent the evening quietly with her sister, for Drew had gone out after dinner, saying that he had some business. Neither Marianne nor Lucy had minded being alone for once and they had spent their time talking about things they had always enjoyed, and embroidering.

Marianne was making a beautiful smocked gown for her daughter, and Lucy had begun to make a bonnet of soft wool for her niece. They said goodnight at just after nine and went up to their rooms, for they were to rise early on the morrow. However, Lucy found it difficult to sleep at first and she sat for some time at the window, gazing down at the street, which was lit with lamps tended by the night watchman.

If she married Jack, it might not be long before she too had a child to make pretty garments for, and Lucy knew that she longed for a babe of her own. She had always been very attached to her sisters and hoped that she would have at least three or four children—and after today she was certain that Jack would make a good father for those children. But would he be a wise choice as a husband? She wished that Lady West had never spoken to her, because she did not wish to doubt him, but it was very difficult to put her doubts from her mind.

Sighing, Lucy went to bed and snuffed out her candle. She was to spend some time at Jack's home, and she was sure that when she met him in his natural environment she would be able to make up her mind. Perhaps, if she were truthful, it was already made up, because in her heart she knew that Jack was the only man she could ever love. She smiled as she settled down to sleep, suddenly impatient to be with him once more.

Jack had returned home ahead of them so as to be there to greet his sister and visitors when they arrived. Drew was escort enough for the ladies, and he always travelled with sufficient grooms and servants to make a journey as comfortable and smooth for his family as possible.

Marianne and Lucy shared a coach, the maids following in a second, though for a part of the journey Andrea's nurse joined them with the child. They all took it in turns to nurse her, for she was a little fractious, and in the end it was Lucy's singing of a nursery rhyme that settled her.

'You will make an excellent mother, Lucy,' Marianne said. 'Andrea has been a little out of sorts the past two days. I do not know if it is a tummy ache or if she has a tooth coming.'

'I think it is a tooth, my lady,' the nurse said. 'Shall I take her now, Miss Horne? She will sleep for a while now she's off.'

Lucy handed the child over to her nurse. 'She is so lovely,' she said. 'I adore her, Marianne. I know gentlemen always wish for a boy first, but Drew seems not to mind.'

'He fell in love with her from the start,' Marianne told her. 'I dare say we shall have a son next time.'

Lucy nodded, but said no more, retreating into thought.

She could not forget the dramatic rescue she had seen the previous day, but what had made an even bigger impression on her was the way Jack had handled the lad after he had pulled him clear of the thrashing hooves. He might have been angry, because what the child had done had been dangerous, but he had been so kind and gentle, soothing the boy until he was over his fright.

Lucy smiled to herself. It had given her a welcome insight into his true character, especially as he had no idea that she had witnessed the incident. Thinking it over these past few hours, she had understood that a man who could do such a thing would never desert a child he had fathered, even if for some reason he could not marry its mother.

Indeed, she would think less of him if he did. It was odd, for she could not explain it, but somehow the small incident had reconciled her to the idea that he might have an illegitimate child somewhere. She still had a lingering doubt, for it would not suit her if her husband retained an attachment to his former mistress. Lucy had surprised herself by discovering that she had developed a possessive attitude towards Harcourt. She would not wish to share him with any woman!

Was that very selfish of her? She could not think it, because he would certainly not expect to share her with another man. The coming visit promised a great deal and she was very much looking forward to the next few days.

'Amelia, my dear one,' Jack said and kissed his sister's cheek as he welcomed her to his house. 'I am so glad you came. I was afraid you might withdraw at the last moment.'

'You know why I do not visit you here,' Amelia told him. She was an elegant woman, tall and slender with a face that was attractive rather than pretty. Sometimes she could look beautiful, but she dressed soberly and did not smile as often as she might. In reflection, her eyes could often look sad, but at that moment they reflected uncertainty rather than sadness. 'However, I could not resist the chance to meet Miss Lucy Horne. I had almost given up hope of your ever marrying, Jack.'

'My work did not allow for such things, and then there was David...' Jack looked at her, witnessing the flash of swiftly hidden pain in her eyes. 'He may rest in peace now, Amelia. His death has been avenged. Collingwood will rot in prison for the rest of his days if they do not hang him. And you have the ring.' His meeting with George Garrick had brought up something far more important and perhaps dangerous, but Jack was not yet certain enough of his facts to mention something that must have distressed her.

'Yes, I have it,' Amelia said, the shine of unshed tears in her eyes. 'I have told you before that I do not wish to discuss this, Jack. I have come here because you wished me to meet Miss Horne, which I am delighted to do—but do not expect more. My mind has not altered about that other business.'

'I think you punish yourself too much,' Jack told her. 'But we shall say no more, my dear sister. I have never wished to cause you pain.'

'No...' Amelia smiled at him with affection. 'You have been the best of brothers, done more than anyone could ever ask or expect. I can never thank you enough, Jack.'

'I want no thanks,' he told her. 'I would see you happy, Amelia.'

'I am happy enough,' she lied, glancing away from his eyes, which saw too much. 'I have my little David and I am content with that—I must be content, for there is nothing more for me in this life.'

Jack's heart ached for her. 'Oh, Amelia. If only you would speak to Staunton. He might release you if you are so wretched.'

'You do not know him, Jack.' Amelia's eyes sparkled with the tears she was too proud to shed, except when alone in her room. 'He enjoys having power over others—and his wife in particular.'

'If he hurts you...'

Amelia shook her head, knowing that she must lie to him. 'No, Jack. His punishments are subtler these days, I assure you. I could never justify leaving him in the eyes of the law—besides, he would take David from me, and I can bear anything but that.'

Jack nodded, his mouth firming into a grim line. He was well aware that Staunton would be within his rights to remove the boy from Amelia's care if she left him. For the moment she was safe enough, here in England, because Staunton had been anxious for his son's life when he allowed them to leave India. However, it was only a matter of time before he returned and then she would be forced to return to him.

'Well, I shall say no more on that other matter,' Jack said, 'though I believe something could be arranged if you wished it.'

'It would be too dangerous,' Amelia told him, a note of despair in her voice. 'Do you think I have not considered...but I dare not. If Staunton ever learned that I came here when he has forbidden it...' a shudder ran through her '...I think he might kill me—but he might do worse.'

'Surely he would not harm his own son?'

'I do not know. I dare not take the risk,' Amelia said. 'I have come to meet your lady, Jack—but as for the rest, it must remain as it is.'

'Very well, it shall be as you wish,' Jack told her. 'Say no more, Amelia.' He turned his head as he heard the crunch of carriage wheels outside the house. 'I believe that may be Lucy and her family now. Of course you have met Drew Marlbeck and his wife before—but not Marianne's sister.'

'She must be quite young,' Amelia said, a teasing look in her eye now. 'I am curious what it is about the beautiful Miss Horne that has caught my brother, for I thought you a confirmed bachelor, Jack.'

'And so I might have been,' Jack said, grinning at her. 'I suppose I should have married in time for the sake of an heir—but I never expected to fall in love.'

'You truly love her?'

'Yes.' Jack gave her a rueful smile. 'Lucy is not your average young lady, Amelia. She wishes to know me better before she listens to a proposal of marriage.'

'Unusual,' Amelia said with a lift of her brows. 'You are one of the most eligible gentlemen around, Jack. Is she aware of that?'

'I honestly don't think it matters to Lucy,' he told her with a smile. 'But come and meet her, Amelia, and then you may form your own opinion.'

'If you love her, then I am sure I shall,' his sister told him. 'Go and greet her, Jack, and I shall meet her when you bring her in, my dearest.'

Jack nodded and left her to gaze out of the French windows in the front parlour, while he went to welcome his guests.

Drew helped Marianne down from the carriage, and then turned to assist Lucy. Even as she was making her descent she saw Jack come out of the house to greet them, and her heart began to beat faster, for he looked so right here. Dressed with casual elegance, he was an impressive figure, at home with himself and his surroundings. His house was not as large as Marlbeck's house, but it was attractive and built of red bricks. The park was large, the gardens well kept and pretty rather than formal, with several herbaceous borders and roses everywhere.

'I am glad to see you arrived safely,' Jack said, addressing his guests in general, but his eyes were on Lucy. 'Marianne, you and Drew have visited me here before, but this is your first time, Lucy. I am very happy to welcome you to Harcourt.'

'I am very pleased to be here,' Lucy said, giving him a mesmerising smile that made him catch his breath. 'We were admiring some deer in your park, Harcourt. I have not seen them so clearly before. I thought they would run away as we passed in the carriage, but they did not.'

'They are quite used to human company,' Jack told her. 'Years ago my mother used to feed them, but these days they are mostly left to feed themselves. My keepers put food out in the cold weather and perhaps that is why they stay. We have to cull them occasionally to keep the herd healthy, but we do not keep them to shoot. My mother would not have approved.'

'Then I should have approved of her,' Lucy said and smiled as he ushered her inside. The hall was spacious with a rather grand staircase leading to the upper landing, but they did not immediately go upstairs, for he turned towards his right, taking them into the front parlour.

'We like to use this parlour on warm days,' Jack told her. 'It has a good view of the park and it is nice to simply walk out into the gardens—we use the drawing room in the evenings. When I am alone here I more often sit in the library, which is at the back of the house.'

Lucy looked about her. The house had a warm, welcoming atmosphere and she liked the way it was furnished, because the wood had a soft gleam that came from years of diligent polishing. Curtains and furnishings had been renewed at some time in the recent past, but it wasn't a smart house where everything looked as if it had just been placed there and must not be touched. Indeed, she had noticed that a bowl on the hall table was filled with all kinds of bits and pieces, including a whip and some gloves. She thought that Jack must have thrown them there earlier and it made her smile, for it told her something about him and his household—something she could not have learned from meeting him in someone else's house.

As they walked into the parlour, Lucy immediately noticed a woman standing by the fireplace. She was quite tall, slender and rather pretty with hair that some might describe as dark blonde, and blue eyes. How sad her eyes were! Lucy knew at once that she was not a happy person and it made her look at Jack, wanting to see his reaction to this lady.

'Amelia, my dearest, please come and meet Miss Lucy Horne,' Jack said, giving his sister a warm smile. 'Lucy, I hope very much that you will be happy to meet Amelia—my sister, Lady Staunton.'

Lucy made a slight curtsy, but Amelia shook her head and reached forward to kiss her cheek. 'I am delighted to meet you, Miss Horne—or may I call you Lucy?'

'Yes, of course, if you wish, Lady Staunton.'

'But you must call me Amelia, of course. I hope very much that we shall be good friends, Lucy. I am always pleased to meet friends of my brother's.'

'Thank you, that is very kind, Amelia.' Lucy smiled at her. She saw the glance Amelia directed at her brother, and knew at once that they were close. It was not Jack who had put that look of sadness in her eyes. 'When I was younger I often wished that I might have a brother—as well as my sisters, of course, not instead of, for I love them dearly.'

'And I often wished that I might have a sister,' Amelia told her with a smile that lit up her face, but did not quite reach her eyes. 'I should like it very much if we could get to know each other well while you are staying here, Lucy. Tell me, do you ride?'

'I have not done so for ages,' Lucy replied, her eyes moving to Jack, who was speaking to Marianne and the housekeeper who had come into the room at that moment. Drew had not yet come in, because he had stopped to speak to some of his servants about the horses. 'But Harcourt has been teaching me to drive.'

'Jack allows you to drive his horses?' Amelia looked startled. 'Surely not the blacks? They are very devils!'

'Oh, no, he borrowed a lady's rig and some very well-mannered horses for my benefit, did you not, Harcourt?'

'Borrowed?' Amelia quizzed her brother with a look. 'Jack, that does not sound like you.'

'Well, I must confess that I actually bought them,' Jack replied, his mouth softening in a smile of apology. 'I wanted Lucy to have the right start, but now that she is here on the estate, we might progress to something with a little more spirit.'

'You shall drive me about the park tomorrow,' Amelia promised her. 'I love to ride and perhaps I shall persuade you to take it up again, Lucy—but tomorrow we shall drive about the park and get to know one another.'

'I am not certain that Lucy is ready to drive with anyone but me,' Jack said. 'But now I am sure that Marianne wants to go up to her room. Mrs March will take you all up, and we shall have some tea as soon as you come down.'

'Thank you,' Marianne said. 'I want to see if Nurse has Andrea settled—and my gown is sadly crushed. I should like to change before I come down—perhaps in half an hour?'

'Yes, of course,' Jack agreed. He turned to smile at Lucy. 'Will that give you enough time?'

'Oh, yes,' Lucy replied. 'I should like to have a little walk about the gardens after tea—if I may?'

'Of course,' Jack said. 'I shall be delighted to take you for a stroll later, Lucy.'

Lucy nodded, following her sister and the housekeeper

from the room. She heard a murmur of voices as she began to walk upstairs, and wondered if they were talking about her.

'She is delightful,' Amelia told her brother as the door closed behind them. 'Yes, I like her very much and I am sure she will make you an excellent wife.'

'If she will have me,' Jack said ruefully. 'I am not certain that she has made up her mind yet.'

'Nonsense,' his sister said. 'How could she refuse? You may not be as wealthy as Drew Marlbeck, but you have more than you could ever need, Jack—and you are attractive, a kind, generous man. What possible reason could she have to refuse you?'

Jack turned away, for he would not distress his sister by telling her that Lucy had heard tales concerning his illegitimate child. 'Oh, I do not know,' he said. 'But I am hoping that she will decide that I am a good fellow once she knows me a little better.'

Amelia looked at him, her gaze narrowing. 'What is it, Jack? Why are you hiding something from me?'

'Pray do not be foolish,' Jack said. 'Why should I wish to hide anything from you? I can assure you—' He broke off as the door opened again and Drew entered, transferring his attention. 'The others have gone upstairs, Drew—but perhaps you would like a glass of Madeira?'

'Thank you,' Drew said. 'It is very good to see you again, Lady Staunton. Are you pleased to be back in England?'

'Yes, indeed I am,' Amelia said, frowning slightly. 'My husband says that this will be his last tour of duty overseas, and we shall make our home here once he returns.' She glanced at her brother, who was pouring wine for himself and Drew. 'I do not wish for anything until tea, Jack. I should go up and see if David is settling in.'

Drew watched her walk from the room, frowning a little as Jack brought him the glass. 'Is Amelia well, Jack? She seems a little strained and I know that things have not always gone well for her.'

'Staunton is a devil to live with,' Jack said and for a moment his eyes glinted with anger. 'I have tried to persuade her to leave him, but of course she will not, though I have hopes—' He broke off, for at the moment all he truly had was suspicion.

'No, I dare say she could not,' Drew said—he believed he understood the situation. 'You do not think he might be persuaded?'

'If he used force against her, I would make him pay for it. But she swears he does not, though I know he makes her very unhappy at times.'

Drew nodded. 'I was surprised that she married him. I should have thought you would warn her against it?'

'I might have had I been at home—but the late Lady Harcourt pushed her into it, because she said it was Amelia's last chance. My stepmother was not a nice person, Drew. I believe my sister married to escape her, and there were other reasons…' He shook his head as Drew questioned with a lift of his brows. 'No, there is no sense in raking over old troubles. It is done and she must make the best she can of it for the moment.'

'Yes, I see. Well, I am sorry for it. If ever I can be of service…'

'Yes, I know,' Jack said and lifted his glass in salute. 'We have been through many a difficult situation together, Drew. Here's to friendship!'

'To friendship,' Drew said and lifted his glass. 'And to closer family ties.'

'Yes,' Jack agreed, though he wondered whether Lucy would take him if she learned his secret, which he must tell her before they became engaged—at least he would tell her the part that was his to disclose.

* * *

'There you are, miss,' the housekeeper said, showing Lucy into the room that was to be hers while she stayed here. 'This is the chamber his lordship requested be yours. It was refurbished a few months ago and I think it is the nicest, though perhaps not the largest, guest room in the house. I hope you will be comfortable; if you need anything, you have only to pull the bell rope by the bed.'

'Thank you,' Lucy said, looking around her with pleasure, for the décor was very fresh and bright, and the colour combination of greens shading to darker blues appealed to her. The furniture was made from a light wood that she imagined must be satinwood, banded with a thin strip of ebony and inlaid with various fruitwoods that had been stained in pinks and greens. 'It is delightful. I am sure I shall be very comfortable here.'

As the door closed behind the housekeeper, Lucy went to smell the posy of flowers, which had been placed on the dressing chest near the window. The roses were a dark, velvety red in colour and their perfume was delicious. She looked out of the window, discovering that she had a wonderful view, for she was at the side of the house and could see trees and, in the distance, a shimmering lake. As she looked away towards the lake, she saw a woman and a young boy, followed by two dogs. She could not see the faces of the woman or the boy, but thought that they must live on the estate somewhere.

Lucy imagined that there must be many beautiful walks on the estate, which she was glad of because she loved to walk, even though she very much enjoyed driving herself. It must be possible for anyone to be happy in a place like this, she thought as she undid the little buttons at the front of her bodice. She looked through the armoire for her clothes, which had been sent on a little ahead in the baggage coach and were already unpacked and awaiting her. Divesting herself of her carriage dress, she chose a pale yellow muslin teagown and had changed into it by the time a knock sounded at her door.

'Come in,' she called and turned as a young maid entered. 'Hello—have you come to help me?'

'Yes, miss. Mrs March sent me. I am Millie and I am to wait on you while you are here.'

'Thank you, Millie,' Lucy said. 'As you see, I am used to waiting on myself, though at my sister's I did have a maid to help me dress for the evening. But if you wouldn't mind, the dress I was wearing when I arrived is sadly creased and in need of a flat iron.'

'Yes, of course, miss,' Millie said. 'I shall be happy to do whatever you wish. I hung your things up for you when they arrived and some of them are a little creased. I could press the gown you need for this evening, if you wish.'

'Oh, how kind,' Lucy said. 'I think the yellow silk—if you are sure?'

'Quite sure, miss. Is there anything I can do for you now?'

Lucy assured her that she could manage, and Millie went away to spread the word below stairs that Miss Lucy Horne was a real lady, and if his lordship was going to marry her—which was the tale brought by his London servants—they were all very lucky. Millie remembered the late Lady Harcourt, his lordship's stepmother, and a right selfish one she'd been! It looked as if the new lady of the manor was going to be a whole lot easier to serve.

Unaware that she had passed some sort of a test by simply being herself, Lucy brushed her hair loose and tied it back with a ribbon that matched her gown. She picked up a paisley shawl and draped it over her arms in case it was cold outside after tea, and went down to join the others in the front parlour.

She found that Jack was alone in the parlour. The French windows were open and he was standing on the threshold, as if wondering whether he should be tempted out into the sunshine.

'Am I the first down?' Lucy asked, and he turned to look at her, his eyes going over her hungrily, their hot gaze sending delicious little tingles down her spine. 'Thank you for my room, Harcourt. It is lovely.'

'I am glad you like it,' Jack said, coming towards her. Her heart raced as he reached her side and she looked up into his face, understanding the passion that lay beneath the polite mask he had shown to her in society. In that moment Lucy knew that she had been right to wait; it was best that they became accustomed to this feeling between them slowly, for otherwise it might have frightened her. No one had ever looked at her this way before, and while it thrilled her, made her aware of all kinds of needs and longings she had never felt before, it also frightened her a little. 'You look beautiful with your hair like that, but so young. I feel that I am so much older.'

'But not too old,' Lucy assured him. 'I like you very well as you are, Harcourt.'

'Do you think you might call me Jack—at least when we are alone?'

'Yes, if you wish, Jack.' Her heart raced as he gazed down at her, his eyes seeming to burn into her, and she knew that he meant to kiss her. She parted her lips on a little sigh, wanting him to take her in his arms, to know the touch of his lips on hers.

'Jack…' Amelia's voice brought them both back to earth with a bump. 'Oh, forgive me. Have I interrupted something private?'

Lucy turned to see her hovering just inside the door,

looking awkward. 'No, of course not,' she said. 'Jack was just asking if I liked my room, and of course I do. It is lovely. Did you help him choose the colours?' She moved away and sat down on a small sofa.

'No, not at all,' Amelia said, throwing her brother an apologetic look. 'Jack chose it all himself. I was in India with my husband at the time. I rarely come here. Staunton is still in India, or I dare say I should not be here now. I returned because my son was sickly and the doctors feared he might die if I did not immediately bring him to a cooler climate.'

'Oh, I am so sorry,' Lucy said. 'Is your son better now?'

'Much better, thank you,' Amelia said and smiled. 'I have met Lady Marlbeck, of course, but I believe you have another sister?'

'Jo is younger than Marianne, and older than me by two years,' Lucy said. 'Well, nearly three really, but only at certain times of the year, if you know what I mean.'

'Just after her birthday and before yours,' Amelia said and nodded. Lucy was a vivacious and charming young lady, and she understood why her brother had fallen for her. 'I remember that I used to count like that once…' She looked sad, as if something had touched a chord in her memory, but then they heard voices and Marianne came in, followed by Drew.

The conversation became general, the ladies talking about the latest fashions shown in the journals to which they subscribed, and the gentlemen talking of politics. With Napoleon finally defeated, the Corn Laws were fast becoming the most-discussed topic in the houses of landowners and cottagers alike.

After tea, Marianne said she wished to look in on her daughter again, and Amelia offered to go with her. Drew went off to talk to a groom about a horse he thought might have picked up a stone on the journey and Jack invited Lucy to walk with him in the garden.

'Yes, I should like that of all things,' she told him. 'Do you think we should content ourselves with the immediate gardens, or may we walk as far as the lake?'

'You do not think it would tire you after the journey?'

'No, I do not,' Lucy assured him. 'I am not in the least tired and I saw the lake from my window. Aunt Bertha has some lovely walks at Sawlebridge, but she does not have a lake, though, as you know, Drew does...' A faint blush touched her cheeks. 'I was still very naïve that day, I think?'

'Perhaps,' Jack said. 'No one but a rogue would have tried to take advantage of your innocence, Lucy.'

'It was fortunate for me that you were there—and when Mr Lawrence tried to abduct me.' She looked at him uncertainly as they went out into the gardens, and turned in the direction of the lake. 'I was told that you fought a duel for my sake, Jack. I am very sorry that it happened.'

'You were not to blame,' he dismissed it with a shake of the head. 'I have faced worse under enemy fire—in Spain and France.'

'Yes, I know,' Lucy agreed. 'But I should have been distressed if you had been hurt badly.'

'Please do not think of it,' Jack told her with a smile. 'We are here now and all that is behind us. I was about to tell you how happy I was to have you in my home when Amelia came in earlier.' He had been about to kiss her for the first time, but with his sister's interruption that moment had passed.

'Thank you. I am very happy to be here,' Lucy said. He offered her his arm and they walked leisurely towards the lake, a comfortable silence between them.

'It is not a large lake,' Jack told her as they approached it, 'as you can see, but it is a natural source. I have improved it with some landscaping, but I fear there is no island for you to explore.'

'I do not mind,' she assured him. 'It has a lovely wild feeling, Jack—oh, do look, there are a family of black swans. I have not seen them before, though I had heard of them.'

'My father imported them for my mother,' Jack told her. 'As you may already suspect, she had a great love of animals and that is why we have the swans—and the deer.'

'I noticed you have several dogs too,' Lucy said. 'Are they simply for hunting or do you keep them as pets?'

'I have no dogs other than Brutus, who is usually kept in the stable block and is not suitable for a house pet,' Jack said and was thoughtful as he looked at her. 'Have you seen another dog on the estate?'

'As I looked from my window I saw a woman and a child,' Lucy said. 'Two dogs were following them and I imagined they must belong to the estate.'

'They are not my dogs,' Jack said and frowned. 'I have thought of buying another dog as a companion, something of the retriever type to take with me when shooting game in our woods and to live in the house, but felt it would not be fair when I was so much away, but now that I intend to settle here…'

'Oh…' Lucy looked at him curiously. 'Were those people trespassing? I thought they must live on the estate?'

'Perhaps—I do not know,' he replied in a dismissive tone. 'It is not important. I shall speak to my bailiff in case it was someone who had no right here.'

Lucy was puzzled by his manner, which was half-careless, half-annoyed. 'Perhaps they came from the village,' she said. 'They were too far away for me to see them properly. You should not be angry, Jack. I dare say they did no harm.'

'I have been away for too long,' he said. 'While there was a threat from Napoleon I believed my duty lay with my country, but that is over and I must attend to my affairs. There are certain things that have been allowed to drift. I must make changes.'

Lucy saw that he was thoughtful. She had believed that he would kiss her when they were far enough from the house not to be seen, but his mood had changed. He talked to her of his plans for the estate and the house, because his renovations had only just begun and he wanted to improve and perhaps build on another wing—but there was nothing romantic in what he said or did, and Lucy could not help wondering why.

At the back of her mind a tiny seed of doubt had begun to emerge. Was it possible that Jack's bastard and his mistress lived somewhere on the estate?

Lucy tried very hard to dismiss the idea from her mind, but it haunted her as she changed for dinner that evening. She wore her new yellow silk gown, and Millie dressed her hair in a soft style that swept up at the back and made her look very sophisticated. She wore a string of pearls about her throat, and pearl drops on her earlobes, and decided that she looked as she would wish to as she went downstairs to join the others.

'You look very much the lady,' Drew greeted her with a smile. 'I like that gown, Lucy. It becomes you.'

Lucy smiled and thanked him. Turning to Jack, she saw that his eyes were on her, and there was a hungry expression in them that made her tingle all the way down her spine. Whatever shadow had fallen over him earlier had obviously gone, and she decided that she would put the incident from her mind.

Dinner was a pleasant affair, with everyone laughing and talking over the delicious meal that Jack's chef had prepared for them. Even Amelia seemed to have shaken off her cares, joining in the teasing and witty conversation that carried them through the meal and into the drawing room.

The ladies retired when the port was brought in, preferring tea in the comfortable drawing room. However, it was not long before the gentlemen joined them. Marianne was asked if she would play for them, and Lucy joined her in a duet, and then Drew sang with Marianne while Lucy played. Everyone was content to have a lazy evening, and no one wanted to play cards—the gentlemen deferring a game of billiards until another time.

The ladies retired at just after ten-thirty, Drew promising his wife that he would not be long behind. Lucy said goodnight to Amelia and the others, and went into her room. Millie had waited for her to come up, but once she had unhooked the back of her gown, Lucy told her that she might go to bed.

She unpinned her long hair herself and sat brushing it for some minutes, in what her sisters would once have called her daydreams. In fact, Lucy was deep in thought. Already she had glimpsed how pleasant life could be as Jack's wife, for they could entertain as often as they pleased, sharing their home with countless friends. And she thought that sometimes it would be nice just to be alone, or simply have her mother to stay. Had there been no lingering doubts in her mind about the situation concerning Jack's bastard and his mistress, she would have told him that she wished to marry him the next day. At least, she would have hinted at it rather than saying it straight out, but she knew that Jack would understand.

Lucy wandered over to her window in her nightgown, looking out at the moonlight. She frowned as she saw a horseman set out from somewhere close to the house and ride off in the direction of the lake. Her instincts told her that it was Jack, and she could not help wondering where he was going. Could he be going to call on his mistress? At this hour?

Lucy turned away from the window, drawing her curtains

to shut out the bright moonlight. She was frowning as she got into bed and snuffed her candle. She was so close to telling Jack that she would marry him, but what she had just seen had made her wonder once more. If he was in the habit of visiting his child's mother at this hour… The pictures her mind conjured up were disturbing and she felt some distress. Supposing the visits continued after they were married? It was not a pretty thought or one that she wished to entertain for long.

Lucy knew that she could not live with such a situation. She had been prepared to accept the existence of a child somewhere, but she had not thought it would be here on his estate, where she would be living as his wife. She had not imagined that he would visit his mistress on the very evening that she came to stay. No, surely he would not? She could not believe such a thing of him. She was sure that he was an honourable man. But what was he doing? She could think of no sensible explanation for him to have left the house at this hour.

Lucy was a little uneasy. If Jack truly cared for her, he would surely not visit the bed of another woman while she was staying with him? And yet she was not a great heiress—so why did he wish to marry her if it was not for love?

It was a mystery, and one that she must solve if she were ever to be completely happy about marrying Jack.

Chapter Seven

Lucy surprised herself by falling asleep soon after her head touched the pillow. She was woken by the sun streaming in at the window, and sat up to see that Millie had brought her a tray of hot chocolate and soft rolls with a pot of clear honey.

'His lordship thought you might like to have breakfast in bed, miss,' the girl said. 'I wondered whether to wake you, but he said that you would wish to go driving this morning and that I should bring your tray at eight.'

'Is it so late?' Lucy asked, sitting up against her feather pillows. 'The bed was very comfortable and I slept all night. I am usually awake before this hour. It was kind of you to bring me all this, and I shall enjoy it—though as a rule a pot of chocolate is enough, for I take breakfast downstairs.'

'I dare say his lordship thought you would like to rest as you'd had a long journey, miss.'

'Yes, I expect that is why I slept so well,' Lucy agreed. 'These rolls look delicious, Millie. Please tell the chef that I shall enjoy them.'

'Yes, miss, he will be pleased,' Millie said. 'I'll bring your hot water in ten minutes, shall I?'

'Yes, thank you, that will do very well.'

Lucy poured some of the rich dark chocolate into her cup, sweetening it with some of the honey, because it could be very bitter. She sipped it and then ate one of her rolls, spreading more of the honey on the soft white bread, which was still warm from the oven. It tasted as delicious as it looked and she ate another before getting up. However, when Millie returned with the water, she was out of bed and brushing her hair, still wearing her nightgown.

'What would you like to wear this morning, miss?'

'I think the green carriage gown,' Lucy said. 'I shall need a shawl and my straw bonnet with the matching ribbons—but I do not think I need a pelisse because it looks as if it will be warm.'

'Old Rubens—he's the gardener, miss—he says the weather is set fair for some days, and he's as good a judge as any. My grandfather always used to hang a piece of seaweed outside his door, but Rubens says he knows by his bones. I think he suffers with the rheumy, miss.'

'Oh, the poor man,' Lucy said. 'I know one of my aunt's servants has bad rheumatics and it is painful. I believe there is some sort of rub that one can put on to help.'

'Rubens uses horse liniment and he smells awful at times,' Millie said with a giggle. 'But don't let him know I said it, because I like him and I wouldn't offend him for the world.'

'Then it shall be our secret,' Lucy said and looked at her thoughtfully. 'I saw some people yesterday afternoon, Millie—a woman, child and two dogs. They were walking near the lake and I could not see them clearly. Do you know who they might be?'

'No, miss, I can't say as I do,' Millie said, laying Lucy's gown on the bed for her. 'I dare say it was someone from the village. They sometimes cut across his lordship's land if they've been to the market. I should say that was what you saw.'

'Yes, I expect so,' Lucy said, though she was not convinced. However, she did not think that Millie would deliberately lie to her so that meant that she did not know anything about Jack's mistress and child—if he had one and if she lived nearby, it had been kept as secret as possible. 'Thank you, Millie. I shall wear my hair loose this morning. You may go now.'

'Yes, miss. I'll come back and tidy your room when you've gone out.'

Lucy nodded absentmindedly. She knew that she must make an effort to put what she had seen from her mind. If Millie knew nothing of the woman and child, it might be that Jack was quite innocent of any deception. She did not know where he had gone the previous night, but it might have been on some kind of business. Perhaps he would tell her. She hoped he might, for it was not the kind of thing that she could ask of him.

Lucy went downstairs when she was ready. She discovered Jack talking to Drew in the parlour on the ground floor. It seemed to be the most generally-used room in the house, though there were many others that were just as pleasant, but it did have the best view of the park.

Jack looked at her as she entered the room, his eyes lighting up with pleasure and something more that she believed was desire.

'You look lovely,' he said. 'Did you sleep well?'

'Very well,' Lucy replied and waited.

'I was called out just after you retired,' Jack told her. 'One of my tenants was close to death and he wanted me to witness his last will—and to confirm that I would allow his sons to continue to farm the acres they rent from me.'

'Oh…' Lucy blushed faintly, for such an idea had not occurred to her. 'That was not a pleasant task for you.'

'It was my duty as a landowner,' Jack said 'Tom Cartwright has been a good tenant and I knew that he was close to death. He had not made a proper will. I think he was superstitious and thought that if he put down his bequests in writing he would die; it is a fear many share, and he knew that if I witnessed his last request it would be good enough. It was sad to see him die, but he had his family about him.'

'I dare say he was well cared for,' Lucy said. 'But I am sorry that your night was not as restful as mine.'

'I am used to it,' Jack assured her. 'In Spain we slept on the ground and snatched what sleep we could get. I need only a few hours a night.'

'Yes, I see.' Lucy wondered why he was telling her this, but resolutely shut out her doubts. He had offered her an explanation for leaving the house the previous night—but why? Did he know that she had seen him leave? A candle had been burning in her room, and he might have seen that she had not yet drawn her curtains.

'Are you ready to go?' Jack asked and nodded to Drew. 'I shall see you later. Please feel free to talk to my bailiff about that matter you were interested in. I am sure he will be pleased to show you.'

Lucy turned and walked from the room, Jack following her outside. She saw that the usual lightweight rig was waiting for them, but this time it was to be drawn by two beautiful chestnut horses. They were a matched pair and clearly much livelier than the horses she had been used to driving.

'Oh, aren't they lovely? What are their names?' she asked, going to stand at their heads and smoothing her gloved hand over their soft noses. They snickered and tossed their heads, showing their spirit and impatience to be off. 'Are you sure you trust me to drive them?'

'I think that you are ready,' he said. 'Rajah and Rusty are spirited, but well trained. I shall take the reins for a start, just to let them work off a little of their high spirits, and then you may take over—if you wish?'

'Oh, yes, please,' Lucy said at once. 'I should enjoy that very much. They are so gorgeous. I never expected that you would let me drive such wonderful horses.'

'Why not?' he asked, giving her his hand to help her into the carriage. For a moment she looked into his eyes, and her heart raced as she saw the passion that burned deep within. 'Do you not know that I would give you anything you asked of me?'

'Jack…' Lucy's lips parted breathlessly, because when he looked at her that way she felt she might melt with love for him. 'I…do not know what to say.'

'Say nothing for the moment,' Jack said. 'You know what I would have of you, Lucy, but I shall not press you for an answer, my dearest. There is plenty of time. We are merely going for a drive, as we did in London.'

Lucy climbed into the carriage. They were merely going for a drive, as Jack said, but it felt very different. She had become so much more aware of him as a person—as a man—these past few hours. She had believed she knew her own heart before, but now she was aware of a longing to know him even better deep down inside her. She wanted him to kiss her and hold her, to tell her that he loved her—and to tell him of her love. She thought that the last of her doubts were fast disappearing, and if Jack had asked her now she would have said yes. However, he did not say or do anything that he would not have done in public gaze, and after a while Lucy felt calm enough to take the reins from him.

The sensation of driving such fine horses was above anything that Lucy had experienced before. She had enjoyed tooling the reins in London, but here in Jack's park it was far more pleasurable. They were in no danger of meeting another vehicle and she was able to give the horses their head and let them trot instead of keeping to a discreet walk. It brought the glow of excitement to her eyes, her cheeks a delicate rose and a smile on her lips as she realised that she now had the skill to handle such spirited horses. She felt a glow of pride because she would never have thought that she could do something like this until Jack had begun to teach her, and it had opened up a whole new world to her.

For his part, Jack was content to watch her and allow her to drive through the park and back round by the lake, coming in a full circle to the front of the house an hour or more later.

'Oh, that was wonderful,' she said as they came to a halt at last and Jack jumped down to help her descend. A groom had come running to take the horses and lead them away. For a moment Jack stood with his hands about her waist, and once again Lucy felt drawn to him, wanting him to kiss her so badly that she was almost forced to tell him. But then he released her, and she saw that Drew had come out of the house. 'I shall go in now. I dare say Drew wants to talk to you about something.'

However, it was Lucy that Drew had come out to meet, and he greeted her with the news that her mother had arrived while she was out.

'Mama is here?' Lucy said and glanced at Jack. 'I must go in at once. I was not expecting her so soon, for I was not sure that she would feel able to leave my aunt.'

'She is in the parlour, Lucy,' Drew said. 'I dare say she may have seen you arrive.'

'Thank you.' She went on ahead of the gentlemen, hurrying

into the house in search of her mama, and finding her with Marianne and Lady Staunton in the parlour. 'Mama…how good it is to see you here!'

'Lucy, my dearest,' Mrs Horne said, feeling a sense of relief as she saw her daughter's glowing face. 'Marianne told me that you had gone driving with Lord Harcourt. I see that you have enjoyed yourself, my love.'

'Yes, very much,' Lucy said. 'I have been driving some beautiful horses—so spirited! Jack says that I acquitted myself so well that he thinks I am ready to go driving with you, Amelia.'

'That is a huge compliment from my brother,' Amelia said. 'It was a long time before he would allow me to drive his horses—and nothing as spirited as those chestnuts. You must be a remarkable whip.'

'She is,' Jack said, coming in at that moment. 'Mrs Horne, I am glad that you could join us. Forgive me for not being here to greet you, but I am sure that my sister has made you welcome.'

'Yes, certainly,' Mrs Horne said. 'I am happy to accept your invitation, sir. Lady Edgeworthy is feeling much better and she insisted that I come to join you all. I sent word, but I believe I have arrived before my letter?'

'You are all the more welcome, for it was a pleasant surprise,' Jack said gallantly. 'Please order some refreshment, Amelia. I have some business I must attend to for the moment, but I shall return to eat my nuncheon with you.'

'You must do whatever you need to do,' Mrs Horne said. 'Perhaps we shall have time for some conversation later, sir?'

'Yes, of course. I shall be at your disposal this afternoon, ma'am,' Jack told her. 'Excuse me.' He exited the room and Drew followed, leaving the ladies together.

'Jack is a conscientious landlord,' Amelia said. 'I know he feels that he was forced to neglect the estate while he was serving under Wellington, but now he intends to put that right. I believe he has put some extensive measures underway, improvements to the labourer's cottages, new farming methods and various things of that nature.'

'Yes,' Marianne agreed. 'That is what Drew was so interested in—these advanced farming methods. There is a whole new school of thought, which he believes will improve the yield a great deal without making the soil poorer.'

'I must admit that I have no knowledge of these things,' Mrs Horne said. 'Bertha rents her arable land to a tenant now. She was able to reopen the mine last year and so far the yields have been very worthwhile. It was Drew who discovered the new seam of copper when he was looking for smuggled goods, you know.'

'Jack told me something of that in one of his letters,' Amelia said. She looked up as the housekeeper entered, two maids following behind with trays of beverages and sweet cakes for the ladies' benefit. 'Ah, refreshments. Thank you, Mrs March, that will be very welcome.'

Lucy got up to help pass the cups and plates. She was a little quiet, reflective as she sipped her tea and nibbled a sweet biscuit. She was delighted to see her mama, but wished that she might have had a few days longer to think about her answer. Her mother was sure to ask her what her intentions were, and though she was almost sure, she could not quite forget that she had seen a well-dressed woman and child walking near the lake. They might have been villagers, and yet she could not be certain.

'Well, my dearest,' Mrs Horne said when they went upstairs to tidy themselves before nuncheon. 'Have you come to a decision?'

'I think I may have,' Lucy told her honestly. 'I do love him, Mama—but I have not forgotten what you told me.'

'I have been thinking it over,' Mrs Horne said, surprising her. 'I still believe the wedding should not be for—shall we say three months? But I would consent to an engagement immediately. These tales are merely gossip, Lucy, and though there may be a child, from what Marianne tells me, Jack is not the kind of gentleman to carry on an illicit relationship once you are married. When I spoke to you, I had only just heard the rumours and my judgement may have been too harsh.'

'I have never thought he would,' Lucy said. 'I was told by a lady who shall be nameless that she had once been his mistress, and that the story of the child was true—but I do not believe that Jack is still in love with the child's mother. He loves me. I feel it, Mama. I think that I should not mind about the child, as long as he no longer saw its mother.'

'Then I do not think there is anything to prevent your becoming engaged—do you?'

Lucy was silent for a moment, and then she smiled. 'No, Mama, I do not. I love Jack very much. I knew it in London, but coming here, seeing the affection he has for his sister, the kindness he shows to his people, these things have convinced me that I should like to be his wife.'

'Then I shall tell Lord Harcourt my feelings on the matter if he asks me,' her mama said. She reached for her daughter, embracing her. 'I am happy for you, dearest, because I believe that he is a decent man and I think you will be loved. And that is the greatest gift that any woman can receive of life, believe me.'

Her mother's revised opinion weighed heavily with Lucy, for most of her doubts had begun with Mrs Horne's warning. She decided that she would forget the woman and child; they were unlikely to be important, and she knew that if she did not take this chance she might lose it altogether.

* * *

It was after dinner that evening, when everyone else was settled in the drawing room, that Jack asked Lucy if she would like to look at some family portraits. She acquiesced instantly, sensing that it was merely an excuse to get her alone for a while. They went to look at the portraits of long-dead members of the Harcourt family, but Jack was not much interested in discussing their history.

'Your mama tells me that she would consent to an engagement, the wedding to be in three months, Lucy,' he said, gazing down at her intently. 'Are you of the same mind, my dearest? I believe you know that I am very much in love with you, for you could not have failed to notice. It would give me great happiness if you would do me the honour of becoming my wife.'

Lucy looked up. 'Yes, I do know that you have strong feelings towards me,' she told him, 'and I must tell you that I...have them too. I shall marry you, Jack, because I love you.'

'Then may I tell your family that you have consented to become my wife?'

'Yes, I believe you may,' Lucy said, her heart giving a great leap of joy. She smiled up at him, wondering why she had delayed this moment, for she could never be happy without him and must trust his love for her. 'I should be very happy to marry you, Jack.'

'Then you have made me the happiest man alive,' Jack told her. He looked down at her for a moment longer, and then drew her into his arms, his head bending so that their lips met in a kiss. Sweet and gentle at first, it gradually deepened until Lucy felt as if she would melt into him, and she longed for the moment when she would truly be his. He drew away from her at last, touching her face with his fingertips. 'I think that must do for now, for otherwise I shall not be able to wait for three months to make you my own. I adore you, my dearest Lucy, and I want you in every way possible.'

Lucy's eyes were glowing as she returned his look. 'I love you very much, Jack. I know that you think me innocent, and perhaps I am too much a child, for Mama has been protective of me—but I know that I want to be yours in every way. Teach me to become the wife you want me to be, Jack. Let it be slowly, but take me along that path to the delights that will be ours one day. I would not come to you on my wedding night completely ignorant of what you expect of me.'

'Yes, that would be best,' Jack agreed, his eyes filled with tenderness. 'I know that there is passion in you, Lucy my love, but you are right when you say we should go slowly. I am glad that we are to have a three-month engagement, because we shall spend as much of that time together as possible, and in that way we shall know each other much better.'

'Then we shall tell Mama and Marianne, for I am sure they all expect it.' Lucy dimpled up at him.

Jack reached into his coat pocket and brought out a velvet pouch, from which he took a ring. It was fashioned in the shape of a daisy, the beautiful diamonds set in silver on gold to give them more shine, and it fitted Lucy's hand perfectly.

'I wanted you to have this for now,' Jack told her. 'It has never been worn by any other lady and is yours alone. The Harcourt jewels are in the bank and many of them are old fashioned; they will need to be reset for you. You shall choose which stones you like best and I shall have them made fit for you, my darling. Some belonged to ladies I would not wish you to emulate.' He grinned at her and pointed out the portrait of a beautiful woman wearing a collar of magnificent rubies. 'She was one of King Charles II's many ladies and some of the Harcourt fortune came from her, because Charles was not her only lover!'

'She sounds very naughty,' Lucy said with a mischievous smile. 'I think we must visit your ancestors again another day, Jack—but I am sure that Mama will be waiting to hear our news.'

'Then we shall not keep her waiting any longer,' Jack said and took her hand. 'Come, my love, we shall tell our families the good news.'

Lucy went happily to bed that evening with the congratulations from her family still ringing in her ears. Everyone was very pleased that the engagement had happened, and Jack planned to announce in *The Times* in a day or so, but they wanted to let Jo, Hal and Aunt Bertha know the good news before it was public knowledge.

'I shall write to your Uncle Wainwright,' Mrs Horne said to her daughter before they said goodnight. 'I have not forgiven my sister for the unkind things she said about Jo, but your uncle has always been good to us and I am sure you will want to invite them to your wedding.'

'Oh, yes, I like my Uncle Wainwright,' Lucy told her with a smile. 'Aunt Wainwright was unkind to Jo, Mama, but it is best forgotten now—do you not think so?'

'Yes, I suppose so,' Mrs Horne agreed. 'I was very angry with her, but I suppose it does not matter now. Jo and Hal are married—and I am sure your sister will want to come and stay once she knows. Do you think Jack would mind if I asked her?'

'I am sure that he would welcome all my family,' Lucy said. 'I hope that you and my sisters and their families—and, of course, Aunt Bertha—will all come and stay with us often when we are married.'

'To think that I once worried what would become of my

daughters,' Mrs Horne said with a little shake of her head. 'After your papa died and we had to leave the Vicarage, I did not know what to do for the best, but you are all nicely settled and I can be at rest in my mind.'

'Yes, Mama,' Lucy said and kissed her. 'Jack has some business that will keep him busy for much of the day tomorrow, but I must be up early—Amelia has promised to take me riding. She says that Jack has a horse that will suit me very well, and I am eager to try, for it is a long while since I rode Papa's pony.'

'Yes, of course, my love,' Mrs Horne said. 'Goodnight, dearest.'

Lucy went into her bedchamber, singing softly to herself. She asked Millie to unhook her, sending her to bed afterwards as she sat in front of her dressing mirror in her shift and brushed her hair. Getting up when she had finished her *toilette,* she went to look out of the window at the gardens. She was just about to turn away when she saw a horseman set out from the house, just as she had once before.

Where was Jack going at this hour? Surely it could not be to the bedside of a dying man yet again? She frowned as she went to bed, for she had discovered that the doubts lingered on, even though she had done her best to dismiss them. Oh, it was so wrong of her to think like this! Lucy did not like what she must in honesty admit was jealousy rearing its ugly head. She loved Jack and she had given him her promise. She was wearing the beautiful ring he had given her, and it was wicked of her to think such thoughts.

He would not have kissed her as he had and told her that he adored her if he had planned on visiting his mistress's bed that night. She would not think so ill of him. Yet there was something that he wished to keep secret—something that took him from the house after everyone else had retired.

Lucy wondered what it could be and if she dared to ask him. And yet she feared to make him angry, to spoil the magical time that being here with him had brought. She must simply trust him and wait until he was ready to tell her his secret.

The next morning Lucy had a riding lesson with Amelia. She found that it came naturally to her, for she had ridden as a child. They kept to the park, because Amelia said that it would be unwise to go too far until Lucy had become comfortable in the saddle.

'You may suffer some soreness,' she said, 'and you will probably be stiff this evening. It is best to do these things gradually, that way you avoid too much discomfort.'

Lucy did not argue, though she would have loved to ride farther afield. She was curious as to what lay beyond the lake and the woods that bounded it to one side.

The afternoon was warm and sultry and Amelia had ordered that some comfortable chairs be brought outside into the rose gardens so that the ladies might be comfortable outdoors. Refreshments were served, and everyone settled down to enjoy the summer, which finally seemed to have settled for a few days.

After a while, Lucy got up and wandered away from the others. She found herself walking in the direction of the lake. She had meant only to stroll for a few minutes, but it looked so enchanting that she was tempted to walk all the way there, and she was thrilled on arrival to see that the black swans were swimming close to the near side of the small lake. She wished that she had brought some bread; even as she regretted her lack, she saw a woman and a small boy of perhaps four or five years come to the far side of the shimmering water and begin to throw some bread to a bevy of ducks. The swans craned their heads round and began to make their leisurely way across to the other side, making Lucy suspect that the woman and child had done this before.

She looked at them across the water, but was still too far away to see their faces clearly. The child seemed to be having fun feeding the ducks, and the swans when they arrived, and she could hear his laughter, which had a merry, happy sound. She hesitated, and then, as the child seemed to become aware of her, she put up her arm and waved to them. He waved back, but the woman looked startled. She took the rest of the bread from him, tossed it into the water and started to drag him away, though he was clearly protesting.

'Oh, don't take him away,' Lucy called. 'I like to see him happy.'

She did not know if they had heard her, but the woman continued to drag the child away, and she could hear his protests as she turned and began to walk back the way she had come. The little incident had made her feel that they knew themselves to be trespassing, which meant that Jack had probably been right when he said they came from the village. It was obviously a favourite place for them, but they should not have been on private land without permission. And if they had been given permission to come here, the woman would not have hurried the child away when she saw Lucy.

Lucy was smiling as she walked back to join her family. Whatever the reason Jack had ridden off late last evening, it was not to see the mystery woman. She had been foolish to let it cloud her happiness and she would put it from her mind.

As she walked to join her sister and mother, she saw Jack come out of the house. He smiled as he saw her, an intimate smile that promised much and made her heart beat faster.

* * *

'Shall we go for a walk before dinner?' Jack asked a little later. Everyone else had gone in for tea, and they were the last to leave the garden. 'I do not think you have been to the summerhouse yet, have you?'

'No, I haven't,' Lucy said, 'though I believe I may have caught a glimpse of it when we drove out the other day. It lies over that way, I think.' She nodded in the opposite direction to the lake. 'Yes, I should like to go there, Jack, though we must not be too long, for it will soon be time to change for dinner.'

'We have an hour,' he said and the expression in his eyes made Lucy tingle all over. He draped her arm over his, giving her a look that spoke volumes as they began to stroll in the direction he had indicated. 'I have been talking to a designer today, Lucy. I want to have our apartments refurbished before our wedding. He has agreed to work for us, and will call tomorrow so that we may tell him what changes we would wish for. You have not yet seen the master suite. I have never used it, for I had other rooms I preferred, but we can make what changes we need.'

'Oh, how interesting that will be,' Lucy said. 'I have many things at Aunt Bertha's that I would wish to bring with me, but it will be fun to choose colours—though the scheme you settled on for my present room could hardly be bettered.'

'Well, you may choose similar colours if you wish,' Jack told her with a smile. 'I want you to be happy with your home, Lucy, and we may as well have it done almost immediately. If we stay here for some weeks, we can see it underway, and then you may wish to go home for a while. I dare say you would wish to be married from your home. Unless you would prefer a big society wedding in town?'

'Oh, no, I do not think so, I would prefer a quiet family affair,' Lucy told him. 'It is so much cooler here in the park,

Jack. The afternoon has been very warm. I took a little walk to the park...' She hesitated, but decided that she would not mention seeing the woman and child again.

'You are not cold?' Jack looked at her in concern. 'Shall I put my coat about your shoulders, dearest?'

'Oh, no,' Lucy said, gazing up at him. 'I am not in the least cold...' and yet she was suddenly shivering.

He drew her into his arms, holding her pressed tight against his chest for a moment, and then he kissed her, his mouth soft at first, becoming demanding, hungry as the kiss deepened. Lucy trembled, giving herself up to the tingling desire that flooded her body, making her very aware of the longing deep within. Her lips parted to allow his tongue to enter, his heat arousing a wild need in her that she had never known, and as his mouth sought her throat, and then the hollow at the base of her throat, she gave a groan of need that echoed his.

His kiss travelled lower, as he pushed aside the flimsy muslin of her gown, his tongue flicking delicately at the sweet mounds of her breasts exposed by his seeking hands. He pushed the gown a little lower still, kissing her softness and taking the tip of her nipple into his mouth, sucking it gently and circling it with his tongue as she trembled and arched against him, her breath coming in sighing gasps of pleasure.

Lucy wanted it to go on and on; she wanted so much more, things she did not understand but instinctively knew would be as sweet as this, if not sweeter. Her body was tingling with desire, weak with longing as she surrendered herself into his keep.

'Lucy, my darling girl,' Jack gasped, for she had aroused such need in him with her willing submission that he burned to take her down and know her in every way. However, his was the stronger will for he sensed that Lucy had no defence against him if he took her too far. 'That is enough for now, my love, or I shall not be able to wait another day, let alone three months.'

'Oh, Jack,' Lucy whispered. 'When you touch me like that…kiss me so deeply…I do not want to wait either.'

'Slowly, my dearest,' Jack reminded her. 'I was to teach you slowly, initiate you in to the delights of love so that when we marry you are not afraid—but I think that perhaps you need very little teaching, for it is there within you instinctively.'

'Yes, perhaps,' Lucy agreed and laughed softly, huskily. 'I think it will be very hard to wait, Jack—and perhaps we need not?'

'You do not know what you are saying,' Jack said, 'and that is my fault. I want you, need you, Lucy—but I love you too much to overstep the bounds. We must and shall wait for the consummation of our love until we marry. Supposing something were to happen…' He shook his head as she looked at him because he did not want to remind her of the things that could go wrong. 'I can wait, my dearest. No matter how tempted I am to love you now, I shall not abuse your sweet trust.'

Lucy gazed at him trustingly. How honourable and considerate he was! Had she suspected that this man had gone out late at night to meet his mistress? She would be a fool to doubt him, for he had proved his love more than once.

Over the next two days Lucy was almost constantly in Jack's company. His designer turned out to be a small, fussy man with olive-toned skin and a large black moustache. He was Italian and expressed himself with his hands, waving them about madly when he got excited. He had brought drawings and swatches of material in so many shades that Lucy was confused.

Jack had taken them both up to the suite of rooms that would be his and Lucy's when they married, and she realised how pleasant they were; they comprised a sitting room that looked out on to the front of the house, two large airy bedrooms, and two dressing rooms, which were almost as big as the bedroom she had at Aunt Bertha's house. The bedrooms stretched the width of the house and were light because they had three windows, two at the back and one at the front, which gave them such an airy feeling.

'I think we will begin with a plaster frieze that will take away the plainness in Miss Horne's room,' Signor Manzarini said. 'The ceiling will be a pale duck-egg blue, the walls a striped silk paper of a slightly deeper shade and the furnishings rich gold and cream. It will give a restful feeling and yet be warm and rich.'

'Yes, perhaps,' Lucy said, willing to be guided, but with her own opinions. 'But I would like a touch of rose somewhere, because that is one of my favourite colours.'

'Ah, yes, pink for the beautiful young lady,' he said, nodding his head. 'I think we can arrange this in the curtains at the windows and the covers for the bed—no?'

'Yes, perhaps,' Lucy said. 'Will you leave the materials here for a day or so, Signor Manzarini? I should like to think about it carefully.'

'Of a surety,' he said, looking pleased. 'It is something so personal that one should take time...and now the matter of Lord Harcourt's room.'

The details of Jack's bedchamber were more easily resolved—they all agreed on dark blue, gold and red, which were rich and luxurious, but more masculine than the more delicate pastels.

After some hours spent in happy discussions of furnishings and fabrics, Signor Manzarini took his leave, promising to return the day after the morrow. In the afternoon, Jack took Lucy driving. He drove himself this time and Lucy admired the spirited blacks, which she acknowledged needed a man's hand on the rein. It no longer mattered, because she knew that she was free to order her own rig whenever she pleased and drive about the estate.

However, it was not until three days later that she did just that and set out for a drive by herself. They had settled the details of the extensive refurbishment, which was to begin almost immediately, and Jack had gone off with Drew to investigate something to do with the new methods of farming that had begun to become more popular amongst enlightened landowners.

Marianne was in the nursery, because Andrea was getting another tooth and a little fretful, and Mrs Horne was helping Amelia to order one of the guest rooms in preparation for a visit from Jo and Hal. Lucy had tried to help, but had been told that she should go for a walk and enjoy the nice weather.

She had decided to order her rig and drive out to see what lay beyond the lake, for she had never been in that direction. Oddly enough, both Amelia and Jack seemed to avoid it when they drove out with her. She found a road that was obviously used to come this way and it led her round to the right of the lake. She had thought that the woods began at once, but she discovered that there was a well-used bridle path leading through them, and she turned her horses in that direction, letting them trot, but not canter, until she came out the other side and saw that she had arrived at what looked as if it might be the dower house.

It was a substantial house built of red brick, but not as old as the main house. There was a large garden at the front and it was filled with perennials that she thought very pretty, and obviously well cared for. As she passed, she saw that a young boy was playing in the garden with a wooden hobbyhorse. Something about him looked familiar, and Lucy slowed her horses, backing them up so that she finally halted directly in front of the house. The boy looked up, smiling at her, his eyes very dark and wide. He came running to the gate.

'Hello, lady,' he said. 'Have you come to play with me?'

'Not today,' Lucy said, smiling at him. 'It looks fun. Perhaps I could come another day?'

At that moment a young woman appeared at the front door. She was wearing a gown that was stylish, but not quite that of a lady, for it looked a little too bright, too fussy, not English somehow. But perhaps she was not English, for when she called to the boy her voice sound odd—foreign.

'Come in, Antonio,' she called, a hint of anger or fear in her tone. 'You know you should not play here.'

'Oh, why stop him?' Lucy said. 'He is a beautiful child. I shall not harm him. I only wished to say hello.'

The woman came out of the house to stand behind the boy, her hand on his shoulder. Her eyes were even darker than the boy's and they flashed with what was clearly anger now. Two dogs had followed her out and started to bark, as if sensing the woman's hostility. Lucy had to calm her horses, for the dogs had made them restive.

'We do not wish for visitors,' the woman said, pushing the boy in front of her, towards the house. 'Go away now. You are not welcome here.'

'I am sorry. I did not mean to intrude.'

Lucy drove on, feeling a little upset. Why had the woman been so hostile—and why had she taken the boy inside? She was almost certain that they were the woman and child she had seen twice on the estate and she could not help being curious. She had tried to put them from her mind, but she decided that she must ask Jack about them when she saw him later that evening.

'I wondered who they are,' Lucy said as she told Jack her story that evening when they were alone. 'I think I have seen them walking about the estate, Jack, but the woman was very unfriendly. She told me that they did not want visitors.'

'Oh, that is Rosa,' Jack said. 'She lives there with the child and I dare say you may have seen them walking on the estate, for the house belongs to me.'

'Yes, I thought I had seen them,' Lucy said, looking at him. Something was wrong about the way he had told her who the woman was, as if he had been forced to give her an answer he did not wish to. 'But who are they, and why do they live on your estate?'

'The child belongs to a distant cousin,' Jack said, but his eyes did not meet hers. 'She had him when she was very young and wanted to be sure he would be well cared for.' Jack frowned. 'I gave her child and his nurse a home. Is there something wrong with that?'

'No, of course not,' Lucy said, but she was aware of a small pinprick of hurt, because she felt that he was lying to her. If the answer were as simple as that, why had he not told her the first time? Why let her find the house and its occupants herself? 'I just wondered why they lived here.'

'Well, now you know,' Jack said and there was a hint of impatience in his voice. 'If you do not believe me, ask my sister.'

'I shall do no such thing,' Lucy said, a little indignant. 'I see no reason why you should lie to me, Jack—indeed, I wish that you will always tell me the truth, for I should never mind what you had to tell me, as long as you did not lie.'

'I have told you, let it be,' Jack said and pulled her into his arms. His kiss was ruthless, hard and passionate, demanding that she surrender to him. Lucy resisted for a moment, because she sensed that he had lied, and he was angry because he had lied. However, her body betrayed her, robbing her of the will to resist his passion and she found herself drowning it, melting into him, giving herself up to him as his hands moved over her breasts, stroking her in a way that inflamed her senses, making her want to give herself up to love. Their intimacy went further than ever before, and she could feel the throbbing urgency of his need, as he held her pressed hard against him, his leg between hers, his lips at her throat. 'I adore you, Lucy. No woman has ever had this overwhelming effect on me. Please believe me when I say that I would never lie to you about anything that concerned us. I shall not betray you, my darling. Know it, believe it. I am yours as you are mine.'

His words were so passionate, his desire so needy that she could not doubt his love. However, she knew that Jack had not told her the truth about the woman and child. There was some mystery here, and somehow she was going to discover the truth of it.

Chapter Eight

Lucy sensed that Jack had slightly withdrawn from her. Despite his passionate kisses, his manner had changed a little. He was still as polite and concerned for her comfort and pleasure as always, but she felt that something was missing. He did not send her those teasing, intimate looks that made her melt inside, but instead appeared thoughtful, brooding. She sensed that his emotions were mixed, part-rueful, hurt even. Of course he had reason to be hurt, for she had questioned his veracity, his honesty.

She did not sleep quite as easily that evening. She was torn between wanting to believe Jack implicitly and sensing that he had lied and was uneasy because of it. He had a secret. Lucy was certain that he was hiding something from her and could not help but feel a little hurt. He should know that he could tell her anything. If the child she had seen was his, she could accept it. Somehow she did not believe that the woman she had seen with the child was his mistress. Jack could surely never have loved her?

Of course it might have happened when he was fighting in Spain. She suspected that the woman might be from a foreign country, and she did have very dark hair and eyes—as the child did, of course. Lucy was prepared to accept that the man she loved might have had a romantic fling when he was a young officer, fighting the enemy—and she believed that he was too generous a man to desert his child. Would he have brought his mistress here to his own estate? If he had, it was hardly any wonder that people gossiped, for such an action would be thought highly improper. A discreet affair with a lady of his own standing in society would be tolerated, even the acknowledgement of an illegitimate child—but a continuing liaison with a woman, who was clearly not his equal in any way, would be frowned upon.

Finding herself awake early, before the rest of the household was stirring, Lucy dressed and went downstairs, letting herself out of the French windows. She could not rest in the house, and needed to walk to clear her head. It was a little cooler that morning, though the sun looked as if it might come through later, but the air was fresh, bracing as she walked in the direction of the lake. She had saved a piece of bread from the previous day and intended to feed the swans if they were there.

They were at the far edge of the lake, but once Lucy started to feed some of the ducks, the family of majestic birds swam lazily towards her, certain that she would save some for them. She smiled as they lifted their heads, as if asking for tribute, and threw a few pieces to them.

It was peaceful standing by the water and it was a few minutes before Lucy became aware that someone was standing at the other side of the lake, apparently watching her. This time it was a man, not a woman. He was dressed in breeches and boots, a dark-coloured shirt opened at the neck, and he carried a riding whip. Lucy was not close enough to see his face, but she knew it was not Jack. She turned away, wondering who he was and why he had seemed to stare at her. He did not look like one of the estate workers and there was something different about him, though she could not have told anyone what it was that struck her as being…not English. Yes, that was it. Something about him looked foreign.

Walking back to the house, she saw Jack coming towards her. He was dressed for riding, and she thought that perhaps he had not slept as well as he might.

'You are out early, Lucy.'

'Yes, I like to walk early in the mornings sometimes. It was very warm last night, and seems cooler this morning.'

'I think it will be just as hot this afternoon,' he said. 'Did you walk to the lake?'

'Yes, I took a piece of bread for the swans. They are such magnificent creatures, Jack. One day I should like to see if I can get near enough to feed the deer.'

'My keeper has some puppies. I want a dog to take shooting, because Brutus needs company,' Jack said, looking at her with thoughtful eyes. 'Would you like to help me choose one? We could go this morning, if you wish?'

'Yes, thank you, that would be nice,' Lucy said, smiling at him a little uncertainly. 'What kind of dogs are they?'

'Working dogs—a crossbreed, I believe. These particular dogs would not be suitable as a lady's pet, but we could find a spaniel if you wish to have one for yourself.'

'Oh, no, I prefer the kind of dog you have described,' Lucy said. 'Hal has a black Labrador retriever. He told me that the breed is new to this country, brought from Newfoundland only a few years ago by fishermen. I believe it is a very good sort of dog for shooting—and also has a gentle nature.'

'Once again you have surprised me,' Jack said, an odd smile on his lips. 'We must ask my keeper what he thinks of the breed, for he will know if they are to be found in this area.'

'Oh, you must not take notice of me,' Lucy said, blushing. 'I am not an expert on these things.'

'But you observe, don't you? You notice things and take note of what people say. When we first met you appeared to be a pretty butterfly, flitting from one social event to the next, sweet, a little bit of a dreamer—but I was wrong. You are a deep thinker. Unfortunately, sometimes you think about things more than is perhaps wise, Lucy.' He slapped his boot with his riding whip. 'I am about to go riding, but if you are ready in an hour's time, we shall visit my keeper at the Lodge.'

'I shall be ready,' Lucy said. She walked on towards the house, feeling her heartbeat quicken. What had Jack meant just now? Had he imagined she was a foolish little thing that he could twist around his finger? Was that why he had asked her to marry him? Had he believed that he could carry on just as he always had, and that his silly little wife would not know?

Jack frowned as he walked towards the stables. Lucy's character had been a revelation these past few days. He had fallen in love with the charming picture she presented to the world almost against his will, for he had wondered if they would suit once the first flush of desire had worn thin. However, each day they were together she surprised him more, her thoughts and observations so much sharper than he had expected—and it delighted him. She was so much more than he had imagined. He had thought himself caught in the toils of a pretty little kitten, but now he understood that he was gaining more and more respect for her as a woman.

She seemed to have blossomed and grown so much since she came to stay here—or perhaps it was because she had revealed more of her true self to him.

He knew that he was deeply in love. It was not just a case of desiring her so much that his loins ached with need and he lay restless in bed, wanting her, imagining her laying beside him so that he could turn to her and take her in his arms, burying himself deep within her willing flesh. He wanted to see her smile at him every day, to hear her laughter, see that thoughtful expression in her eyes as she sat quietly, watching and listening. She was not a dreamer, but a woman with keen powers of observation—and it had been inevitable that she would discover Rosa and Anthony in time.

Jack had not expected it to happen so quickly. He had hoped to keep his secret for a little longer, because nothing had changed. He was still unable to tell Lucy the truth. It had been in his mind that he would tell Lucy before they were married; indeed, he ought to have told her before they became engaged, had meant to do so, but at the last moment he had held back. He had not wanted to tell her a half-truth, but in the end that was just what he had done—and the lie was heavy on his conscience. He knew that Lucy had sensed he was lying, and it was there between them, but for the moment he could do nothing.

Jack had given his word that he would always care for the child. He had no intention of breaking that promise, or of revealing the secret of his birth to anyone. In actual fact, he had grown attached to the child and liked to visit him sometimes. But that might have to change. Perhaps he should have sent both Rosa and the child away before inviting Lucy to stay?

Jack frowned as his horse was brought out of the stable. He had suggested to Rosa that he would find them another house somewhere—a house as good as the one they had now, in a pleasant area, perhaps nearer to a town. She had wept and begged him not to send them away, and he had given in—for the moment.

He mounted, still thoughtful, undecided. Here the child was under his eye, cared for and happy. He could not be certain what might happen if he insisted on sending them elsewhere. It was a quandary, for Jack was not a man to break his word—and yet if he did nothing, it might mean a rift with the woman he loved.

Lucy spent a happy couple of hours with Jack later that morning. They drove out to the Lodge to see Briggs, Jack's keeper. He was a tall man dressed in worn breeches and a coat that had seen better days, and from his speech and manner towards Jack—whom he addressed as Captain Harcourt—she suspected that he had served under Jack in the army.

'I've got two pups that might suit you, Captain,' he told them. 'They've good soft mouths and keen noses.'

'May we see them?' Lucy asked and he smiled at her.

'Yes, miss, of course. They look like balls of fluff at the moment, but don't be fooled. These are hunting dogs.'

'My fiancée was asking about Labrador retrievers,' Jack said. 'She has heard that they have lovely natures that fit them as house dogs as well as hunters.'

'Ah, know a thing or two about dogs, do you, miss?' Briggs looked at her and nodded. 'Well, it happens I do know of a couple of pups going—but they are expensive, mind. They have become popular and these belong to a neighbour of yours, Captain. Sir John Hastings. I am sure he would let you have one if you asked, but he was asking five guineas for them.'

'Buy them both,' Jack said, taking some coins from his pocket. 'We'll look at the pups you have, and you can keep the Labradors here for us until we come again.'

'Just as you wish, sir,' Briggs agreed. 'I was thinking of getting one myself for breeding, but your lady can have her pick—one or both, as she pleases.'

'Then we have struck a deal,' Jack said as they followed the keeper to a large shed at the back of the house. Several dogs were running free and one of them barked and rushed up to them, but a word from Briggs had it sitting, though it watched as the shed was opened and two pups came trotting out to rub noses with their mother. They were black and white collie crossbreeds, and looked adorable. 'Attractive chaps—and full of themselves. Yes, they will do very well as shooting dogs. I'll leave it to you to get them trained, Briggs—but I'll visit often enough for them to get to know me. You will have the Labrador pups here by the end of the week?'

'Yes, of course, Captain.'

'Come, Lucy. I think we have done our business here.'

'Yes, I think so for the moment. Thank you, Mr Briggs. I shall look forward to seeing the new pups.'

'Yes, miss,' he said. 'May I wish you happy? I never thought to see the Captain in the petticoat line, but I can see why. Congratulations, Captain. You've got a prize there and no mistake.'

'You will make her blush, Sergeant Briggs,' Jack said, grinning as he helped her back into the carriage. 'We shall call again in a few days.'

Lucy laughed softly, her eyes sparkling with mischief as they drove away, but she did not answer his teasing. They had been driving in silence for some five minutes when she saw a man at the side of the road, and instinctively knew him as the one she had glimpsed at the far side of the lake earlier that day. Now she could see that he was young, in his mid-twenties perhaps, rather handsome in a stern, forbidding way, with black hair and eyes, and olive-toned skin.

'Do look, Jack,' she said urgently. 'Who is that man? I am sure he was out near the lake this morning.'

Jack glanced at the man, but caught only a brief glimpse as he was turning away. 'I have no idea, Lucy. I do not think he works for me, and should probably not have been there. We sometimes have trespassers on the estate, often journeymen travelling from one place to another. He may have come to the estate looking for work.' He shot an inquiring look at her. 'Did he do something to annoy you?'

'Oh, no, nothing like that,' Lucy said, feeling happier because she knew that Jack had told her the truth this time. He had no more idea of the stranger's identity than she had. 'I thought he looked as if he might be foreign—perhaps Spanish?'

'I did not see him that well,' Jack said but looked thoughtful, a little annoyed. 'If that is so, I shall tell my men to keep an eye out for strangers. I do not refuse travelling workers access, for we sometimes have work to offer them, and he may already have asked. My bailiff will probably know. However, it should have been noticed and reported to me or dealt with by someone. I fear discipline may have slipped in my absence and it cannot be allowed to continue. When my uncle left the estate to me I was too busy with my work to do more than pay a brief visit every now and then, but it must certainly be put right now. I cannot have your security put at risk, Lucy.'

'It hardly matters,' she said. 'I do not think he means any harm—I just wondered, for he did not look like an estate worker.'

'Journeymen come from all walks of life,' Jack told her. 'He may be a master at his trade, perhaps a carpenter or metal worker—he could even be a lawyer or a house builder. Even so, he should not be at liberty to come and go on my land without my knowledge. This must be investigated.'

'Yes, perhaps,' Lucy said, looking thoughtful. 'But I thought… he looked as if he might once have been a soldier.'

'If that is your opinion, I shall certainly speak to my bailiff when we return, for I should like to know that young man's business here.' Jack frowned, because he had begun to think there was more to this than he had first thought.

Jack had decided that he would give a dinner to celebrate their engagement. As yet Lucy had met only a few of his neighbours, who had called on business and were therefore gentlemen.

'You must meet some of the ladies living nearby, for they will be your friends,' Jack told her later that day. 'We shall hold our dinner on Friday night, before Drew and Marianne go home. Jo and Hal will be here by then, and it will be a good chance for everyone to meet.'

'Is it not a little short notice?' Lucy asked, for there were only two days in which to send out invitations and make the arrangements.

'My chef has been ready for days,' Jack told her with a smile. 'I sent the invitations out yesterday, and I think that you will discover most of them will be accepted. Invitations are not as frequent here as in town and seldom refused.'

'Then I shall look forward to meeting your friends,' Lucy told him. 'Jo will be here by tomorrow evening, and I am looking forward to seeing her so much. It seems ages since we parted, though it is only a few weeks.'

'Well, you will be able to gossip as much as you like for the next few days,' Jack teased and bent to kiss her cheek. 'I have some business I must attend to, my love. I shall see you this evening.'

'Yes, of course,' Lucy said, watching as he walked from the room.

* * *

A little later she saw him ride away, and she got to her feet, feeling oddly restless. She was sure that Jack had something on his mind, something that was bothering him more than he would admit. 'I think I shall go for a walk—would you like to come, Marianne? Amelia?' Her sister and Lady Staunton both declined, saying that it was too hot. 'I may not be back for tea, Mama, but do not worry. I shall be back in time to change for dinner.'

Lucy had not deliberately intended to walk beyond the lake, which was one of her favourite spots, but somehow she found herself turning towards the bridle path through the woods. She did not know why she was drawn back to the house and its mysterious occupants, for she had been warned to stay away. However, it was as if a mysterious thread was pulling her, compelling her to go on even though her nerves were tingling.

After all, if the child belonged to a cousin, and the woman—Rosa—was merely his nurse, there was surely no reason why Lucy should not visit him. Jack had not forbidden her. She knew he was hiding something—but he had not asked her to stay away from the house or the boy. She was aware that he might not be pleased if he knew that she had deliberately set out to visit the child, but he had not forbidden it.

As she drew closer, she heard voices and laughter. The child was shrieking, obviously playing at the front of the house again, but he was not alone. Lucy stopped as the house and garden came into her view and she saw what was going on. The child was being tossed into the air, which was making him shriek with laughter—but the man throwing him and catching him in his strong arms was Jack Harcourt.

Lucy was stunned. She stood watching, her breath catching in her throat, because she was torn between a feeling of pleasure in the scene and dismay. Jack was clearly on good terms with the child. Indeed, there was warmth and affection between them, even love, which was pleasant to see. In other circumstances Lucy would have thought it charming, but Jack had lied to her. He had dismissed the boy as being a cousin's child to whom he had given a home—but this was far more than an act of charity. He was obviously fond of the child.

The boy must be Jack's son! There was no other explanation for what was taking place. He had lied to Lucy, not once but several times. He had lied about the child and he had lied about the reason he had gone out that afternoon—which meant that he was capable of lying about anything.

At that moment, the woman saw her, and there was a gleam of triumph in her eyes, as if she was pleased that Lucy had witnessed this little scene. She did not speak to Jack, and it was clear that he had not noticed her. Lucy turned away, her eyes stinging with tears she was too proud to shed. How could Jack have deceived her in this way?

She walked swiftly back the way she had come, the unshed tears blinding her eyes. Because she was so distressed, she did not see the stranger standing just a little way from her. He too was watching the man playing with the child, and the look on his face was angry, his dark eyes narrowed, his mouth hard. As Lucy walked away, he began to follow her. He made no attempt to speak or catch up with her, walking a steady pace behind her, shadowing her until she reached the other side of the lake and began to gather pace until she was running towards the house.

José Domingues frowned as he watched the young English girl run the last few paces to the house. A lot that was happening here puzzled him, for his grasp of the English language was not yet as good as he would like, and he was not sure what the situation was here. It had taken him a long time to find this place and now that he had, he was not sure what to do.

Lucy went straight up to her room. Her eyes felt heavy and stung with the tears she was holding back, her heart was aching. Jack had lied to her. He had lied to her not once but several times, and she did not know what to do, because it hurt so very much to discover that he was not the honest, decent man she had believed him.

If only she had waited a little longer before agreeing to marry him! She knew that Jack had sent the advertisement of their engagement to the London papers, which made it difficult for her to withdraw. She would be branded a jilt and everyone would laugh at her. She might never be able to go into society and she would never marry...but she did not wish to marry anyone but Jack!

The realisation that she was caught in a trap and that whatever she did now was sure to bring heartbreak brought on the tears she had tried so hard not to shed. She threw herself on the bed and wept, sobbing for some minutes.

At last her tears dried and she got up to wash her face in cold water. It was a while before her face stopped looking patchy and red and she decided to stay in her room, preferring to miss tea rather than let anyone see her misery.

After an hour or so she rang for Millie, who came to help her change her gown for the evening. Millie looked at her in concern, asking if something was the matter.

'Oh, no,' Lucy said, hiding her distress. 'I had something in my eye—some dust, I think—and it made them water.'

'Should we put a little *poudre* on your nose?' Millie asked, though she knew that Lucy's complexion was usually so clear that she needed none. 'Just so that it is not red?'

'Yes, perhaps we should,' Lucy said. She opened the tiny box and took out the little pad, dabbing it on the end of her nose and then brushing most of it away again, for it looked unnaturally white. 'I do not like it much, though some ladies wear it, and rouge, I think.'

'Oh, yes, the *poudre* was very fashionable some years ago,' Millie told her. 'Though some say it is not good to use it often, for it is whispered that it makes people ill. I am sure it will not harm you, Miss Lucy, for you use it so seldom.'

Lucy frowned. 'I think that was a long time ago, when it was made from lead and ladies painted their maquillage so thickly, and I dare say this is not the same at all—Mama would not have let me have it if it were.'

'It has taken the redness from your nose,' Millie said as she finished dressing her hair. 'No one will know you have been crying now, miss.'

'I have not been crying, it was just the dust,' Lucy said, but did not look her maid in the eye. 'Thank you, Millie. I shall go down now.'

Millie went away. For once she did not tell her fellow servants what she had learned. She was very fond of her mistress, and she knew she had been weeping, whatever she said. Just what had his lordship been up to, to upset her like that? Millie would very much like to know! She had always admired him, but she would not if he upset her Miss Lucy!

Lucy went downstairs. For once she was the last to arrive, and she was glad that she had taken her maid's advice and powdered her nose, because everyone looked at her curiously. She put on a bright smile and apologised for keeping them waiting, though it was noticeable that she was making an effort. Mrs Horne wondered what had upset her, but decided not to ask, because Lucy would come to her if she wished to confide in her.

However, Jack was not as diplomatic. He frowned as he escorted Mrs Horne into dinner, his eyes on Lucy.

'Has something upset Lucy?'

'I do not know,' Mrs Horne replied. 'She seemed happy enough earlier, but she went for a long walk—towards the lake, I believe. Perhaps she may have seen something she did not like...she can be sensitive, though she does not say much about her feelings. Lucy is either happy and full of life or quiet, sir. I have learned that is usually best to leave her until she is ready to talk.'

Jack nodded but did not answer. It was clear that Lucy was either upset or angry, and it seemed to be on his account, for she was studiously avoiding his eyes. He held his tongue throughout dinner, for he did not wish to provoke a public disagreement, but after the gentlemen rejoined the ladies in the drawing room that evening, he sought her out.

'Would you take a little stroll in the gardens with me?'

'I do not think I care for a walk this evening,' Lucy replied in a polite, cool voice.

'Then let me show you the family jewels, which arrived this afternoon. I sent for them so that we may decide what you would like to have reset for your own use.

'I shall leave the choice to you.'

'Lucy!' Something in his voice warned her and she looked up, surprised by the angry gleam in his eyes. 'If you do not come with me, I shall be forced to have this out in front of your family.'

'Since you wish it,' Lucy said, her eyes glinting. Her hurt had turned to anger. She had been trying to avoid a confrontation, but since he was set on it, she would give him his wish, though he might regret it. 'We shall go somewhere we can be private—perhaps the garden is best, for we shall not be overheard.'

Lucy walked a little ahead of him down the stairs and out through the long French windows in the front parlour. Her back was straight, her head held proudly. He caught up with her, taking her arm and swinging her round to face him.

'What is all this?' he demanded. 'You have been sulking all evening.'

'I do not sulk!' Lucy retorted angrily. 'I have been behaving with dignity, for I did not wish to provoke a quarrel—but if you wish for the truth, I shall tell you. I do not like lies or liars. You told me that you went out on business this afternoon.'

'I did.' Jack's gaze narrowed as she turned away from him. 'Lucy, what is wrong?'

'If by business you meant paying a visit to your bastard and his mother, then I acquit you of lying.' Her face was very pale, her eyes glittering with the temper he had not suspected lay beneath her sweet manner.

'She is not my mistress!' Jack said in a quiet voice that made her blood run cold. 'I am not in the habit of lying and I have told you that Rosa is the boy's nurse.'

'She looks at you as if you were hers,' Lucy said, 'and she hates me. If she is not your mistress why should she feel hostility towards me?'

'I do not know,' Jack said. 'Unless…' He shook his head as Lucy questioned with her eyes, because he was not sure how to answer her. If Rosa was resentful towards her, it must be because he had told her that she would have to go away unless she kept out of sight of the main house. 'I swear to you that she is not my mistress.'

'Then why keep her and the boy here? Do not tell me he is merely the child of a distant cousin, because I saw you playing with him, Jack. It was clear that you loved him, were close to him. Is he your son?'

'I know that you have heard tales of a bastard child,' Jack said, looking uncertain. 'I cannot tell you the truth of his birth, Lucy. It is a secret—a secret I promised never to reveal.'

'But is he yours? Surely you can tell me that?'

'Why should I?' Jack's expression had gone cold, his eyes proud, angry. 'If you loved me as you say, you would trust me. I should not need to reveal something that I have already told you I am sworn never to reveal. You must learn to trust me and not to spy on me.'

'I was not spying on you. The child wanted me to play with him. He is innocent and beautiful. I wondered why the woman was hostile, particularly if she was just his nurse and I wanted to discover why—but you were there with them, playing with him…and you told me you had to go out on business.'

'A part of my business was to tell Rosa that I was still looking for another house for her.'

'So that you could hide them away, pretend that they did not exist?' Lucy said scornfully. 'I would have accepted your son had you told me the truth—but I shall never accept a mistress that you keep near you so that you may visit her when you have time. You must choose—it is her or me.'

'Must I, Lucy?' Jack's eyes narrowed, his tone soft but menacing. 'I do not take kindly to threats.' He seized hold of her, pulling her hard against him and taking possession of her lips. This kiss had no tenderness, but was a bruising, hungry, angry kiss that took her breath and left her weak as he suddenly let her go. 'I love you, want you as my wife, but I shall not be threatened, Lucy. Think about what you feel, because as yet we are merely engaged and an engagement may be broken—but if you marry me, I shall not allow you to dictate to me.'

He turned and walked away from her, striding off into the

shadows, leaving Lucy alone and close to tears. She knew that he was very angry, and in his anger he had become someone else—a man she did not know.

Lucy had spent a restless night, unable to sleep as she lay tossing on her pillows. The thoughts kept going round and round in her mind—could she really trust Jack? Was the child his son? Would he make a habit of lying to her when they were married, and could she bear it if *that* woman was his mistress?

There was a point during the night when at last sleep had come to her, but it was fitful, causing her to start up and cry out more than once. In the morning when she woke, she felt heavy eyed and tired, her heart aching because a night of searching her thoughts had led her nowhere.

Jack had refused to tell her the truth, but perhaps Rosa would not hold back. Dressing hurriedly so that she could leave before anyone was stirring, Lucy left her bedchamber and went downstairs. She had decided that she must speak to Rosa, even if the woman was hostile once more. She could not marry Jack with this shadow hanging over her, and it was clear that he would tell her nothing.

She took a heavy paisley shawl with her, wrapping it around her because the early morning was chilly and the sky looked overcast. She thought there might be a break in the weather, and she walked swiftly, hoping that she might complete her mission and return before the skies broke and the impending rain came down.

It did not occur to Lucy that she was storing up more trouble for herself. She had spent such a miserable night that she could only think of one thing and that was discovering the truth for herself from Rosa's lips. She walked fast, running sometimes because her emotions were high, driving her on though at the back of her mind she understood that Jack would be angry again if he discovered that she had been here. She did not wish to provoke his anger, but how could she bear to live here and not know the truth?

She reached the house, her courage almost deserting her as she hesitated outside the garden gate, wondering if she ought even now to turn back. A part of her wanted to trust Jack, to go back to where they had been before their quarrel, but another part of her refused to accept what he had told her. As she hesitated, the door of the house opened and Rosa came down the path towards her. She stopped a few feet away, staring at Lucy, her eyes cold and hostile.

'What are you doing here?'

'I came to ask you something,' Lucy said, shivering, though not from cold. She hugged her thick shawl about her, wishing that she had not come and almost turned away—and then from somewhere her anger and spirit returned. 'Are you Antonio's mother?'

'Of course I am his mama,' Rosa said, lifting her head proudly, her eyes flashing. 'Does he not look like me?'

'Yes, he does a little,' Lucy agreed. She felt the pain strike her heart, because Jack had lied again. 'Who is his father?'

'But you know the answer,' Rosa said and her eyes gleamed with spiteful glee. 'You saw him playing with the boy. It was obvious that they love each other. Why would such a man come here if he were the child of another?' She tossed her long dark hair defiantly. 'You are the one he will marry for the sake of his name and family—but he will always come back to me, because he loves me.'

'No! He loves me,' Lucy cried as the pain struck her like a dagger in her breast. 'You are lying! Jack does not love you—he could not. He comes to visit the child, but he does not want you.'

'Perhaps for now you have him,' Rosa told her scornfully. 'For a little while he finds your pale skin and hair fascinating and he will come to your bed every night and speak of love—but he knows that I can give him the passion you cannot. When he has tired of you, he will return to me. You cannot hold him for he belongs to me…he needs what only I can give him.'

'No! You are a liar!' Lucy cried, but her heart felt as if it were breaking. There was a wild beauty about Rosa at that moment, the kind of appeal that would bind a man to her—something that Lucy knew she could never offer Jack, however much she loved him. 'I shall not believe you. He loves me…'

She turned to run away with Rosa's laughter ringing in her ears. 'Run away, little English rose. A rose lives but a day or two at most, but I have the blood of the flamenco in my veins and the hot sun of Spain. He will come to me when he has had enough of your pale flesh and lose himself in the joys of mine.'

Lucy was weeping as she ran, her heart breaking bit by bit, for how could she deny the truth of Rosa's words? It was clear that the woman knew she had a hold on Jack, a hold that Lucy could never break. How could she marry him knowing that he would be hers for only a short time? And yet how could she not marry him when her heart was his alone?

She did not know which way to turn in her distress. Her mama would support her, take her away from this place so that she need never see Jack again—but that would break her heart. She wanted Jack to love her and sometimes she believed that he did, but how could she believe his passionate declaration now?

The child was his son and Rosa was its mother. Surely he would not have brought them here unless he cared for them both… The thought was sheer torment, but it would not leave her as she sped towards the house. It seemed that she must be doomed to unhappiness whatever she did.

Jack saw Lucy running towards the house from an upper window. He had been about to go riding, feeling that he needed some hard exercise to work off his frustration. It was clear to him at that moment that his fiancée was distressed, and instinctively he knew that she had been to the house. What lies had Rosa been telling her now?

Cursing himself for a fool, he went downstairs to intercept Lucy before she could disappear. This thing had to be settled between them one way or the other!

She saw him as he left the house and swerved, as if she meant to avoid him, but he went after her, sprinting to catch her, then swing her round to face him. Her eyes were defiant, angry, and he felt his own temper rising. Why would she not accept his word? She ought to know that he would not betray the love he felt for her.

'You've been there again,' he said harshly. 'What did Rosa say to you? Whatever it was you should ignore it. She is a liar and if Anthony did not need her I should have sent her away long ago.'

'Is she the liar?' Lucy flashed, too hurt to be cautious. 'Why did you try to hide them from me? If you had told me he was your son, I would have accepted it. But you cannot expect me to accept your mistress. Rosa told me that you love her; she swore that you will go back to her when you have tired of me.'

'And you believe her?' Jack's eyes flashed with anger, though he was not sure whether he was most angry with Rosa, Lucy or himself for being a fool. 'I do not think we can go on like this, Lucy. Clearly you take her word above mine. You believe nothing I say, and no marriage can succeed like that—indeed, there should be none between us.'

'Jack…' Lucy drew back as if she had been struck. Was he saying that he no longer wished to marry her? 'What do you mean?'

'Damn it! I hardly know,' Jack exclaimed. 'Go back to the house, Lucy. I must think about this, because at the moment I cannot see a future for us. You do not trust me and I do not care to spend the rest of my life explaining myself to you.'

With that, he turned and strode away. Lucy stood staring after him for a few moments, then whirled and ran into the house and up the stairs to her own room.

Chapter Nine

Lucy sat at her dressing table, staring at herself in the mirror. Her face was very pale, but she had not wept since she left Jack. His parting words to her had left her feeling cold and shivery. Jack was so angry! She could not blame him in her heart, because she knew that she had behaved badly. What she had done that morning was not the behaviour of a properly brought-up young lady. In her position many girls would have pretended to know nothing about his mistress; they would have accepted the situation and pretended not to know as long as he was discreet—but she was not marrying him for position or wealth! She would have married him if he had none of those things, providing that he loved her and was honest with her.

Lucy was too much the Reverend Horne's child to tolerate liars and cheats. She hated the thought that Jack had deceived her over the boy and a part of her longed to believe him. He had accused her of taking Rosa's word over his, and, when she thought about it, she had done so…and that was both wrong-headed and foolish. She had invited Jack to tell her the truth, but he had stubbornly refused—why was that? Surely it would have been easier to come straight out and say, 'Yes, he is my son, but the woman means nothing to me.'

He had not done that...but he had sworn to Lucy that he loved her. Perhaps she ought to have been content with that, Lucy thought, beginning to understand that to an honourable man her words would be like poisoned barbs. Supposing that he was telling her the truth...supposing the child was not his, but belonged to someone he had cared for?

Rosa had sworn that she was the boy's mother and that Jack was her lover, but she was clearly jealous and perhaps in love with him herself. Her spiteful words had been meant to hurt, to cause distress and perhaps destroy Lucy's love for Jack—and his for her.

Oh, how foolish she had been to put herself in this position! Lucy realised that she had pushed Jack too far. He had said some harsh things to her in anger, but she had brought them on herself by accusing him of lying. Suddenly, she could not bear to leave the situation as it was. She had to speak to him at once!

Jumping up, she pulled her riding habit from the armoire and changed into it, collecting her whip and gloves and rushing down the stairs. She would ride out towards the lake, for she was sure it was in that direction Jack had gone earlier.

When Lucy arrived at the stables, she found that none of the grooms was anywhere to be seen. Only the stable lad was there, brushing out an empty stable. She called to him, asking him to saddle a horse for her.

'Which one shall I saddle for you, miss?' Jeremiah asked.

'Oh, any...that lovely chestnut,' Lucy said. 'Please be quick, because I am in a hurry.'

'Yes, miss, if you say so...' Jeremiah was puzzled because he knew the chestnut was a very spirited beast and usually only ridden by his lordship, but he did not dare to disobey the lady he knew was to be mistress here.

Lucy was impatient to be off, accepting the lad's hand to help her mount the chestnut. She felt its restiveness at once, but felt confident enough to canter out of the yard, because she had no fear of horses and did not realise that one of Jack's favourite thoroughbreds had not been exercised for two days.

Feeling the springy turf beneath its hooves, the chestnut pulled at the reins and Lucy, in a reckless mood, gave it its head. The wind lifted her hair so that it streamed back from her face, and a feeling of excitement overcame her as she allowed the horse to gallop at headlong pace towards the lake. For the moment she had forgotten the reason she had come out, forgotten her distress in the glory of this wonderful feeling of freedom. Nothing seemed to matter but the exhilaration of riding the magnificent animal beneath her as they flew across the turf.

She was enjoying the experience so much as she raced round the perimeter of the lake that she did not see the eyes peering from amongst a clump of dense trees. When the fox suddenly darted out in front of her and her startled mount snorted, and shied, she pulled desperately on the reins, causing the chestnut to rear up on its hind legs. Lucy had not been prepared for it and she was thrown from the saddle, striking her head hard against the ground. A little moan escaped her, but then she lost consciousness as the horse went careering off into the trees.

Jack had been to the village. He had decided that it was best not to confront Rosa at the moment, because he might lose his temper. However, he was going to have to make other arrangements for the boy's education and care. It would no longer suit him to allow Anthony to remain in his nurse's charge.

He had allowed it this long, because Rosa loved the child and Anthony had become attached to her, but he had known for a while that the Spanish girl had ideas and dreams that he had no intention of fulfilling. She saw herself as Lady Harcourt, and had declared her love for him when he had told her that she could no longer live on his estate.

'If you send me away, I shall kill myself!' she had declared dramatically. 'I love you, Jack. I love you as no one else will ever love you. This pale girl you would marry is no good for you.'

'Stop that at once!' Jack had ordered. 'You forget your place. You are Anthony's nurse, no more. You will abide by my decision and until then you will keep away from the lake.'

Rosa had looked at him sullenly, making no answer. He knew that she had taken her revenge when Lucy had given her the chance. In his anger he had blamed Lucy for not trusting him, but he knew that he should have told her the truth long ago. He had hoped that he would be able to do so by now, but he was still bound by his promise—a promise he could never break without the permission of the person involved. He had hoped Lucy would accept that the boy belonged to a relation and that that would be the end of it, but he knew that she had the right to the truth. He would have to speak to the child's mother, tell her that his happiness depended on his being able to tell his future wife the whole story…

It was as he came through the park that he saw the chestnut running wild. He frowned, because he had given orders that it was to be exercised only by his head groom, who was an excellent rider, or himself. Urging his horse forward, he cut across the path of the thoroughbred, making it shy and then suddenly stop. It was panting, clearly having run its course, the panic that had caused it to bolt now forgotten as it recognised the scent and the soothing voice of its master.

Jack was off the back of his mount, taking charge of the

reins and soothing the chestnut as he stroked its quivering neck.

'Whoa then, boy,' he murmured softly. 'Had a fright, have you? It must have taken something to shake Brent off—but you're the boy to do it. He should have known to take it easy...there, then, it's all over now.'

Jack caught the reins of both horses. He could see that the chestnut was heaving, obviously having blown itself in its panic. There was no way he could ride and take the horse with him. He would have walk them both back to the stable and then start a search for Brent, unless he had managed to make it back himself. One thing had suddenly struck him—the saddle on Firethorn's back was for a lady. Surely his sister hadn't been foolish enough to saddle the chestnut? Amelia was usually a good judge of horses and she rode well, but she ought to have known she couldn't handle this beast.

It was more than twenty minutes before Jack finally reached the stable. The first person he saw was his head groom, calmly combing one of the mares. He frowned, because he knew Brent too well to think that he would be here if he knew the chestnut was running wild—and, thinking about it, he would never have used a lady's saddle!

At that moment, the groom turned to look and his expression confirmed Jack's assumption that he had known nothing of what happened. He came to Jack at once, looking at the chestnut in concern.

'He looks as if he has been running wild, sir—there's a scratch or two on his legs, nothing that can't be treated—but what happened?'

'That is what I would like to know,' Jack said. 'I caught him as I returned from the village. He looked blown. Something must have made him bolt and run himself ragged—but if you weren't riding him, who was?'

'I have no idea, sir. The grooms know that no one but you or me rides Firethorn.' He frowned. 'I was out of the stable for a few minutes earlier…' He glanced round the yard and his gaze fell on the lad. 'Here, lad, do you know who took the chestnut out this morning?'

Jeremiah looked scared, kicking at the ground with the toe of his boot. 'It was Miss Horne,' he said. 'She told me to saddle him for her.'

'Lucy!' Jack felt the ice trickle down his spine. 'Damn it! How could you let her take this beast out? You had been told that only Brent or I were to ride him!'

'I'm sorry, sir,' the lad snivelled, wiping his nose with the back of his hand. 'She picked him and I didn't like to say no.'

Brent cuffed him across the ear. 'Perhaps that will teach you to think, if there's anything between those ears,' he growled. 'If anything has happened to that young lady, you will be in big trouble!'

'No, it isn't his fault,' Jack said, because despite the feeling of horror running through him he could not in all honesty blame the boy. 'In future, remember that no lady may ride my special horses—do you hear?'

'Yes, my lord. Sorry, sir. I didn't know what to do.'

'In future, think,' Brent said. He looked at Jack. 'We had best organise a search for her, my lord. Do you have any idea where she might have gone?'

'She went towards the lake, sir,' Jeremiah said. 'Shall I fetch the others?'

'We must rouse everyone from the stables,' Jack said. 'I know where she might have gone. Jeremiah, look after these horses and mind you do it properly!'

'Yes, sir.' The lad caught the reins and led them away,

suitably chastened. He knew he was lucky to get away so lightly. Almost any other master would have had him thrashed or turned him off, or both.

Jack went into the stable, leading out another of his best horses and saddling it himself. 'I'm going to look for her,' he said. 'Get the others together. Bring the chaise in case she is hurt and send someone for the doctor.'

'Yes, sir. I am sorry, sir. Had I been here, it would not have happened.'

'If anyone is to blame, it is me,' Jack said grimly. He mounted his horse and set off to look for Lucy. It was obvious that she had fallen and there was only one person to blame. He had lied to her and quarrelled with her, and because of that she had been reckless. If she was badly hurt or injured, he would never forgive himself.

Lucy stirred as she felt the coolness touch her face. Her eyelashes flickered and then she opened her eyes, giving a little start of fear as she looked up into the face of a stranger. She tried to sit up and felt the soreness at the back of her head, and, turning dizzy, she lay back again.

'Please, you do not try to move for a moment,' the man said. 'You bang your head as you fall from horse. I think you dead, but I come running and I bring water. You not dead, but your head hurts—no?'

Lucy tried opening her eyes again. This time they focused properly and she saw the man's face clearly. 'I've seen you before about the estate,' she said in a whispery voice. 'Who are you?'

'My name it does not matter,' the man said. 'Forgive me, I speak only little English. I come here from Spain two months ago and I look for someone. I no harm you, English miss.'

'I am not afraid of you,' Lucy said. She sat up gingerly, feeling slightly less dizzy now. 'Thank you for helping me. If you could help me to stand…' He gave her his hand, pulling her to her feet. For a moment she swayed as everything went round and round. She might have fallen if he had not held her arm to steady her. 'Oh… that's better. I'm all right now…' She took a step forward and stumbled as her ankle almost gave way. 'It hurts…I don't think I can walk.'

'You hurt ankle as you fall,' he said and frowned. 'It is long way to house. I think you stay here, I go fetch help.'

'No, please don't go,' Lucy said. 'I might be able to get home if you will help me…please?'

He looked doubtful, but did not move away as she attempted to hop on one leg, but again she stumbled. The stranger put an arm about her waist, steadying her as she tried again, and this time she managed to move a little way.

Lucy gave a little moan of despair. It hurt her too much to put her foot to the ground and she was feeling dizzy again. 'I think perhaps you had better go and fetch help,' she whispered. 'I feel terrible…' She gave a little moan and fainted again, her fall eased this time by the man who caught her in his arms, lowering her gently to the ground.

He knelt down beside her, torn between trying to revive her once more or fetch help. Hearing the sound of hooves approaching fast, he turned just as Jack came riding up to them. He raised his arm, beckoning him, and in another moment Jack had dismounted and raced to Lucy's side.

'What happened?' he asked. 'Did you see her fall?'

'I am over there,' the man said, pointing to the road that led through the trees. 'I see animal dart from trees and horse rear up. She fall and hurt herself. I bathe head and in time she come round, but she not able to walk—ankle hurt bad.'

'Thank you for caring for her,' Jack said. His eyes

narrowed as he looked at the man. 'You're Spanish, aren't you? Why are you here?'

'I no do harm. I look for work…' He saw that several men on horse back and a chaise were coming towards them, and he shook his head, taking a step back. 'I no do harm,' he said and then turned and fled into the trees.

'Come back,' Jack called. 'I only wanted to know who you are.' He frowned because he had wished to thank the man properly for caring for Lucy while she lay unconscious, which must have been for several minutes. However, at that moment some of his men arrived and his attention was turned to the problem of getting Lucy home without injuring her more.

'Is she conscious, my lord?' Brent asked.

'I think she has been,' Jack said, frowning as Lucy moaned, her lashes fluttering against her pale cheeks. 'I believe she's had a bang on the head and injured her ankle. You've sent for the doctor?'

'Yes, my lord. Sam went for him straight away. I told him to say it was urgent.'

'Open the carriage door,' Jack said, bending to lift Lucy in his arms. 'The sooner we have her home and in bed the better…'

Lucy was hardly conscious as they carried her home, though she moaned a few times as the movement caused her pain, and it was some time later that she opened her eyes to find her mama at her bedside.

'Mama,' she whispered as Mrs Horne touched her shoulder. 'What happened? Where am I?'

'You fell from your horse,' her mother said, soothing her damp hair from her forehead with a cloth wrung out in cool water. 'Someone helped you, but I think you must have fainted again. The doctor is here and he would like to examine your head and your ankle.'

'It hurts,' Lucy said. She looked uncertainly as the elderly man came forward and peered down at her over his gold-rimmed spectacles. 'My ankle is painful, but my head feels sore.'

'It may be that the manner of your fall saved you from worse harm,' the doctor said as he gently moved her head to one side to look at the spot she indicated. 'The skin is not broken and there is no blood, but I think you have a small lump and I am sure it will be sore for a day or two. May I look at your ankle, Miss Horne?'

'Yes, please,' Lucy said. 'It is the left one, doctor.'

He made a gentle but thorough examination, then nodded as he drew the cover back over her legs. 'I do not believe you have broken anything, but you have bruised yourself badly, and you may have a nasty sprain. You will feel unwell for a few days, and I advise you to stay in bed. I shall leave you some powders that may help to ease any pain you feel.'

'Thank you,' Lucy said and smiled. 'It was so foolish. I did not see the fox.' She closed her eyes again, because her head was aching. 'I am so tired…'

Mrs Horne accompanied the doctor to the door. Outside, she spoke to him, her expression anxious. 'Do you think there is any lasting damage, sir? I believe she lost her senses for some minutes.'

'These things are not always straightforward,' the doctor told her. 'She seems to have recovered her wits, and to know what caused her fall, but I cannot tell you with any certainty that she will not have a further relapse. However, if she gets through the next few days with no troubles, I think you may take it that she has been lucky.'

'Thank you for coming, sir,' Lucy's mother said, though

she was less than reassured by his words. It seemed that there was nothing they could do but let Lucy rest and pray that she was not badly harmed.

'May I come in?' Jack asked some minutes later. He looked towards the bed, where Lucy lay with her eyes closed. 'I have been told very little—except that she must rest for some days.'

'He could offer us no comfort,' Mrs Horne said, her expression anxious. 'It seems that a bang to the head is something he has no idea how to treat—and he said only that if she seems well in a few days she probably will be fine.'

'It is disturbing, but I think we must trust his judgement,' Jack said. 'Doctor Heron has always been reliable—but I will send for a doctor from London if you wish it.' He joined her at the bedside, gazing down at Lucy, his eyes intent on her face, a little nerve flicking at his temple. 'I am so sorry, my dearest...so very sorry.' He bent to kiss Lucy's forehead and her eyelids flickered for a moment. 'Forgive me.'

Mrs Horne stared at him as he stepped back from the bed. 'You ask her forgiveness. Am I to assume that it was your fault she was riding that horse?'

'I fear it may be,' Jack said, a catch in his voice. 'We had had cross words and I left her without...' He shook his head, because it was impossible to explain. 'If she should die...I shall never forgive myself. Oh, God! I cannot bear it...this is all my fault.'

'Lucy is not a child,' Mrs Horne told him softly. 'I think sometimes you may have thought it, sir—but she is a woman and she makes her own decisions. I shall not blame you until I hear it from Lucy's own lips, and I think you should not blame yourself either. We must both pray that Lucy recovers.'

'You are generous, ma'am. You will allow me to sit with her?'

'Yes, of course.' Mrs Horne got to her feet. 'I shall return in an hour.'

Jack sat in the chair she vacated, pulling it closer to the bed so that he could take Lucy's hand in his. He pressed it to his cheek, a tear sliding from the corner of his eye as he gazed down at her pale face.

'Forgive me, my dearest Lucy,' he said. 'I love you so much and I have wronged you. Do not leave me, I beg you. I promise that I shall make it up to you. Somehow I shall make you love me again.'

When Lucy opened her eyes later that evening, she saw that her sister Jo was sitting by the bed, looking at her sadly. She yawned and stretched, smiling at her.

'When did you arrive?' she asked, sitting up against the pillows. As she did so, she felt the soreness at the back of her head and the pain in her ankle. 'Oh, it hurts. I remember now. The fox ran out of the trees and my horse reared up. It was such a strong creature and I could not control it. I dare say I should not have taken it, for I knew that it was too strong for me. I hope Jack is not cross with me, for it may have hurt itself.'

'I do not think Jack will be cross, dearest,' Jo said and leaned forward to kiss her cheek. 'We have all been very worried about you, because you banged your head and the doctor thought...but it does not matter. I believe you are perfectly in your senses, and it is no worse than when you fell from a tree as a child and did not recover your senses for some hours.'

'Did I?' Lucy stared at her. 'How strange, I do not recall it.'

'You were very young, and it was my fault that you were in the tree at all,' Jo told her. 'I climbed up to rescue a kitten that Papa had given us, and you decided to come too...but you fell and hurt yourself.'

Lucy shook her head, smiling at her sister. 'It did not stop me climbing trees. I was in a tree when Jack came to Marianne's for the christening...I think that is why he thought I was still a child. And I think he *will* be cross with me, for I knew I ought not to have taken that horse—and we had quarrelled.'

'Jack has been sitting with you for most of the day,' Jo said. 'Indeed, he left only when I came to take his place. He has been very worried about you, dearest. I think he loves you a great deal.'

'Does he?' Lucy frowned. She would have liked to ask Jo what she thought about Jack's behaviour these past few days, but to do so would be a betrayal. She had already hurt him by questioning his honesty, and she would not compound her stupidity by speaking of things that were private, even to her beloved sister. 'Yes, perhaps he does...'

'Why do you question it?' Jo asked. 'I know Jack Harcourt quite well, because he and Hal are great friends. He would not have asked you to marry him unless he cared for you, Lucy. Why should he? I dare say he could have taken his pick of all the young ladies looking for a husband, but he chose you. I know that you are beautiful and your nature is just as lovely, but he would not have chosen you just for that, my dearest sister. Besides, had you seen the look on his face as he sat beside you, you could not doubt it.'

Lucy looked at her thoughtfully. She knew that Jo would never lie to her, and now she was remembering Jack's kisses, his teasing, the way he had done everything to make her happy, and she realised that she had been very foolish to doubt him. Jack had a secret, but it was not necessarily what she had suspected. Indeed, she had begun to think that she might have guessed it, for the clue lay in the child's name. Rosa called him Antonio, but Jack used the name Anthony.

'I know…' Lucy sighed, because she knew that she had hurt Jack and the rift between them would need mending. 'I think—' She broke off as Millie entered, carrying a basket of beautiful red roses. They had a heady perfume and it seemed to fill the room immediately. 'Oh, how lovely.'

'His lordship asked me to bring them up to you,' Millie said and smiled as she saw her young mistress sitting up eagerly. 'I'm glad you're better, miss. We have all been worried about you below stairs.'

'Oh, do put them where I can see them,' Lucy said. 'Yes, in the window. I can smell them from here. The scent is gorgeous. It was so thoughtful of Jack to send them to me.'

'He told the gardener he wanted the best we had to offer, miss,' Millie said. 'They are wonderful, aren't they?'

'Yes, they are,' Lucy said. 'Thank you, Millie, that is just right.'

'Can I bring you anything, miss? Something light—like some nice soup or a glass of milk?'

'Yes, thank you. I should like some tea and sweet biscuits please.' She looked at her sister, the gleam of laughter in her eyes. 'Do you remember when I sat on the edge of your bed and stole your biscuits? You were so sure that romantic love did not exist then, Jo.'

'But I learned differently when I met Hal,' Jo said. 'I believe that Jack loves you, Lucy—but if you are unhappy, if you do not believe that he loves you as you would wish, you must withdraw. Mama will not be cross and I shall stand by you, dearest.'

'Oh, no,' Lucy said. 'I do not wish to withdraw—but I have made Jack angry and I am afraid that he may have changed his mind.'

* * *

'Lucy seems much better,' Jo told Jack when she went downstairs later. 'She is drinking tea and eating biscuits—but she told me that she is afraid you are very cross with her. I hope you will not be too angry because she took that horse without your permission?'

'I am not angry with her, only myself,' Jack told her with a rueful look. 'We quarreled, as she may have told you. As for the horse, I should have warned her against taking the thoroughbreds. Lucy is a natural whip, but she is not strong enough to handle such high-spirited beasts.'

'Her fall was caused by a fox,' Jo told him. 'If she got as far as the lake before she was thrown, I think that she must have handled the horse rather well. Do not underestimate my sister, Jack. I know she appears fragile and dreamy, but she is much stronger than you may imagine—and though she does not shout or get angry very often, she usually manages to get what she wants in the end. She has a strong will.'

He looked thoughtful. 'Yes, perhaps you are right. It had not occurred to me, but I see what you mean—had she been completely out of her depth, she would not have got so far. I see that I must buy her a horse with spirit that she can manage.'

Jo smiled at him. 'We have all spoiled her, Jack, and I think you as much as the rest of us, but despite that she retains the sweetest nature. She would not tell me why you had quarrelled, but I hope you will not let it stand between you?'

'No, it shall not,' Jack said. 'And now, if you will excuse me, I shall go up to see her.'

He nodded to her and went past her, up the stairs and along the landing to the room that was Lucy's. Tapping at the door, he put his head round and saw that Lucy was sitting up against her pillows, her eyes closed.

'May I come in?' he asked and she turned her head to look at him.

'Yes, please do,' she said. 'I think I must apologise to you for taking that horse. I do hope that he has suffered no lasting harm?'

'Had you died, I think I should have shot him,' Jack told her. 'But thank you for your concern, he will recover.'

'Oh, no, you must not shoot him, poor thing!' Lucy looked horrified. 'It was such fun riding him, but the fox came and he was startled and I was not quick enough. I think he is a little too strong for me, but I should like to ride again—if you will allow me?'

'Have I not told you that you may do anything you please—as long as you bring no harm to yourself? I was very frightened, Lucy. When I realised that he had thrown you, I thought that you might be dead.'

'I am very sorry to have distressed everyone,' Lucy said. 'I was restless and I wanted to find you, to talk to you. I know that I have behaved badly, Jack. It was improper of me to accuse you of…' She faltered, pleating the bedcover with nervous fingers. 'Only, I find that I have a possessive nature and I should not like to share you with anyone else.'

Jack smiled ruefully. 'It is because you are the way you are that I love you so much, my dearest Lucy. I would not wish you to be meek and accepting, but you must trust me. I am not yet at liberty to tell you everything, but please believe that I am not betraying you.'

'Yes, I think I do believe it,' Lucy said. 'I have been very foolish to listen to Rosa. She told me that she was Anthony's mother and that you loved her even though you would marry me for the sake of your family.'

'Rosa is not his mother,' Jack said. 'I am not at liberty to tell you more, but she is not his mother—and she has never been my mistress. And surely you cannot believe that I asked you to marry me simply because you were suitable?'

'I have been foolish, haven't I?' Lucy said, giving him a shy smile. 'Can you forgive me?'

'It is my fault,' he said. 'I kept them there because I have promised to care for the boy, but I should have sent them away. I wish that I could tell you everything, Lucy, but I cannot. Will you accept my word that I love only you? I shall not say that I have never had a mistress for that would be a lie, but there is no one now—and there will not be while I have you, my dearest.'

'Oh, Jack…' Lucy's eyes pricked with tears, but she held them back. 'I do love you so and I don't know how you can love such a foolish girl.'

'Do you not, my darling?' Jack's voice was husky with passion. 'If you knew how difficult it was for me to sit here without climbing into bed with you and making love to you this instant, you would not say such an idiotic thing! I assure you that I have suffered these past days as much and more than you can know.'

Lucy's laugh was soft, her eyes lighting with amusement as she felt a return of her confidence. 'I do love you so much, Jack. I cannot help wishing that Mama would relent and allow us to marry sooner.'

'She has been generous enough not to blame me for your accident,' Jack told her, 'though I blamed myself. However, she has seen you unhappy and I do not think it will make her inclined to relent. We must hope that she does not see fit to make us wait even longer.'

'Oh, I am sure she would not,' Lucy said, though she knew he was right. Her mama was sure to insist that the engagement continue, because Lucy had shown herself to be unhappy. She was determined that from now on she would let nothing distress her. 'Did you see him?' she asked as something suddenly occurred to her. 'Did you see the man who helped me? He bathed my head and helped me to stand, and then I fainted again.'

'Yes, he was kneeling by your side when I arrived,' Jack said and frowned. 'I was grateful for what he had done, but he took fright and ran off before I could thank him properly. He said he was looking for work.'

'Did he?' Lucy wrinkled her brow as she tried to think. 'I cannot recall what he said to me, though I am not sure he is English.'

'I think he must be Spanish,' Jack said. 'He would not give his name, but I think he was afraid I might blame him for your accident. He ran away before I could offer him help. If he needs work I am sure we could provide something on the estate.'

'I wondered…' Lucy shook her head. Something had occurred to her, but she thought it best to keep it to herself, because she might be wrong. She had promised Jack to trust him, and she did—but she thought that when she was well again she might go to the house through the trees once more.

'What is it?' Jack asked, eyes narrowed. 'If you have something on your mind, please tell me.'

'No, it is nothing,' she said and smiled. 'Do you think we can go to look at the puppies tomorrow?'

'If you are feeling well enough to come down,' Jack said uncertainly. 'Doctor Heron said your ankle was sprained but not broken, but it may take a few days to heal. No, you must continue to rest and I shall bring the puppies to you, and you may choose which one you wish to have for your own.'

'Thank you,' Lucy said. 'You are very kind to me, Jack.'

'Kindness does not come into it,' he told her gruffly. 'I want to make you happy, Lucy, and I feel that I have failed so far. You must give me a second chance, my dearest.' His expression was grave, sending a little chill down her spine. Jack said that he had forgiven her, but something was missing. She felt that he was holding back from her. The old easy manner, the teasing smile had gone—and she wanted them back!

Lucy tried to get up the next morning, but was unable to walk despite her best efforts. She was forced to stay in bed, but later on that day she heard squeaking sounds coming from outside her room and then Jack entered carrying two adorable puppies in his arms. Both puppies had black coats, but one had a brownish patch around his eye, which was both endearing and amusing. Lucy smiled as they struggled to get free of his grip on them.

'Oh, how beautiful they are,' Lucy said as she looked at them. 'Do let them come on my bed, Jack.'

He obliged her, depositing them beside her. The pups made the most of their freedom by pouncing on Lucy and covering her face with enthusiastic licks, tumbling and squealing as they made themselves entirely at home. They settled on her lap at last as she sat propped up against the pillows.

'Clearly, they know who they have to impress,' Jack said. 'The one with the patch is the male, the other is a bitch and not quite as boisterous as her cousin. They are from two different litters. Briggs thought it best because we may wish to breed from them if they prove as reliable as their reputation suggests.'

'I do not know which to choose,' Lucy said. 'They are both gorgeous.'

'Then we shall have them both,' Jack said. 'Briggs may have some of their puppies if they have a litter. Do you wish him to train them for you, Lucy? At the moment they are ill-mannered little beasts, for they wet my breeches as I carried them here, and I must go and change before I am fit for company.'

'Yes, perhaps it would be best,' Lucy said, because she suspected that in their excitement one of the pups had wet her bed and that meant poor Millie would have to change all the clothes as well as the sheets. 'But I shall visit them as often as I can, and when we are married they will live in the house with us.'

Jack scooped up both bundles of wriggling mischief and carried them off with him. Lucy waited until he had left the room before throwing back the covers and putting her foot to the floor. Her ankle still hurt, but she managed to take a few rather tentative steps across to the window. As she looked out towards the lake, she saw a woman, child and two dogs walking towards the trees.

It seemed that Rosa continued to walk about the estate as she pleased. Lucy smothered the tiny doubts instantly. She would not let them creep in again whatever happened; besides, she thought she might know the truth of Jack's secret, even though he had told her nothing. She decided to sit by the window, for she did not wish to return to bed, though she was not yet ready to go downstairs.

'Should you be down?' Amelia asked Lucy later the following afternoon when she joined her for tea on the lawn. 'The doctor said that you ought to stay in bed for several more days.'

'Oh, I cannot bear to lie there when the weather is so lovely,' Lucy told her and smiled appealingly. 'Do not scold me, Amelia. I shall not ride or walk far again until my ankle is truly better.'

'I do not know how you managed to stay on Firethorn's back

so long,' Amelia told her. 'I would not have dared to take that horse out, especially when it had not been exercised for a while.'

'No, I knew that he was restive,' Lucy confessed. 'I suppose I ought to have turned back, but my pride made me go on. I think I should have managed him had it not been for the fox.'

'Well, it was lucky that you did not harm yourself more,' Amelia said. 'You were reckless, Lucy…but then, as a young girl, I was too.' A look of deep sadness came to her eyes. 'Had I been more careful…' She shook her head. 'I must tell you that I am returning to my husband's house in London at the end of next week. I have had a letter informing me that he will be arriving in England a day or so after that and expects me to be there. He must have followed me almost immediately. I had hoped he would not return to England just yet.'

'Oh…' Lucy looked at her, sensing the hidden emotions. Amelia was struggling against fear, regret and something else. 'I shall miss you. I do hope you will come and stay with us when we are married.'

'If my husband permits it, I shall,' Amelia said. 'However, he may not do so very often—though he would allow me to visit you in London.'

Lucy was not sure what to say. She had sensed for a long time that Amelia was nursing a secret sorrow. She thought that she might have guessed at least a part of it, but she was not sure enough to come out and say anything, for she did not wish to distress Jack's sister.

She looked round as her mother and sisters came out to join them. Marianne and Drew had delayed returning to their home, because they could not think of leaving until they were sure that Lucy was fully recovered.

'Have you seen Jack?' she asked as Jo sat down next to her. 'I haven't seen him since this morning.'

'I think he had some important business,' Marianne said. 'Drew and Hal went with him. I believe it may have concerned a horse, Lucy. Drew did not say exactly, but I imagine it was something important.'

'Oh, I see.' Lucy nodded and smiled, for there was nothing more important than the purchase of fresh bloodstock, especially when there was a breeding stable. 'Then I do not suppose we shall see them until later.'

'Drew said he would see me this evening,' Marianne told her and smiled. 'I think we shall go home at the beginning of next week. Jack had to cancel the dinner for his neighbours, because you were unwell, Lucy—but he has rearranged it for Monday. We shall leave the next day. I think Drew has been very patient, because he has things he must do at home.'

'Yes, I expect so,' Lucy said. 'I think the refurbishing work is due to begin here next week, and we shall stay to see it started, but after that I think Mama will want to go home?' She raised her brows at her mother, who nodded. 'We have preparations to make, and Jack said he will escort us and stay a few days, though he will return here for a while to see that everything goes smoothly.'

'Have you set the date of your wedding yet?' Jo asked, placing a hand on her gently swelling stomach. 'Do not leave it too long, Lucy, or I may not be able to attend.'

'I think perhaps another two months,' Lucy said, glancing at her mother.

'Why so long?' Jo asked. 'You both know your own minds. I should have thought you could arrange for the banns to be called almost at once when you get home.'

'I am not sure…' Lucy looked at her mama. 'I have not yet discussed it with Jack.'

'Then do so as soon as possible,' Jo implored her. 'This

rascal is taking over my life and I should hate to miss your wedding, Lucy.'

'Oh, no, you must be there!'

Lucy glanced at her mother again, but Mrs Horne did not say anything one way or the other. Lucy was thoughtful as the conversation became general, letting the others talk as she so often had in the past, listening and absorbing all that went on around her, while following her own thoughts.

She had decided that nothing stood between her and Jack, therefore she did not see why they should wait any longer than the time necessary to have the banns called in church.

'May we walk together in the garden?' Lucy asked Jack that evening when everyone had settled in the drawing room. 'There is something I wish to say to you, Jack.'

His gaze narrowed, for she looked serious and he wondered what had made her so thoughtful, but he stood up and offered her his hand. 'Of course, Lucy. I am at your disposal entirely.'

She took his hand, which he placed on his arm as they left the others and went downstairs, going out through the French doors in the small parlour to the lawn beyond. They strolled away from the house and the lights streaming from the upstairs windows, to the shadows of the rose arbour.

'Is there something important you have to tell me, Lucy?' Jack said, turning to look at her. 'Are you troubled about anything?'

'No, I am not troubled, Jack,' Lucy said. She gazed up at him, her expression earnest, intent. 'Jo asked me when we were to be married. She begged me not to delay it too long, for she fears that she might not be able to attend. As she says, we might be married in the time it takes to have the banns called when we return home.'

Jack studied her face. 'What do you want, Lucy? Is it your wish that we should be married in a month from now?'

'Yes, it is,' she told him. 'I know that Mama asked for a three-month engagement, but I believe she might relent if we asked her.'

'You know that it is what I want,' Jack said and his voice was husky with desire as he reached out for her, drawing her to him. His mouth touched hers, his kiss gentle at first, tender, searching, but then as she gave herself to him, it deepened, becoming passionate, hungry, demanding. His lips moved lower, down her slender neck, his tongue delicately flicking at the little hollow in her throat. Lucy arched her head back and moaned as he ignited a flame of desire. She ran her hands into his hair, pressing her lips against his throat, nibbling at his earlobe. Jack groaned, holding her closer still so that she felt the burn of his throbbing manhood through the thin silk of her gown. His hand moved over her right breast, caressing it, his thumb circling the nipple as it became peaked and sensitised under his touch. 'God, how I want you!'

'Take me now if you wish,' Lucy said huskily. 'I want to be yours, Jack. I love you so much.'

He pushed the bodice of her gown downward so that he could see the soft mounds of her breast, lowering his head to kiss and suck at them one after the other, nudging at them with his lips, licking delicately with his tongue and just grazing them with his teeth. The fire burned ever fiercer between them. Lucy shivered with pleasure, feeling the moistness run between her thighs and the melting sensation within her, which made her want to lose herself in him, become one with him as never before.

'Enough...enough,' Jack said, restoring order to her gown. 'Any more of this and I shall not be responsible for my actions. I know that you would give yourself to me, my darling, but I am not such a rogue as to take advantage of you, even though I am tempted beyond bearing. We shall wait until my wedding ring is on your finger, my love.'

'Then ask Mama if we can set the banns a month sooner,' Lucy whispered against his chest as he stroked the back of her neck with his fingertips. 'For otherwise, I do not see how we can endure the waiting.'

'I have told Jack that I shall think it over,' Mrs Horne said the following day when her daughter came downstairs mid-morning. 'Have you definitely made up your mind, Lucy? I know that you are in love—but you were upset about something, were you not?'

'Yes, I was, Mama,' Lucy agreed. 'But I was very foolish and we have resolved it now. I love Jack and he loves me.'

'Yes, I believe he does,' Mrs Horne said and looked thoughtful. 'I shall think about it carefully and give you my answer this evening. Will that do?'

'Yes, of course, Mama,' Lucy said. 'I shall abide by your decision, for you have always been so generous and good to me.'

'Well, you shall have your answer this evening,' Mrs Horne said. 'What are you going to do today? It is warm enough to sit in the garden, I believe.'

'I thought that I should like to go for a drive,' Lucy said. 'I have not seen Jack this morning—do you happen to know where he is?'

'I believe he had some business on the estate,' Mrs Horne said. 'Drew and Hal went with him. Why do you not drive one of your sisters out, dearest? You must not be afraid because you had a tumble.'

'Oh, no, I am not,' Lucy said. 'I shall see if either of them would like to drive out with me. In the meantime, I must send word to the stables that I would like my rig brought round. I do not think I am ready to ride yet for my ankle still hurts a little, but I can drive perfectly well.'

Lucy went off to request that her rig be made ready and then looked for her sisters. Marianne was in the nursery because Andrea had a tooth coming and was fretful, and Jo was lying in bed because she felt a little tired.

'Perhaps I should stay with you instead,' Lucy suggested. 'Or would you rather sleep, Jo?'

'I think I shall sleep for a while,' Jo told her. 'I am feeling very lazy these days. You go for a drive, Lucy. It will do you good to get out for a while. Perhaps Amelia would go with you?'

'I think Amelia went out walking half an hour ago,' Lucy said. 'I do not mind driving out alone. I am not afraid of my horses, Jo.'

She left her sister to rest and went downstairs. Her rig had been brought round, and the lad Jeremiah was holding her horses. He looked at her a little uncertainly.

'Mr Brent says that I am to come with you, miss—just in case.'

'Yes, of course, if you wish,' Lucy said. She smiled because she did not mind that the boy had been sent to keep an eye on her. She knew that she was capable of managing her horses, because they were well-trained creatures, almost as spirited as the chestnut, but more reliable.

'I'm sorry I let you take that devil out, miss,' Jeremiah told her as he hopped up beside her. 'I should have said something, but I didn't like to.'

'I hope your master was not angry,' Lucy said, looking round at him in concern. 'It was not your fault. I knew at once that he was restive, but I did not turn back.'

'I reckon you rode him well, miss,' the lad said, falling immediately under her spell. 'His lordship were angry, but fair. Mr Brent cuffed my ear and made me do all the worst jobs, but it could've been worse.'

'Well, in future you must tell me if I pick the wrong horse,' Lucy said and let her horses go.

They set off at a good canter towards the park. Lucy had no intention of going to the house in the trees. If Jack had a secret she must learn to live with it, because she had decided that in future she would do nothing to risk causing a breach with him.

Chapter Ten

Lucy enjoyed her drive through the park, following the well-used bridle paths. However, she did not know them well enough to be certain of her direction, and when she discovered that she had somehow driven out on to the open road she was a little dismayed.

She turned her head to glance at Jeremiah. 'Where are we, do you know?' she asked him.

'Yes, miss, it's all right,' he told her cheerfully. 'If you follow this road for a bit, it takes you through the village and, if we turn right by the church, we shall soon be back on his lordship's land.'

Lucy smiled gratefully. 'It is just as well you came with me,' she said, 'for I should have had to stop and ask someone the way.'

They were approaching the village now, which consisted of a main street with cottages on either side facing each other, an inn and a little baker's shop, also a forge where a man was shoeing a horse. At the end of the street was the church and the Vicarage, a large well-built house with a front garden that reminded Lucy of her father's living. She came upon the road leading to the right and turned her horses. After they had been driving for a while she saw what she thought was the wood that bordered the lake, and a few minutes after that she realised that she had come round in a circle. Ahead of her was the house where Rosa lived with the child.

Lucy hesitated, wondering if she could make a detour so that she did not have to pass it, but as she hesitated two dogs dashed out into the road, forcing her to pull her horses up. A moment later the boy came dashing after them...followed by a woman, who was laughing as she caught him up and lifted him into her arms, hugging him to her. Hearing the child's laughter, and seeing the way he responded, brought a lump to Lucy's throat, for she knew the woman well, and she was suddenly quite sure of the truth. Now she understood why Jack had done his best to hide his secret. She handed the reins to Jeremiah and got down, because Amelia had become aware of her and was staring at her, her face white with shock.

'Walk the horses a little, Jeremiah,' she said. 'I may be a little time.'

The boy obeyed, getting down and leading the rig a little farther along the narrow road. Lucy waited for Amelia to come up to her, giving her a reassuring smile.

'Lucy,' Amelia said as she recovered herself. 'What are you doing here? Are you sure you should be driving yet?'

'I had Jeremiah with me,' Lucy said. 'It was just as well, for I lost my way in the park and had to go through the village. Jeremiah directed me here.' She looked at Amelia and then at the child. Despite the difference in their colouring, she could see a strong likeness about their features. It was something in the set of their eyes and their noses—and the reason Lucy had felt so deeply that the child was Jack's, because it was a family likeness. 'I did not realise that the road would bring us this way, for I had not come by that route before. I promise that I was not spying on you, Amelia. And I shall keep your secret, believe me. No one shall hear of it from me.'

'My secret…' Amelia's face was very pale. 'You imagine that you know, but you can have no idea of the truth. Anthony *is* my son, but I have stayed away for such a long, long time…' She could not stop the sob escaping her as she gave the boy a little push. 'Go to Rosa, my precious.'

The child looked up at her, seeming reluctant to leave her, but Rosa had come to the front of the house and was staring at them with resentful eyes. However, she did not attempt to come to them, merely taking the boy's hand and leading him to the back of the house.

'If Staunton should learn that I was here, he would take David away from me,' Amelia said in a shaking voice. 'You do not know how cruel he can be, Lucy. You quarrelled with Jack over that girl, I know, for he told me. He begged me to let him tell you my secret—only you and no one else—but I refused, because I was so afraid of what you might think or say.'

'I do not condemn you,' Lucy said immediately. 'Why should I? I do not know your story, Amelia, and you must not feel obliged to tell me. I came here unintentionally, because I have decided that Jack would not lie to me. If he deceived me it was for your sake and I cannot blame him for that.'

'I shall—must—tell you my story,' Amelia said. 'But not here, not at this minute. Please drive on now and let me say goodbye to my eldest son. This may be the last time I am able to see him for months, years—perhaps ever.'

'I am sorry,' Lucy said, feeling distressed. 'I would not have caused you more grief for the world.'

'You will keep my secret? Give me your promise, Lucy!'

'You have it,' Lucy said. 'Perhaps we may talk later?'

'I shall return shortly and we will speak in private.'

'Yes, of course,' Lucy said. She went back to her rig, climbing up to the driving box again. 'Come, Jeremiah. We must go now…'

They drove in silence until they reached the house, because Lucy had much to think about. When she halted the curricle at the front of the house, the lad jumped down and held the horses. She looked at him as she climbed down to join him.

'You will say nothing of anything you may have heard or seen this morning, Jeremiah.'

'I didn't hear nothing, miss,' the lad said. 'Weren't nothing to see but some dogs and a lad playing, miss—was there?'

Lucy smiled at him, sensing that he spoke nothing but the truth. He had stayed with the rig, and she was fairly certain that he could not have heard what Amelia was saying to her, but she was sure that even if he had chanced to hear a few words, he would say nothing. 'Thank you,' she said. 'I have no money with me, but you shall have a guinea for yourself next time I see you.'

'Me ma will be glad of it, miss,' he said and grinned at her. 'Shall we go driving often when you're his lordship's wife, miss? It beats mucking the stables out.'

Lucy laughed and left him, returning to the house. She suspected that Jeremiah would become a favourite with her in the years to come. A shadow had lifted and she felt so much better, because she now knew that Jack had told her as much of the truth as he could right from the start.

Lucy had changed into a pretty muslin gown when Amelia returned to the house an hour later. She saw her coming and went out to meet her. Amelia nodded as she reached Lucy, and they turned towards the rose arbour, finding a wooden bench where they could sit and talk in peace.

'I know that you thought Anthony was Jack's son,'

Amelia told her. She had taken off her white gloves and was twisting them nervously in her hands. 'He was protecting me, because when I first had the child I wanted to give it away—I was so ashamed.'

'But Jack wanted to keep him?' Lucy looked at her and she nodded, a little smile on her lips.

'I was seventeen when it happened,' Amelia said. 'I must tell you that I was a spirited girl then, much as you are, Lucy. My mother had died when I was very young and my father remarried. I did not like my stepmother and she hated me. She could not bear to have me in her sight, and I was left here while she and my father were in London or at another estate, which she preferred. I think my mother's influence was too strong for her here.'

'Yes, perhaps it might have been, for I have seen it in many small things,' Lucy said, looking thoughtful. 'I like it—I like the feeling of another woman having been happy here. But please continue. You were telling me that you were much alone?'

'Yes. I had a governess who could not control me; in truth, she did not try very hard, and when I was seventeen my father dismissed her. I think he intended to send me to someone—a friend who would help me become a proper young lady—but he died. My brother was away in Spain at that time and I was alone with my stepmother. She did everything she could to make my life miserable—and then I met *him*. His name was George, Captain George Garrick, and he told me he was a friend of Jack's. He brought me a letter from him, telling me that he would visit as soon as he could.' Amelia paused for a moment, an odd look in her eyes, and then, 'George was such fun to be with. He was gallant, teasing me, giving me small gifts and flowers—and then he made love to me. I was young and innocent, Lucy. I liked to be kissed, and when he went further I did not stop him. It happened so gradually that I was not aware of what he intended, but then one day he did not stop at kisses and caresses. I gave myself to him, for I loved him, but a few days later he went away and I never saw him again.'

'Oh, how wicked,' Lucy cried, horrified at the way Amelia had been treated. 'You poor thing. You must have been so upset.'

'Yes, I was,' Amelia said. 'I believed he had deserted me. I did not know until much later that my stepmother made him leave, made him believe that I was promised to another. I was so innocent that at first I did not know what had happened to me. It did not occur to me to wonder why I no longer had my monthly courses. It was only when my stepmother heard me being sick that she told me I was with child.'

'You must have been shocked and distressed,' Lucy said, understanding so many things now. 'What else did she say to you?'

'You can imagine the things she said to me,' Amelia whispered. Her face was very pale and her eyes dark with remembered shame and grief. The pain of that betrayal had been put away, but she had suffered deeply because of it. 'I did not know what to do. She threatened to put me away, into an asylum, which she said was the proper place for wicked girls.'

'Oh, no! How could she?' Lucy was stunned, hardly able to credit that any woman could be so cruel to her stepdaughter, but believing it because Amelia told her it was so. 'Could you not have written to your lover, told him the truth?'

'I still believed that he had deserted me. I did not discover her part in it until it was too late.'

'Oh, you poor thing. How unkind that was in her!'

'Jack came home before she could do anything,' Amelia said, her hands trembling. 'He knew at once that something was wrong, and my stepmother told him I was wanton and had brought it on myself. Jack did not believe her. He asked me for the truth and believed me when I told him. He went after his friend, but George had become engaged to someone else and would not break his word to her. Jack was furious and they fought, but I do not know what happened—he never told me. When he came back he took me to Spain with him, and my child was born there. I lived with Rosa in a house quite privately and no one knew that I had had a child. Some months after my son was born, Jack brought us all back to England. He installed Rosa with Anthony in the dower house so that I could visit him, and for a year or more I saw him regularly…' Amelia paused, seeming as though it was too difficult to go on.

'What happened then? Can you bear to tell me?'

'Jack had to leave England, going to France to rejoin his regiment. My stepmother did not dare to send me to the asylum as she had threatened, because she feared what Jack might do when he came back—but she made my life difficult in every way she could, and when Staunton started to court me, she forced me to marry him.'

'You did not care for him?'

'I liked him well enough,' Amelia said, her eyes dark with sorrow. 'I did not know his true nature. Besides, my stepmother told me that if I did not take him I would never marry. She said that she would expose me as a whore and I should be shunned by all decent company.'

'How wicked she was!' Lucy cried looking at her in horror. 'To be so cruel to you.'

'I was not afraid of her, for I knew Jack would protect me, but I thought if I were married I need not see her again, and Staunton was attractive in his way at that time. He had money and I wanted to live instead of being at home with her.' Amelia shuddered. 'I discovered my mistake on my wedding night when he understood that I was not a virgin bride. I shall not go into details of what he did to me, but he forced me to tell him about the child—and he warned me of what would happen if I ever saw him again. He said that if the truth ever got out he would kill me and…he beat me and then he raped me.'

'Oh, Amelia…' Lucy's eyes filled with tears, for she was shocked that any man could be so cruel to his wife. 'I am so very sorry.'

'I could not leave him, because I was afraid of what he might do,' Amelia said. 'I was his slave rather than his wife, and he did not leave me alone even when I carried his child.' She closed her eyes, tears trickling down her cheeks. 'I wish I had left him before he got me with child, because I love my son…both my sons.' She opened her eyes and looked at Lucy. 'I had to choose between my sons, Lucy. I could have one or the other.'

'That is terrible,' Lucy said. 'It must have torn you apart.'

'Yes, it has…' Amelia sighed. 'And then I met someone—a gentle, kind man who loved me as I loved him. His name was David Middleton. He wanted to take me away from my husband, but I knew that if I left Staunton he would take my son from me. I was torn between them, and I did not dare to visit Anthony. My husband made me go with him to India and I told David that I could not leave him. And then…a few months ago David was murdered.'

'No!' Lucy looked at her in horror. 'It was not…?'

'Staunton?' Amelia shook her head. 'He does not have the courage to do such a thing, Lucy. Jack told me he was killed because of a game of cards…but I knew that it was the end of all hope for me. While David lived there was a chance that I might have escaped, but now…'

'I am so very sorry,' Lucy said, finally understanding so

many things that had puzzled her, not only concerning Amelia but also Jack. 'You may trust me to keep your secret.'

'Thank you, I am grateful,' Amelia said. 'I know that I should stand up to him. Anthony is mine and Jack has borne the brunt of all the gossip, letting people believe that he has a bastard…and that is not fair to you, Lucy. It was wrong of me not to let him tell at least you. Please forgive me?'

'Do not be concerned for us,' Lucy said. 'Your son is a beautiful little boy and if Jack wanted to adopt him and take him into our home I should not mind in the least. It is true that I was jealous when I thought Rosa was his mistress, but—'

'Good grief! Did she tell you that?' Amelia looked astonished and then angry. 'That is ridiculous. I think that Jack must dismiss her and find someone else to take her place. I believe we can no longer trust her.'

'Do not dismiss her for my sake,' Lucy said at once. 'While I mistakenly thought her Anthony's mother and Jack his father I was hurt, but now I know how foolish I have been. She has no power to hurt me any more.'

'Then perhaps we shall keep her for the time being,' Amelia said and looked thoughtful. 'I wish that I had the courage to leave Staunton, but I think that he would fetch me back. I could bear his punishment for myself, but I could not bear it if he hurt David—or Anthony. It is the reason I seldom come here.'

'If Jack adopted him, would your husband allow you to visit us sometimes?'

'I do not know,' Amelia said. 'He might if people believed that Anthony was truly Jack's son…if he admitted it openly.'

'You must ask Jack to do it,' Lucy said generously. 'I shall speak to him myself, because I think it may be the only way to set you free of your husband's tyranny.'

'You are very kind,' Amelia said, linking arms with her. 'I am so glad that Jack found you. At one time I believed that he would never marry.'

'Thank you for telling me your secret,' Lucy said and smiled at her.

'I should have told you before or allowed Jack to do so,' Amelia apologised. 'I would have given my baby away, but afterwards I came to love him. I have protected him in the only way I knew how.'

'We had best return to the house now,' Lucy said. 'I do not think the men will return in time for lunch, but the others will be waiting.

Lucy noticed that Amelia was very quiet during lunch. Afterwards, she excused herself and went up to the nursery to be with David. Lucy could only guess at the pain she must have been feeling inside, because to be forced to choose between her sons was a terrible thing for any mother. It must be tearing her heart in two.

After lunch the chairs were placed outside so that the ladies might enjoy the return of the fine weather. Amelia did not come down immediately, and Jo was still feeling tired. Marianne and Mrs Horne were making baby gowns, and after a while Lucy decided that she would go for a little walk. Her ankle was not strong enough to carry her as far as the lake, but she could walk in the formal gardens, because there were benches here and there where she might sit and rest if it began to pain her.

At the moment it hardly hurt at all, and Lucy was encouraged to walk farther than she had with Amelia that morning. She walked beneath a rose arch, which took her through to a wild garden; enclosed by walls of box hedging, it was secret and pleasant, many of the flowers self-set, rambling everywhere as if they had been carried by birds or the wind. However, it was so beautiful that she thought a gardener had artfully arranged it so, and she stood watching dragonflies darting over a pool where lilies and other delicate plants grew. It was several minutes before she became aware that she was being watched.

She turned around, finding that Rosa had come up behind her. She was alone, her hands behind her back, her dark eyes hostile as she looked at Lucy.

'What are you doing here?' Lucy asked, a shiver running down her spine. Something about Rosa's attitude had warned her to be alert. 'Where is Anthony? Why is he not with you? You are his nurse. You should be looking after him.'

'He is sleeping,' Rosa said. 'He will not wake until I return—perhaps for some hours. I gave him something with his milk.'

'You did what?' Lucy was stunned. 'How could you? That is wicked! Have you done it before?' She saw the expression in Rosa's eyes and knew that she had. 'You are not fit to have the care of a child! I shall tell Jack to bring him here. He will send you away—and it is what you deserve.'

'You stole him from me,' Rosa went on, her eyes glittering. Lucy realised that she had not listened to a word she said. She was ill...under some strain that had turned her mind. 'Everything I love is taken from me. It is not fair...why should you have what is mine? I am the child's mother. He was my lover and we were happy until you came.'

'You are not Anthony's mother,' Lucy told her. 'And Lord Harcourt was never your lover. You have made it up in your head, Rosa—it is all a lie. You are merely the boy's nurse and now you are no longer fit to care for him. I think that you are ill.'

'You lie!' Rosa suddenly raised her right arm and Lucy saw something flash silver in the sunlight. The woman ran at her, the knife at the ready, and she realised that Rosa meant to kill her. 'You stole him from me—and when you are dead, he will come back to me...'

'No!' Lucy screamed, holding her hands before her as Rosa rushed on her. She made a grab for Rosa's wrist, gripping it and struggling with her as the other woman attempted to stab her, all the while screaming and yelling that Lucy had stolen her man. 'Help...help me, someone...'

Suddenly, a man came running. He grabbed Rosa from behind, his arms enclosing her in a powerful grip as she fought and struggled, continuing to yell abuse at Lucy. She was still holding the knife, but the man had her tight and she could do nothing but scream and shout.

'Lucy...' Another man had entered the wild garden. Lucy saw him and gave a little sob of relief. 'Help him subdue her, Jack...she has a knife.' Even as Lucy spoke, Rosa broke free of her captor and Jack moved to block her path, preventing her from reaching Lucy. In her frenzy, she stabbed him in the arm, and then the stranger had her again, and this time he wrenched the knife from her hand, flinging it in to the pool.

'Stop it, Rosa,' he commanded as she continued to fight against Jack. 'You know this is wrong. This man is not your lover—you were always mine. I should have come to you before this, but I did know not what you do here.'

Rosa's head came up sharply. Her eyes widened as she stared at him, and for a moment it was clear that she did not know him, but then recognition came and she sagged, all the fight going out of her in an instant.

'José...' she moaned and then said something in Spanish that Lucy could not follow.

Understanding that she was no longer dangerous, Jack left her and came to take Lucy in his arms, holding her close. 'Thank God he was near by,' he said. 'I have been looking for him. I believe I know who he is.'

Lucy looked up at him. 'He is Rosa's lover, he just said as much.'

Jack nodded. 'It is as I thought. When Rosa first came to us, she told us that her father had sent the man she loved away. She believed he had joined the army and died fighting the French. She had run away from her home and we took her in to be Anthony's nurse. When we came to England, she begged us to bring her with us, and because she had no home and nowhere to go we brought her. For a long time it was all right, but then she became…well, I have known for a while that she could not continue as Anthony's nurse for much longer.'

'Rosa is mine,' José said, making them turn to look at him. Rosa was standing quietly now, her head bowed. She looked subdued, her eyes dull as if she hardly understood what was going on. 'She has been ill and it is for me to take her with me. We shall go back to Spain and marry. I care for her and perhaps one day she will be my Rosa again.'

'She tried to kill Lucy,' Jack said. 'By rights she ought to stand trial for attempted murder.'

'No, Jack,' Lucy said and touched his arm. 'Let José take her with him. She can never harm me again, for he will not let her—and he did help me, not once but twice.'

'Yes, that is true,' Jack said looking down at her and then at José. It was clear that all the fight had gone out of Rosa. She was subdued, standing quietly with his arm about her. It was not clear whether she truly knew what had happened or who he was, but he was her only chance of salvation. Jack met his steady gaze. 'You must love her a great deal or you would not have come to England to look for her.'

'I have searched for many months,' José said. 'When I saw you at the house with her, and the way she looked at you, I thought she might be your mistress—but then I watched you with your lady and I know you love her. Rosa is not well. We go to Spain and she learn to love me again.'

'Take her, then,' Jack said. 'Make sure that she does not come here again, because if she does I shall not be so lenient next time.'

'Jack, you must have your arm bound. It is bleeding.' Lucy pulled urgently at his sleeve as José led the subdued Rosa away. 'And Anthony is on his own. She gave him something to drug him…you must go and fetch him here so that he is safe.'

Jack looked down at her tenderly. 'No, my love,' he said. 'Anthony is at the house, being cared for by Millie. I went to the dower house to tell Rosa that I had found a good house for them, and I found the boy alone. He was just stirring, but obviously not from a natural sleep. I decided to do what I should have done long ago and brought him home with me.'

'Good, I am glad,' Lucy said and smiled warmly at him. 'You can adopt him, Jack, and we shall bring him up as one of our family.'

'Would you really be happy for me to do that?'

'Yes, of course. I have already said as much to Amelia. She told me, Jack. I saw them together and she decided it was best I should know. I swear I did not intend to go there today. I got lost when out driving and Jeremiah directed me home. I didn't know it would take us past the dower house.'

'There was no reason why you should not drive that way,' Jack told her, his intent gaze on her face. 'I am glad that you know the truth, Lucy. I hated having to deceive you.'

'You did not lie to me, except in the matter of his exact relationship to you, and I understand now why you kept silent. It was for your sister's sake, and I have promised to keep her secret just as you have.'

'Amelia has decided to break her silence,' Jack said. 'When

she learned what had happened, she wept and said that she would never leave her son to the sole care of a nurse again. She has decided that she will leave her husband. I have told her that she may have the dower house so that she can live near us with both her sons.'

'That is wonderful,' Lucy said. 'But will her husband allow her to take his son? He has the power to make her return to him, and if she refuses he can take the child from her—can't he?'

'Perhaps,' Jack said and frowned. 'This must not be repeated to anyone else, Lucy, not even Amelia—but Drew and I have been making inquiries. We told everyone that we were looking for horses, but instead we have been meeting someone. He is the father of Amelia's child and he wanted to make some retribution for what he did years ago.'

'But how can he do that?' Lucy asked. 'He left her to the mercy of your stepmother and she would have been sent to an asylum if you had not come home.'

'Yes, that is true, but George has no children. He deserted Amelia because he was told that she was promised to another. When I discovered what had happened and went after him, he had in his anger and disappointment promised to wed a rich heiress. He married her for her money, but she was a bitter woman and died childless a year ago. He did not know that Amelia had given birth to his child until a few months ago because, when he was stubborn and refused to give up the heiress, I did not tell him. He discovered by chance that Staunton had been beating Amelia and his conscience was roused when he learned the reason for his brutality. After that, he set himself the task of finding a way to get her free of her husband—and I think he has found it.'

Lucy stared at him in wonder. 'Do you think that there is a chance it will work? What does he know that will bring such force to bear on a man like Lord Staunton?'

'I blamed Sir Frederick Collingwood for David Middleton's death, and it was his hand that did the evil deed,' Jack said, his expression grim. 'But George says that Staunton bought Collingwood. He was in debt to him so deeply that he would have ended in the Fleet if Staunton had given the word. Apparently, he struck a bargain with Collingwood—David's death for the promissory notes he had given Staunton. It seems that his whole estate was forfeit at that time and he would have been ruined had Staunton called them in.'

'Can this be proved?'

'Collingwood is in prison, awaiting trial. George has some influence with the judge who is to try him for murder. He has promised that Collingwood's sentence will be transportation rather than hanging if he will make a full confession and a statement, accusing Staunton of his crime.'

Lucy stared at him in wonder. 'And Amelia knows nothing of this?'

'It is not finished yet,' Jack said. 'I do not wish to raise false hopes, but if Collingwood goes against the promise he has given, I shall find some other way to get her free of Staunton. Now that she has made up her mind to leave him, I shall not let her down.'

'Oh, Jack,' Lucy said and reached up to kiss him. 'You are so wonderful! And I am so glad that you have told me,'

'All I hope is that your mama does not set her face against the wedding because of the boy,' Jack said. 'For otherwise I think that we shall have to elope, my darling, for I truly cannot wait much longer.'

'You asked me a question this morning, Jack,' Mrs Horne announced when they had all gathered in the drawing room before dinner that evening. 'I must tell you that I was still undecided, and when you brought Anthony here this afternoon

I was shocked. However, Amelia has seen fit to tell me the truth and I must tell you that I sympathise entirely with her story, for it brought tears to my eyes.'

'Then you no longer insist that we must wait the full three months?' Jack asked, throwing a teasing smile at Lucy. 'I must tell you that we both wish to marry as soon as the banns are called.'

'I see no reason why you should not,' Mrs Horne said, smiling at him warmly. 'Indeed, it strikes me that you have been rather noble, Jack, for you took the blame and shielded your sister in a way I can only admire. I think it speaks volumes for your character that you have never spoken a word in your own defence, when you might have scotched all the rumours had you wished.'

'I could do nothing that would harm my sister,' Jack said and gave her an affectionate look. 'Amelia has had to make up her own mind, for I have never tried to persuade her to break her silence. It is difficult for any of you to know how she is situated. She is very brave to have taken this step, because I know Staunton will try to take some revenge on her.'

'You must not allow that, Jack,' Lucy said and smiled at her future sister-in-law. 'He must be stopped. Amelia has the right to some happiness.'

'Yes, indeed she does, Jack agreed. 'It is my intention to see that she gets what she deserves. She will live here with us, and in time she will take up residence in the dower house, but only when I am sure that she will be safe there.'

'Amelia is welcome to stay with us as much or as long as she likes,' Lucy offered instantly. 'But when it is safe she will have her own home and we shall visit each other every day.'

'You have all been so much kinder than I could have expected,' Amelia said, her eyes sparkling with the tears she was struggling to hold back. 'Jack has urged me to leave my husband for a long time, but instead I stayed away, denied myself the joy of seeing my eldest son—but now I have decided that nothing will part me from either of my sons.'

'Nothing shall part you from them,' Jack promised her. 'If Staunton wishes to cause trouble, he may come to me.'

After that the subject was dropped and they all began to talk about the wedding. Lucy and her mother would return home after the next Monday evening and the dinner Jack was giving for his neighbours. Jack would escort them to Sawlebridge and stay for a few days, returning to make sure that everything was being done as they wished in the matter of the refurbishment. Everyone else would then travel to Sawlebridge House for the wedding.

It made for a happy discussion, which the ladies continued once they had left the gentlemen to their port, because they had all decided they would need new clothes. Jo most of all, because she was fast growing too big around the waist for most of her gowns.

'I should like to make my own wedding dress,' Lucy said, a thoughtful expression in her eyes. 'Do you remember how we used to make things in the front parlour at the Vicarage? Marianne would cut them out and then we would all sew a piece of whatever we were making.'

'Yes, of course I remember,' Marianne said. 'But would you not rather have a gown made especially for you, Lucy? You have become used to stylish gowns now, things you had made for you in town.'

'Yes, and of course I shall have my trousseau made by a talented seamstress,' Lucy said. 'But a wedding gown should be special and nothing could be more special for me than a gown my sisters helped me to make.'

'Well…' Marianne laughed. 'If you feel like that,

dearest…it so happens that I bought some ivory silk that I meant to give you as a wedding gift before we went home. I thought you might have it made up for your wedding gown, but if you wished, I could cut it out tomorrow.'

'Oh, yes,' Lucy said, her eyes bright with pleasure. 'It is exactly what I should like, Marianne. If you did the cutting, it would be perfect. Jo might do a little sewing before we leave and I could finish it at home.'

'I can do better than that,' Jo told her. 'Hal thinks that as the wedding is so close it would be better for me to come home with you and Mama and stay until after the wedding. He will have to go to his father's house for a week or two, but I do not need to accompany him, and it will be less travelling for me. We can work on your dress together and I can be with you until after the wedding. And then I shall go to Papa Beverley's house until my baby is born.'

'Jo! How lovely,' Lucy exclaimed, because she could have asked for nothing better. 'It will be like it used to be before you were married—and I should like it of all things. We can talk about the embroidery and plan it together.'

'Some weeks ago, I asked Ellen to make a beaded panel for the front of your gown,' Jo said. 'You know that my dear sister-in-law does the most exquisite embroidery. Like Marianne, I was keeping it until the right moment, and I shall give it to you tomorrow when we are planning your gown.'

'I have some pretty lace put away somewhere,' Mrs Horne said. 'I shall get it out for you, Lucy, for you may wish to trim a petticoat or the sleeves with lace.'

'It might make me a pretty bonnet,' Lucy said. 'I know that Jack has asked Drew to stand up with him as his best man. I wondered if Hal would give me away, Jo?'

'I am sure he would be honoured,' Jo said and smiled at

her sister as the gentlemen came to join them in the drawing room. 'But you may ask him yourself.'

Hal gave his promise easily and Lucy's smile grew as the evening progressed. Her wedding was going to be exactly as she had always dreamed it would be, in the bosom of her family, for she had invited both Marianne and Amelia to be her matrons of honour and to allow Amelia's two young sons to be page boys. Andrea was too young, and Jo would find it too tiring to stand for a long time, but she would play her part in dressing her sister before the wedding.

It seemed that even the gentlemen had become engrossed in the wedding plans and were discussing who ought to be invited and who should be excluded. Jack asked what flowers everyone liked best, and Drew spoke about a suitable carriage and horses, and promised to bring Marianne down two days before the wedding so that any alterations to the gown could be made after consulting with her.

Marianne played the pianoforte for a while, and Lucy sang a duet with Jack, and then everyone began to yawn and say goodnight. Jack claimed Lucy as she would have gone upstairs, taking her into his library so that they could be alone. He kissed her softly, sweetly, but with an underlying hunger that made her tremble in his arms.

'I am so glad that your mama has agreed to our marriage,' he said huskily. 'I love you so much, my darling, and I cannot wait to make you my own.'

'I am yours,' Lucy said. She laid her hand on his arm, aware of the raised line beneath his sleeve, which she knew was a bandage. 'Is your arm sore, Jack? I know Rosa stabbed you…'

'It was little more than a scratch,' Jack said. 'You must not worry, dearest. I have known much worse.'

'Yes, I dare say,' Lucy said. 'Marianne told me that Drew

was caught up in a lot of fighting in Spain and had found it difficult to forget all the things he had seen. I dare say it was much the same for you?'

'Yes, perhaps,' Jack agreed. He had seen things that he would never describe to anyone, let alone his gentle wife, but he did not wish her to feel as if he were shutting her out. 'War is always horrific, Lucy, and such memories are hard to forget—but it is all over and I have other things to occupy my mind these days. I would rather think of our wedding and the life we shall live afterwards.'

'Oh, yes, much better,' Lucy said, reaching up to touch his face. 'But never forget that I love you enough to share anything you wish to tell me, Jack.'

'Yes, I believe you would,' he said, smiled and kissed her softly. 'Go to bed now, my darling. Tomorrow I shall take you driving if you wish.'

'Yes, I should like that very much,' Lucy said. 'I enjoyed driving myself, but it is even more fun to go out with you—and if I am very good you might let me drive your horses.'

'I might, if you are very good,' Jack said with a teasing look. 'Go up now, my love, or I may sweep you up and carry you off to my lair.'

Lucy's laugh rang out as she said goodnight to him. She was feeling very happy as she went up to bed that night. It seemed that all her troubles had simply melted away. Amelia had both her sons in the nursery and was looking forward to her new life. What more could any of them possibly want?

Chapter Eleven

Jack was as good as his word, having his curricle brought round soon after breakfast and taking Lucy for a drive in the park. They called at the Lodge to see the puppies, because Lucy wanted to get to know hers before she went home. She would have liked to take them with her to Sawlebridge, but knew that it was best to leave them with Brent, because otherwise they would make puddles in Aunt Bertha's parlour.

After they left the Lodge, Jack allowed Lucy to drive for some twenty minutes or so and was complimentary on her ability to control the horses. It was obvious to him that she was ready for something more spirited than the horses he had bought for her use. He had already decided that she should have a new rig and some high-stepping horses as one of her wedding gifts, as well as various other trinkets he had it in mind to buy her. The best of the Harcourt jewels were already being reset for Lucy and she would of course have a generous settlement. He was planning to take her to Paris for a few weeks, and they would visit the fashionable shops there to buy anything that took her eye.

Jack fully intended to spoil his lovely young wife. For some years he had had little time to spare for pleasure, and due to some astute investments and the good stewardship of his agents and lawyers, his estate was considerably more productive now than when he had inherited it. He would enjoy spending his wealth on Lucy and their children. Indeed, he believed that he had never been happier than he was at this moment.

It was such a pleasant afternoon that the chairs were brought out to the lawn and the gentlemen, Lucy and Amelia decided to play an impromptu game of cricket on the lawns. Lucy managed to score five runs before a high ball was caught by Amelia, perhaps because Hal was too sporting to catch her first ball. Hal was in next and he began to hit the ball for sixes, which meant it went farther and farther into the shrubbery, and eventually Lucy was unable to find it. She wandered deeper into the tall bushes of sweet-smelling roses, some of which were trained over arches or pergolas, searching for the ball she was sure had come this way, but without success. She had almost decided to give up and go back when she came face to face with a man.

'Oh…' she said, feeling startled because he was a stranger and it was so unexpected. She could see that he was a gentleman, some years older than Jack or Drew, and there was something about him that sent a shiver down her spine. 'You made me jump, sir. I am sorry, I do not know your name…'

'Who are you?' the man answered in a sharp tone. 'The new bride, I suppose. Harcourt has decided to take the plunge, I hear—well, I wish you joy of him, for it is likely to be short-lived if he does not stop interfering in my business.'

Lucy backed away from him. Something about him had made her feel cold all over and she had a premonition that their perfect afternoon was about to be spoiled. She turned and ran back towards the others, feeling frightened though she did not know why she should.

'What is the matter?' Jack asked, for he sensed immediately that something was wrong. 'What happened to upset you?'

'A man in the shrubbery,' Lucy said. 'He threatened you, Jack.'

'Threatened me?' Jack frowned and started forward, then stopped as the man walked towards them. 'Damn it! He wasn't expected for a few days.'

Lucy happened to be looking at Amelia and saw the colour drain from her face. In that moment she knew who the man was, and why he had made the threat that had frightened her. Jack thrust her behind him and she ran to Amelia, putting an arm about her waist, and feeling her tremble.

'Don't worry, dearest,' she said softly. 'Jack won't let him take you. None of us will.'

'Staunton,' Jack said. 'I had not expected you just yet. Has my letter come to your hand?'

'The ship met good weather and we arrived in Portsmouth some days earlier than expected,' Lord Staunton said. 'I have had nothing from you, Harcourt, but someone told me I might find my wife here.' He shot a look of fury at Amelia. 'Madam, we are leaving at once. Fetch your son and join me now. Your things may be sent on later.'

Amelia was trembling but she raised her head, looking at him proudly. 'I am not leaving with you, Staunton. I have no intention of ever living with you again.'

'No?' His eyes narrowed, glittering, menacing as he stared at her. 'You think your brother will protect you, no doubt? If you wish to be sued for enticement, Harcourt, you may keep the cheating bitch. She was ruined before I ever had her and I care not what she does—but you will fetch my son to me immediately. He belongs to me and shall come with me today.'

'No!' Amelia cried and looked to her brother for support. 'I refuse to give him up. You would abuse him as you have abused me, and I shall never let you have him.'

Staunton moved towards her, but Jack, Hal and Drew took a step forward, united in their determination to stop him. He halted, looking at them uncertainly.

'You may prevent me now,' he said at last, his top lip curling in a snarl of anger. He was a large man, his once-handsome face fleshy and showing the signs of his ill health, for he was a man who indulged too much at the table. 'But the law is on my side. I shall have my son and I'll ruin you, Harcourt.'

Jack moved forward, his mouth set hard as he gave the other man a scornful look. 'You may do your damnedest, Staunton, but I think you may change your mind when I tell you that Collingwood is in prison, standing trial for the murder of David Middleton. He has signed a sworn statement in front of judges that you paid him to carry out that murder—that you were the instigator of the crime and only you.'

The colour washed from Staunton's face, his eyes narrowing as he glared at Jack. 'You think yourself clever, Harcourt, but I was not even in the country when Middleton was murdered.'

'Of course not,' Jack replied smoothly. The contrast between them was marked, the one lean, strong, attractive, and the other overweight and with too high a colour in his mottled cheeks. 'You made sure of that by accepting the commission as a temporary ambassador for the East India Company—but once I expose you and the way you have treated my sister, it will be generally believed. It may not be proved in a court of law, but the scandal will ruin you—and any judge who hears how you have beaten and shamefully used your wife would grant her a divorce.'

'And you would risk that scandal?' Staunton sneered. 'If I could not show my face in society, would it be any better for that bitch I married?'

'We shall always accept and love Amelia,' Lucy said, drawing a sharp look from him as she added her voice to Jack's in Amelia's support. 'She will be accepted by those who love her—and I think if her story was generally known, others would be more understanding than you think, sir.'

'Who asked you?' Staunton growled. 'From what I hear, you are nothing but the daughter of a country parson and have no consequence. Your opinion is worthless.'

'Please be good enough to leave my property,' Jack said, his eyes glittering dangerously at the insult to Lucy. 'Where is your carriage, sir?'

'I rode here. And I'll leave when I choose…with my son.'

'You will leave now,' Jack said. 'Either you leave of your own accord or I shall have some of my men escort you.'

'Leave it to me, Jack,' Drew said and walked towards Staunton. 'I believe Lord Harcourt asked you to leave. In my capacity as a Justice of the Peace, I am giving you notice that, unless you do as he asks, I shall arrest you and you will be imprisoned until such time as a trial may be arranged. You have been accused of complicity in murder, Lord Staunton, and your rank shall not save you. My advice would be to leave now and put your affairs in order, because you will be arrested for the crime you have committed within due course of the law.'

'Take your hands from me!' Staunton said, his face going white and then red. Marlbeck had too much influence to be denied. Together, he and Jack Harcourt would make formidable enemies. 'What do you want of me, Harcourt?'

'You will renounce all right to your son and you will grant Amelia a divorce on the grounds of cruelty.'

'Never! I'll see them both dead first,' Staunton said. He was furious, knowing that they had the upper hand, but unwilling to give way. 'I'm going now—but don't think you've won, because I'm not finished with you yet.' He turned his malicious gaze on Amelia. 'I'll deal with you later.'

Drew looked at Jack. 'Do you want me to deal with him? I'll have him taken to the nearest prison and kept there until his trial, if you wish?'

Staunton was walking away. Once he had put a safe distance between them, he began to run, disappearing into the shrubbery.

'I think we should not become involved personally,' Jack said, frowning. 'The evidence is slight, Drew, because we have only the word of one man, and he is a self-confessed murderer. George Garrick first heard the tale, because Collingwood bragged of it in his cups, but it might be difficult to make the charge stick in a courtroom. However, Staunton may come to terms when he thinks about it, because it would ruin him socially, if nothing more—that is my hope.' He turned to look at his sister. Amelia was very pale as she clung to Lucy's hand. 'Whatever happens, my dearest sister, I shall not let him take you or the boy, believe me.'

'But he said that he would ruin you.' Amelia was visibly shaken. She had suffered too often from her husband's bullying. 'Did he really pay for David to be murdered?'

'I had hoped to keep it from you,' Jack said, looking at her uncertainly, for this was another cut to her heart. 'Forgive me, I only recently learned of it from George.'

'He is so evil…' Amelia looked so distressed that Lucy put both arms around her, holding her as she trembled. 'I would not want to be the cause of harm to you—or Lucy.'

'Nonsense,' Mrs Horne told her firmly. 'It is quite wrong

that a husband should be able to treat his wife as yours did you, my dear. Jack is perfectly right to stand up to him. As for the scandal, that is something we should all live with, but I think you will discover that, despite some initial shock, a great many women will have sympathy for you, Amelia. I dare say you are not the only wife to be unfairly treated. Divorce is a terrible thing, but sometimes it cannot be avoided. You may not be accepted in the highest circles, but you will certainly still be loved by your friends.'

'You are all so kind,' Amelia said and suddenly gave way to tears.

'Come into the house, dearest,' Lucy said. 'You must lie down for a little, but do not fret. Your friends are determined to protect you, and we shall.'

Jack frowned as the other ladies followed them in. He met Drew's raised brows with a nod. 'I could not say much while the ladies were here, but Staunton is a dangerous man. I shall tell my men to be vigilant, because we don't want him coming here again unannounced.'

'You are going to have to do something about him, Jack,' Hal said. 'The man may not have the guts to commit murder himself, but he is not above ordering it. While he is at liberty, none of you will be safe.'

'He has commissioned a murder once,' Drew warned. 'Do you want me to issue a warrant for his arrest?'

'I would prefer to wait and avoid a scandal if I can,' Jack said. 'Collingwood has signed a sworn statement, but if someone got to him he might recant. I still have hope that Staunton will come to terms. If he wished, he could give Amelia her freedom and relinquish his right to the boy and be free to live his own life.'

'But will he?' Drew asked. 'Or will he try to cause more trouble for you?'

'That remains to be seen,' Jack said. 'It is impossible to seal my estate because of the roads that cross it beyond the lake, but I shall alert my men to keep a watch for him—and I shall tell them that if they see anything suspicious, they may shoot.'

It was a rather subdued party that met for dinner that evening. Amelia had recovered her spirits enough to join them, because Jack had managed to convince her that she was quite safe in his house. Clearly, she could not have her own establishment until this unsavoury business had been settled, but he was hopeful that Staunton would see sense and come to a gentleman's agreement without resort to law.

'I am grateful for your help,' Amelia told him. 'But supposing he will not let me go, Jack? If he sued you for enticement, it could cost you dear.'

'If I must pay for your release, I shall do so,' Jack said and smiled at her. 'But we should bring a cross-petition for cruelty. Divorce is very difficult, Amelia, and in the past most ladies have preferred not to seek that remedy—but Mrs Horne was right when she said that people have begun to think it is wrong that a husband should subject his wife to the kind of thing you have had to endure. I believe we should win, not only the case but also public opinion.'

'Perhaps…' Amelia turned away, clasping her hands before her. 'I have not told you, Jack…but Staunton thinks… he suspects that David is not his son.'

'Ah, I see.' Jack nodded. 'It would be a powerful aid to his case. I do not like to ask, dearest—has he cause to think it?'

Amelia turned to look at him. 'David *is* his son. I wish with all my heart that he were not—but he is. David Middleton loved me, but he was never my lover. I learned my lesson the hard way, Jack.'

'Then we have right on our side,' Jack said. 'Have faith, Amelia—I shall not let you down.'

Jack wished that he was as confident of success as he had allowed his sister to think, but he knew that this wretched business could go either way. She could not prove that David was her husband's son, and others might choose to think Staunton a wronged husband. She would probably achieve her divorce, because Jack could bear witness to the bruises he had seen on her after her husband had beaten her, and her maid was willing to swear to it. But Staunton would quite possibly be awarded the custody of his child, unless the sworn statement accusing him of conspiracy to murder swayed the judge to their side.

'I wish there was some other way of getting her free,' Jack confided to his friends that evening when the ladies had retired to the drawing room and they sat over their port. 'I know he is guilty of enticement to murder. George Garrick was certain of it, and he got the statement for us—but I am not sure it is enough.'

'There is one certain way,' Drew said, causing the other two to look at him. 'It has its penalties, Jack. You might have to live abroad for a while…'

'You mean challenge him to a duel and kill him?' Jack nodded. 'I have thought of it—and as a last resort…' He shrugged his shoulders.

'You know you can rely on us,' Hal said. 'I will stand your second and Drew will see fair play.'

'It is a last resort,' Jack emphasised. 'I have killed in battle and in self-defence, but I have never killed in a duel. I would prefer that the law dealt with him.'

'It may be that you have no alternative,' Drew said. 'If it comes to that, I'll see it blows over. You have influential friends, Jack, including the Regent. You won't go to prison—but, as I said, it may mean spending some time abroad.'

Jack nodded. A duel to the death was the last thing he wanted, because he knew that Lucy was looking forward to her new home, and to having her family visit her often. She would be loyal to him, of course, but it would cause her some grief and disappointment if they were forced to live abroad for a few years until the scandal died down.

It was not an ideal solution, but Jack knew that if things did not go as he hoped, he might be driven to it at the last.

Lucy had been a little surprised at the way her mother had championed Amelia's cause, for Mama had always been very strict about matters of propriety, but, as she explained to Lucy the next morning, in Amelia's case she had been punished enough for her indiscretion.

'She was foolish to let that gentleman seduce her as a young girl, but her stepmother was much to blame for allowing her too much freedom. Had she been guided properly, she would never have been in this situation in the first place.'

'It is hard to remember your modesty at times,' Lucy said honestly. 'Amelia thought herself in love with Mr Garrick. Naturally, she believed that he would marry her.'

'Indeed, yes, I can sympathise,' Mrs Horne agreed. 'But she was unwise, Lucy. It may be easy to think the world well lost for love—but had she been wiser, she would have waited until his wedding ring was on her finger.'

'Yes, Mama, I know you are right,' Lucy agreed. But she could not help feeling for Amelia, because she knew that if Jack had been less scrupulous, she would already have been his wife in everything but name.

* * *

When she looked out of the window a little later that day, she saw that Amelia had taken a basket into the rose garden, clearly intending to cut some flowers for the house. They had guests that evening and she had clearly decided to carry on as usual. Lucy went quickly downstairs and followed her, because she knew that her friend was still feeling distressed and perhaps needed some company.

She hurried after Amelia and had just reached the beginning of the rose garden when she heard a scream. She ran towards the sound and saw Amelia wrestling with her husband. Lord Staunton had his hands about her throat and was clearly trying to kill her.

Lucy was horrified. She knew that there was no time to call for help or go in search of the men, and she looked about her for a weapon, her eyes chancing on a spade that had been left by a clump of roses. Swooping on it, she rushed at Lord Staunton's back and brought the flat of it against his head with as much strength as she could muster. He gave a startled oath and slumped to his knees on the ground, letting Amelia go free. She was choking, her hand to her throat, and after a moment she collapsed to the ground.

At that moment a gardener arrived, clearly intending to continue the work he had left unfinished. Lucy brandished her weapon as Lord Staunton rose to his feet only seconds later, and turned to look at her. Her blow had knocked him down, but had not incapacitated him, and now he was in a rage at her.

'Damn you,' he snarled. 'You little bitch. I'll teach you a lesson. Harcourt thinks to cheat me of what is mine—but I'll take what he prizes most from him!'

'Stay away from me!' Lucy cried, holding her spade ready. 'Help me! Get help, someone! Fetch Jack…'

The gardener had been attending to Amelia, who had fainted, but at Lucy's words he got to his feet and stood for a moment, undecided as to whether he should do as she said or help her himself. As the angry Staunton suddenly launched himself at Lucy, trying to wrench the spade from her, the young gardener made up his mind. He took a flying leap at Staunton, bringing him down in a tackle that would not have disgraced the playing fields of Eton.

Lucy backed away as the young man wrestled with the older man for some time, straddling him at the last, and pinning him down with an arm across his throat, just as more help arrived. Jack came running, followed by Drew; they took stock of the situation at once.

'Well done, Nat,' Jack said, going to Lucy's side. 'You may let him up now. You have done me a great service today.'

Drew knelt down by Amelia, who was recovering from her faint. She sat up, coughing a little as she felt the pain in her throat. 'He tried to strangle me… Lucy hit him with a spade and…' She could not go on for her throat hurt too much and she was struggling to speak.

'You have sealed your fate, Staunton.' Drew helped Amelia to stand, turning to look at her husband as he was hauled roughly to his feet by Nat. He was clearly winded, beaten and subdued by the strength of the gardener. 'You will be arrested for the attempted murder of your wife.'

'He meant to have a go at Miss Horne, too,' Nat said. 'I saw him go for her, sir, and I knocked him down. He had tried to strangle Lady Staunton first. I'll swear to it in any court of law.'

'Thank you, Nat,' Jack said. He looked at Staunton, his eyes cold as ice. 'I think we have all we need now, sir. You will hang for what you tried to do today. We no longer need Collingwood's confession.'

'Damn you!' Staunton cried and pulled a pistol from his coat pocket. He aimed it at Lucy, thinking to wound Jack more by killing her, but before he could press the trigger, he gave a strangled cry, his face turning a strange purple colour. His eyes rolled and his body began to shake, the pistol falling to the ground, where it was kicked out of harm's way by the gardener who had been about to try another flying tackle. 'Damn you all to h…'

Staunton fell to the ground and lay twitching, his eyes staring wildly as the spittle bubbled from his mouth mixed with blood. Jack knelt by him, feeling for a pulse as he finally lay still.

'He's dead,' he said and stood up. 'Some kind of fit… possibly apoplexy or his heart.'

Amelia walked over to look down at him, her hand still at her throat, because it was so painful. 'His doctor told him months ago that he ought to change his lifestyle, but he refused to listen,' her voice rasped because she could barely speak.

'It might have been the fight,' Nat said. 'I knocked the stuffing out of him, sir. I'm sorry. I didn't mean to kill him.' He looked anxious, clearly afraid of the consequences.

'He brought it on himself,' Drew said. 'Clearly, he was unfit and his lifestyle was not conducive to health. We must have a doctor to him, but I think I can vouch for it that it was death by natural causes.'

'Yes, of course,' Jack said and his eyes met the young gardener's. 'You have done us all a service, Nat. I shall not forget that you helped to save my lady's life. I am very grateful. It will be as the marquis says, Lord Staunton died of natural causes. We shall have him carried to the house. Please go and fetch some of the others, but say nothing of what happened here. It is best that it remains a secret.'

'Yes, sir. Whatever you say, my lord.' Nat looked at Drew. 'It was a good thing you were here to witness it, sir.'

Lucy had gone to Amelia, and had her arm about her waist. She offered her a handkerchief, because Amelia was crying and could not find her own. 'It is all over now, my dearest,' she comforted. 'He cannot harm you again. I know your poor throat must be very sore, but it will soon feel better. Think of the future and forget what happened here. I shall take you into the house and Mama will make you one of her soothing lemon tisanes. Jack and Drew will see to everything here.'

Amelia nodded, her arm about Lucy's waist. The two ladies walked away, leaving Jack and Drew alone, as the gardener sped off to fetch help.

'A blessing we could not have looked for,' Drew observed when they were alone. 'I am glad I was still here to be of service, Jack. There may be some talk, of course, because people may wonder—but I am confident that we shall brush through it, and no one need ever know what really happened here.'

'He may have some bruising…'

'I dare say it may have occurred when he took a tumble from his horse,' Drew said. 'It happened yesterday, which is why he walked here through the park rather than coming to the house as he ought.'

'I should be grateful if we could keep it all hidden,' Jack said with a rueful look. 'The fewer that know the truth, the less scandal. Amelia says that she does not wish to go into society, but she may one day—and her son does not have to know what his father was.'

'I agree entirely,' Drew said. 'Lord Staunton took an unfortunate tumble yesterday, which brought on the attack today. I am sure the doctor will be happy to agree with my diagnosis.'

Jack smiled at him. 'Thank you, my friend. I shall not forget this day.'

'You have done me favours enough in the past,' Drew said, smiling grimly. 'It is the least I could do. Besides, Marianne would never forgive me if we had had to postpone the wedding.'

The dinner party for Jack's neighbours went ahead as planned that evening. Amelia did not make an appearance. Jack told everyone that she was grieving for her husband, who had died suddenly of an apoplectic fit and was not feeling well enough to come down. Everyone expressed their sympathy, and only the family knew that Amelia's throat was so sore that she could not speak properly.

Lucy was the centre of attention as the prospective bride, and she was so charming and welcoming to all her future neighbours that they gave hardly a thought to the circumstances of Lord Staunton's demise. Indeed, most believed the family was being heroic to carry on at such a time, and accepted Jack's excuse that he had felt it too late to cancel.

After they had enjoyed a good dinner and an evening of cards, music and conversation, the guests took their leave and the family sat down to talk about what must happen next. It was decided that Mrs Horne, Lucy, Jo and Hal would set out for Sawlebridge the next morning as planned. Marianne and Drew would go home as if nothing untoward had happened, and Jack would accompany his sister to her husband's country house, where the funeral would take place almost at once.

'I shall bring Amelia to you as soon as it is over,' Jack said to Mrs Horne. 'Her son will naturally inherit the estate and she will have an income as the dowager Lady Staunton. After the wedding, she will decide whether she wishes to live here as we had agreed, or reside at her husband's home.'

'She is still very distressed,' Lucy said. 'But she will have you, Jack, and perhaps she would like to be alone for a while.'

'I believe Amelia will wish to attend our wedding,' Jack said, 'though of course she will be officially in mourning.'

'She may wear grey rather than black,' Mrs Horne said, looking thoughtful. 'I do not think anyone would censure her for that on such an occasion.'

'Yes, she may,' Jack agreed. He looked around at them and smiled. 'I cannot thank you all enough for the way you have taken Amelia to your hearts. I could not have expected it, and it makes me happy that I am marrying into such a generous family.'

'We all love Amelia,' Mrs Horne said, giving him an approving look. She had decided that he was exactly the kind of man for Lucy. 'And now I should like to retire. We have a long journey in the morning. Jo, you must come too—do not be long, Lucy.'

'No, Mama, I shall not,' she promised. Everyone followed Mrs Horne from the room, leaving them alone. Lucy moved towards Jack, smiling up at him as he took her into his arms and gazed tenderly down at her. 'I am so glad it is all settled without a fuss, Jack. It might have been the blow I struck him, you know, as much as the fight with Nat.'

'I am sure it was his condition that brought on the fit,' Jack said, for he would not have her believe she might have contributed to Staunton's death. 'He drank too much and was stout. Amelia says he had been warned to cut down on his drinking several times. Besides, if you had not done what you did, Lucy, he might have succeeded in killing her.' He gave her a rueful look. 'It was very brave and resourceful, my darling—but it might have rebounded on you had Nat not arrived when he did.'

'I still had my spade,' Lucy said, 'and I should have used it again, but I was grateful for his help—and then you and

Drew came so I knew that I was safe.' She smiled up at him, eyes bright with mischief. 'You must not scold me, Jack. I know that I am impulsive, but sometimes it may be a good thing—do you not think so?'

Jack nodded. 'Yes, but I hope you will not be too impulsive in the future, my love. I do not wish to see you hurt or injured.'

'You may talk, sir!' Lucy told him. 'Did you think of your own safety when you plucked that child from beneath the hooves of those horses in town? You might easily have been injured yourself.'

'You saw that?' Jack's eyebrows went up. 'You said nothing.'

'No, because I did not wish to embarrass you, but it made me think that I should like to marry you. Not so much because of the way you acted when the child was in danger, but what happened afterwards. You were so gentle and kind, Jack—and the child was reassured. I thought that you would make a good father for my children.'

'Indeed?' Jack's mouth twitched at the corners. 'And what kind of a husband did you think I would make?'

'Oh, the very best,' Lucy said, tipping her head to one side, her face alight with mischief. 'I am looking forward to having you prove it to me, Jack.'

'Wicked jade!' he said, and his head came down as he took possession of her lips, his kiss passionate, hungry, demanding. Lucy melted into him, her body melding with his so that they became almost one—but not quite: that would have to wait for their wedding night.

'Oh, you do look so beautiful,' Marianne said, as she twitched the folds of the billowing skirt of ivory silk. 'The dress is even better than I thought when I cut it out for you, my dearest.'

'Yes, it is exactly what I wanted,' Lucy told her, eyes glowing brighter than any diamonds. 'The front panel is exquisite. Jo asked Ellen to make it for me, as you know, and it works perfectly.'

'Ellen would have been famous had she ever become a seamstress in London,' Marianne said decisively. 'I have asked her to do some beading for me once or twice, because I adored what she did for Jo—and she loves doing it. Every time I wear it I am complimented and asked who embroidered the panel for me, but I never tell them because Ellen will only do it for the people she cares about.'

'She has no need to work at all,' Jo said. 'Lord Beverley loves having her and little Mattie with him, and that means that Hal and I can spend some time at our own estate. She was pleased to be invited to your wedding, Lucy—and Beverley wanted her to come. He seems much better at the moment. I think it is because he is determined to see my son born.'

Marianne smiled contentedly as she looked at her. 'I think you will have a boy, Jo. You are carrying your baby differently to the way I carried Andrea. I hope for a boy next time, but Drew says it doesn't matter. He adores his daughter and me—and that is all he cares for.'

'Hal says the same,' Jo said and pushed a lock of her flame-coloured hair back from her eyes. She was looking radiant in green, her hair hanging loose in the way her husband liked it best, and she still looked a little like a beautiful gypsy despite her jewels and her elegant clothes. 'But I want it to be a boy for Papa Beverley, because I know how much it means to him.'

'We are all so lucky,' Lucy said, embracing her sisters fondly. 'When Papa died and we had to move from the Vicarage, I thought I should never be happy again. Then

Aunt Bertha asked us to live with her and Marianne got married—and then you married Hal…' Lucy's eyes lit up with happiness. 'I fell in love with Jack the first time I talked to him at your wedding, Marianne. We did not meet again for years and I did not expect that we should ever marry, for I believed he must have met someone else long ago. When we did meet again, I fell in love with him once more, but I still did not think he would look at me, for he thought me still a child.'

'Did you truly love him all that time?' Jo asked, looking at her curiously. 'You did not tell anyone.'

'No, for you would all have thought that I was a little girl dreaming of her knight on a white horse, and I believed it was just a dream myself.'

'A dream come true,' Marianne said and kissed her sister. 'We are so happy for you, dearest. Jack is a good man, and I know you will be happy.'

'Yes, I shall,' Lucy said. She kissed each of her sisters on the cheeks and then turned as Amelia entered, looking very attractive in a pearly-grey gown with a straw bonnet and matching ribbons. 'Amelia, is it time?'

'Your mama asked me to tell you that the carriages are waiting,' Amelia said and smiled. 'That dress is exactly you, Lucy. How clever you were not to have it made by a fashionable seamstress. It is such a simple creation and yet it hangs so well.'

'Thank you,' Lucy said and kissed her too. 'And now I think we should go down for I do not wish to keep Jack waiting at the church.'

Jack turned his head to watch as the organist began to play and he saw his bride walking to meet him down the aisle. She was so beautiful that it took his breath, because she had such a look about her…an aura of happiness that seemed to shine out from her. Her gown was simple, of ivory silk with a skirt that flowed to a short train at the back, the sleeves rather like the hanging sleeves of a medieval gown, the front panel exquisitely embroidered with sparkling beads that reflected the light like diamonds. Her hair had been dressed simply too, so that it was brushed back from her face and fell on to her shoulders like a cloud of pale silk, just a few fresh flowers pinned into it here and there. She carried the posy of white roses tied with silver ribbons that he had sent her, and she wore a simple strand of pearls about her throat.

Jack thought that she could not have looked lovelier if she had worn a gown created by the best seamstress in London or Paris, and covered herself in diamonds. In truth, Lucy needed nothing to make her beautiful; she was exquisite—and not just in looks. He was well aware that his bride was as lovely in her nature as she was in appearance, and his heart leaped for joy as she took her place at his side, gazing up at him, the glow of love in her eyes.

Because of the secret he had sworn never to reveal, they had quarrelled and she had been exposed to danger more than once. Jack knew that if he had lost her, he would never have married, because she was the only woman he had ever truly loved.

He smiled as she handed her posy to her eldest sister and the ceremony began. They had come through the difficult days, and the future held nothing but the promise of happiness for them both.

Lucy stood at the window of the house Jack had brought her to that night. It belonged to a friend of his and was only a few miles from her aunt's home. They had it to themselves that night, waited on by the servants they had brought with them, and would leave in the morning to make the crossing over the Channel to France. Lucy had taken leave of her family at her aunt's home and now she was alone. Dressed in a filmy nightgown, her hair brushed until it shone with good health, she gazed out at the night sky.

Observing the way the moon turned everything it touched to silver, she had a smile on her face as she thought of her wedding and the reception afterwards. It had not been a large wedding, for she had wanted to invite only her closest friends and family, but there had been many gifts sent to her and Jack from people she hardly knew.

'We shall hold a ball in town when we return,' Jack had told her. 'And then we shall invite all the fashionable people we did not invite to the wedding and thank them for their generous gifts.'

'It was very kind of all those people,' Lucy said, a little overwhelmed by such generosity. 'I only met Lord Kilverton once—and his wife twice. I did not expect them to send me such a beautiful set of twelve magnificent silver-gilt coasters.'

'Oh, Kilverton is grateful for a service I once did for him,' Jack told her with an easy smile. 'When we are married you will meet all of my close friends, for we shall ask them to stay with us, my darling. But I dare say the gift was as much for you as for me, because in London he told me he thought you were a lovely girl and said that he thought I had made a good choice.'

'Oh…' Lucy had blushed because she was surprised. 'I do not think I know who your true friends are, Jack.'

She was smiling to herself as she recalled his reply, and her smile remained in place as she turned to see him enter the bedchamber a moment later. He was wearing a long gown of black brocade shot through with gold, and his feet were bare, his hair slightly damp as if he had bathed before coming to her.

'What were you thinking?' he asked as he came up to her.

'About the wedding and how kind everyone has been to us,' Lucy said gazing up at him. 'I am so happy, Jack. At times I wondered if this day would ever come...'

'You cannot be happier than I,' Jack said and put his arms about her, pulling her closer, gazing down at her, the heat of desire in his eyes. If she had looked beautiful in her wedding gown, she looked alluring now, making him throb with need and desire 'I love you so...want you so...'

'I am yours now,' Lucy told him, her lips parting on a sigh. She arched into his body as he kissed her, giving herself up to the overwhelming surge of desire that rushed through her as his lips touched hers. 'I love you, Jack.'

And then he had scooped her up in his arms and was carrying her to the bed. He lay her down, divesting himself of his robe, revealing that he wore nothing underneath. Lucy let her eyes feast on him, for he had a beautiful body, strong and lean, the muscles rippling as he reached for her. She looked up at him invitingly, the tip of her tongue slowly moistening her lips as he lay down beside her. He drew her nightgown over her head, tossing it to lie on the floor beside the bed, his hand tracing the line from her throat, down between her pert breasts. Then he bent his head and kissed her, first on the lips, softly, tenderly, his passion controlled. He licked gently down her throat, circling the little hollow at the base of the throat with his tongue, and then moved lower to flick at her breasts.

'Jack...' Lucy breathed as her body arched, the thrill of his touch arousing her to new heights. 'Ohhh...that is so good...'

Jack sucked delicately at her breasts, grazing them with his teeth so that she cried out, not with pain, but with the tantalising thrill that shot through her, making the moisture run between her thighs. His kisses moved lower, down her flat naval to the moist patch of golden curls that covered her femininity. He kissed her there, and his hand moved down, parting her legs, his fingers caressing softly, delicately, arousing her so that she arched once more and cried his name aloud. He kissed the tender flesh between her thighs and then stroked her with his finger again, until she called out once more, begging him to take her.

Jack delayed yet, bringing her to a shivering climax with his hands and tongue so that she was half out of her mind with pleasure, and only then did he thrust into her. She was wet and warm, welcoming him. He slid into her, and Lucy cried out, but the pain of losing her maidenhead was a slight thing that was soon forgotten as he kissed her again. Lucy clung to him, arching her back to meet his thrusting, whimpering and crying his name again and again as the pleasure mounted. And then they came together in a shuddering climax that had them gasping and clinging to each other.

Afterwards, they lay for some time, satiated, their bodies slick with sweat, their limbs entwined so that it was hard to discover where one ended and the other began. Lucy was so content that she fell asleep in his arms, feeling that she never wanted to be parted from him again. Jack stroked the satin arch of her back, smiling as her steady breathing told him that she was sleeping. He held her close, closing his eyes, allowing himself to drift into sleep, knowing that he would always wish to sleep like this in future.

Towards dawn they woke and made love again, and if anything it was even better, slower, the exquisite sensations lasting for longer as they discovered more ways of pleasing each other. Lucy learned quickly, as she always did, and Jack discovered that she wished to give as well as take, giving him pleasure with her lips and tongue, as he had her.

* * *

When Lucy woke again, she discovered that the bed was empty. Jack's side felt cold to the touch, and she sat up, wondering where he had gone. It was early yet and she had thought he would stay with her until the morning, but even as she got out of bed, he came through from the dressing room. He was fully clothed in riding dress, and he smiled as he saw she was awake.

'Did I wake you, my love? You were sleeping when I left you, and I had a surprise for you. I wanted to give it to you when you woke.'

'Oh, Jack, you have given me so many gifts,' Lucy said. 'What is it?'

He offered her his hand. 'Come to the window and look out.'

Lucy took his hand, stepping from the bed. She was naked, but she felt no shame. How could she when he already knew every part of her so well? She glanced from the window and gave a cry of surprise as she saw the beautiful lightweight carriage and the matched pair of black horses.

'Oh, Jack, are they for me?' She glanced at him in delight. 'They look as if they are thoroughbreds. And that rig is so elegant!'

'Nothing but the best for my wife,' Jack told her. 'You have proved yourself as a whip and I have never met a woman with as much courage, Lucy. So why should you not drive horses I would be proud to drive myself?'

'Oh, Jack, you spoil me,' she said and turned to hug him. 'I shall get dressed at once and come down, for I cannot wait to drive them.'

'Summon your maid, my love,' he said, feeling that the look in her eyes had more than repaid his generosity. 'I shall go down and wait for you. We shall put them through their paces before we leave for France.'

Jack was smiling as he left her, because he knew that the gift he had given her that morning had pleased her more than anything else he could have chosen. Half-a-dozen diamond necklaces would not have delighted her so well, though she would have those too in time.

Was it only a few short weeks since he had felt that life had nothing worth having to offer him? The future had looked so bleak and empty that he had almost given way to an urge to drink himself into oblivion. With Lucy as his wife, Jack knew that he would never feel that sense of emptiness again. From now on, he would have everything he could possibly desire…

* * * * *

RICK'S APPOINTMENT with his attorney early Wednesday morning went only moderately better than his meeting with social services the day before. The prognosis wasn't great—but at least his attorney was going to file a motion for DNA testing. Just so Rick could petition to see the child...his sister's baby. The sister he didn't know he had until it was too late.

The rest of what his attorney said had been downhill from there.

Cell phone in hand before he'd even reached his Nitro, Rick punched in the speed dial number he'd programmed the day before.

Maybe foster parent Sue Bookman hadn't received his message. Or had lost his number. Maybe she didn't want to talk to him. At this point he didn't much care what she wanted.

"Hello?" She answered before the first ring was complete. And sounded breathless.

Young and breathless.

"Ms. Bookman?"

"Yes. This is Rick Kraynick, right?"

"Yes, ma'am."

"I recognized your number on caller ID," she said, her voice uneven, as though she was still engaged in whatever physical activity had her so breathless to begin with. "I'm sorry I didn't get back to you. I've been a little…distracted."

The words came in more disjointed spurts. Was she jogging?

"No problem," he said, when, in fact, he'd spent the better part of the night before watching his phone. And fretting. "Did I get you at a bad time?"

"No worse than usual," she said, adding, "Better than some. So, how can I help?"

God, if only this could be so easy. He'd ask. She'd help. And life could go well. At least for one little person in his family.

It would be a first.

"Mr. Kraynick?"

"Yes. Sorry. I was…are you sure there isn't a better time to call?"

"I'm bouncing a baby, Mr. Kraynick. It's what I do."

"Is it Carrie?" he asked quickly, his pulse racing.

"How do you know Carrie?" She sounded defensive, which wouldn't do him any good.

"I'm her uncle," he explained, "her mother's—Christy's—older brother, and I know you have her."

"I can neither confirm nor deny your allegations, Mr. Kraynick. Please call social services." She rattled off the number.

"Wait!" he said, unable to hide his urgency. "Please," he said more calmly. "Just hear me out."

"How did you find me?"

"A friend of Christy's."

"I'm sorry I can't help you, Mr. Kraynick," she said softly. "This conversation is over."

"I grew up in foster care," he said, as though that gave him some special privilege. Some insider's edge.

"Then you know you shouldn't be calling me at all."

"Yes… But Carrie is my niece," he said. "I need to see her. To know that she's okay."

"You'll have to go through social services to arrange that."

"I'm sure you know it's not as easy as it sounds. I'm a single man with no real ties and I've no intention of petitioning for custody. They aren't real eager to give me the time of day. I never even knew Carrie's mother. For all intents and purposes, our mother didn't raise either one of us. All I have going for me is half a set of genes. My lawyer's on it, but it could be weeks—months—before this is sorted out. Carrie could be adopted by then. Which would be fine, great for her, but then I'd have lost my chance. I don't want to take her. I won't hurt her. I just have to see her."

"I'm sorry, Mr. Kraynick, but…"

* * * * *

Find out if Rick Kraynick will ever
have a chance to meet his niece.
Look for A DAUGHTER'S TRUST by Tara Taylor Quinn,
available in September 2009.